Praise for *The Longest Night*

"In this touching and stupendously fresh debut, Braden proves that one doesn't have to turn an entire genre on its head to get something new and exciting. Their blossoming is slow, steady, inevitable, and entrancing. Contemporary romance fans will savor every page."

—*Publishers Weekly* STARRED Review

"The depth and intimacy of the relationship is slowly and lovingly revealed by one of the best debuting romance writers in memory, one who can write superb contemporary sex scenes without a hint of coarseness, in which the feelings of both protagonists are made crystal clear. Braden has a genuine gift for this genre, and readers will hope to see many more books carrying her name."

—*Booklist* STARRED Review

"Watching this romance unfold from Ian's point of view is refreshing and insightful. Braden will soon amass a strong readership."

—*Library Journal* STARRED Review

"There's so much to enjoy in Ian and Cecily's story: amazing sexual tension, a remote location, and the utter privacy of having no one around and no electronic distractions. The frigid winter setting is a breath of fresh air...and Ian's unique way of getting under Cecily's skin makes for a compelling read."

—*RT Book Reviews*

"Filled with trauma, survival, compromise, healing, sizzling sensuality, romance, and love, all set in a remote wilderness, this story is certain to captivate readers. With such a winning first novel, Ms. Braden is certain to gain a huge readership."

—*Romance Junkies*

the deepest night

KARA BRADEN

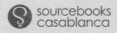
sourcebooks
casablanca

Published by Sourcebooks Casablanca, an imprint of Sourcebooks, Inc.
P.O. Box 4410, Naperville, Illinois 60567-4410
(630) 961-3900
Fax: (630) 961-2168
www.sourcebooks.com

Printed and bound in Canada
WC 10 9 8 7 6 5 4 3 2 1

To Judy Number One, who brings joy to my father every day, and to Judy Number Two, who's shared her three greatest gifts with me: her wisdom, her encouragement, and her daughter, my best friend.

Chapter 1

RAY POWELL KNEW THAT THE CAPTAIN OF THE *Penzance Runner* had sailed the waters off Cornwall for years, but that didn't stop him from surreptitiously bracing himself as the chartered fishing boat heeled to starboard with reckless speed. The darkness stretched around them in three directions, broken only by the silvery white glow of endless stars above and the welcoming lights of St. Mary's harbor ahead. Though it was July, the cold wind off the Celtic Sea slid through the open window to bite at Ray's face, and three or four days' worth of stubble did little to warm his skin.

The boat's captain was an old fisherman based out of the port town of Newlyn, on the mainland. He steered the boat toward a long, narrow dock on the south side of the harbor. All around them, small fishing and pleasure boats rocked on the waves. St. Mary's was the largest island in the Isles of Scilly, thirty miles off the coast of Cornwall. Everything, from furniture to groceries, had to be brought in by ship. Here on the islands, ships were a way of life.

"Hopefully the weather's taken a turn for the better. The rain stopped just yesterday, after almost a solid month. Not that it's stopped the tourists." The captain eased up on the throttle; the bow plunged as their speed slowed to a crawl. "How long are you here for, this time?"

"Just a couple of weeks. Maybe a bit longer," Ray answered. He hadn't yet decided. Maybe he'd just stay until all his bruises and wounds healed. Maybe he wouldn't leave at all.

No, that was just wishful thinking. Much as he loved it here on the island where he'd spent so much of his childhood, he'd made a home for himself across the Atlantic, in Virginia. He had responsibilities to his employees and his best friend turned business partner, Preston Fairchild. Together, they ran Samaritan International Security, a private military contracting company tasked with local security and bodyguard work in a dozen hot spots across the globe. Though their on-site command teams and managers were all competent, Ray was under no illusions about the success of the company. That lay firmly in his and Preston's hands.

Besides, he thought pragmatically, without Ray to carry his share of the load, Preston would bury himself in work and never have a moment's fun. Worse, Ray acted as the senior field troubleshooter when things went disastrously wrong. If Ray quit Samaritan, that responsibility would fall squarely on Preston's shoulders, and Preston hadn't been out in the field for almost five years. He wasn't getting any younger. Then again, neither of them was.

Ray laughed at himself and ducked belowdecks to retrieve the hefty backpack that served as his only luggage. He was thirty-six, not sixty-three, and he had no intention of settling down in any way. He wasn't about to lock himself behind a desk in a corner office,

Copyright © 2014 by Kara Braden
Cover and internal design © 2014 by Sourcebooks, Inc.
Cover design by John Kicksee

Sourcebooks and the colophon are registered trademarks of Sourcebooks, Inc.

The characters and events portrayed in this book are fictitious or are
used fictitiously. Any similarity to real persons, living or dead, is
purely coincidental and not intended by the author.

Published by Sourcebooks Casablanca, an imprint of Sourcebooks, Inc.
P.O. Box 4410, Naperville, Illinois 60567-4410
(630) 961-3900
Fax: (630) 961-2168
www.sourcebooks.com

Printed and bound in Canada
WC 10 9 8 7 6 5 4 3 2 1

the deepest night

KARA BRADEN

sourcebooks
casablanca

"Filled with trauma, survival, compromise, healing, sizzling sensuality, romance, and love, all set in a remote wilderness, this story is certain to captivate readers. With such a winning first novel, Ms. Braden is certain to gain a huge readership."

—*Romance Junkies*

Praise for *The Longest Night*

"In this touching and stupendously fresh debut, Braden proves that one doesn't have to turn an entire genre on its head to get something new and exciting. Their blossoming is slow, steady, inevitable, and entrancing. Contemporary romance fans will savor every page."

—*Publishers Weekly* STARRED Review

"The depth and intimacy of the relationship is slowly and lovingly revealed by one of the best debuting romance writers in memory, one who can write superb contemporary sex scenes without a hint of coarseness, in which the feelings of both protagonists are made crystal clear. Braden has a genuine gift for this genre, and readers will hope to see many more books carrying her name."

—*Booklist* STARRED Review

"Watching this romance unfold from Ian's point of view is refreshing and insightful. Braden will soon amass a strong readership."

—*Library Journal* STARRED Review

"There's so much to enjoy in Ian and Cecily's story: amazing sexual tension, a remote location, and the utter privacy of having no one around and no electronic distractions. The frigid winter setting is a breath of fresh air…and Ian's unique way of getting under Cecily's skin makes for a compelling read."

—*RT Book Reviews*

"But he *always* stays there. I'm certain he'll be no trouble at all, and there's nowhere else he can stay. The island's all booked. It's tourist season, you know. And he's one of ours."

One of ours, Michelle thought, waking up a bit more at that. *As in, from St. Mary's?* Then why would he need a hotel at all, unless it was just for one night? She still wanted to object, but St. Mary's was a small, tight-knit community. Even though Valhalla's Rest wasn't hers, she didn't want to lose the goodwill of the locals.

Hesitantly, she said, "Well—"

"Wonderful," Helen interrupted immediately. Michelle could hear the woman's cheery smile, now that she'd gotten her way. "He's at the pub for a bite now, so you won't even need to make dinner. We'll bring him round in one hour, then?"

"One hour," Michelle confirmed numbly, and they both hung up.

She turned on the light and got out of bed, rubbing her eyes with one hand. She checked the clock on the wall. Just after ten. She'd been asleep for maybe two hours.

Of course, she'd been running a bed and breakfast for years, back in the States. She knew how to deal with troublesome guests on less sleep. Hopefully this particular guest wouldn't be troublesome at all.

He had to be a local who just needed a place to stay for one night. Maybe there was a problem with his house—plumbing leak, electricity went out, something like that. Something in the kitchen, she guessed, since he was having a late dinner at the pub. At least he was polite enough not to expect her to cook for him on no notice.

Yawning, she went to brush her teeth and make herself presentable.

A Cornish pasty and a pint of local ale went a long way toward soothing Ray's post-mission nerves. The familiar pub had been comfortably quiet, with only a few locals at the bar and tourists at the tables near the windows. The bartender, a man Ray knew only in passing, had been happy to serve up a late meal, but he'd spent most of his time cleaning the bar and restocking. Ray was grateful for the silence; he was too tired for any sort of meaningful conversation. St. Mary's was his refuge when the rest of the world turned dark and threatening.

Now, as Ray went out into the cool night, he felt another piece of his combat wariness break away. The wind was bracing, the sky overhead dark and filled with stars even here, in Hugh Town. Ray hefted his backpack and headed for a battered white taxi waiting in the street.

Ray lifted a hand to wave at the man leaning against the passenger side. "Evening, Malcolm."

"Ray! How are—My God, what happened to you?" Malcolm asked as Ray stepped into a pool of light at the curb.

Ray's smile tugged at the cuts on his face. "Never try to shave on an airplane," he deflected with a laugh.

Malcolm smiled back, though the expression was tinged with worry. He hurried to open the back door as he relieved Ray of his backpack. The courtesy wasn't necessary, but tonight Ray appreciated it. He was too tired to do anything but get into the taxi and close his eyes. He'd been on the move for longer than he wanted to consider, crossing eight time zones. He couldn't recall sleeping on the flight from Gatwick to Newquay or the train from Newquay to Penzance.

This time, he was asleep before the taxi started to move.

He woke from his doze to Malcolm softly saying, "Ray? Wake up, mate. We're here."

Ray opened his gritty eyes and looked around. They were parked just outside the familiar white walls of Valhalla's Rest. If Virginia was now his home, Valhalla's Rest was his sanctuary. Once, it had been his grandparents' house—the place where he'd spent every summer holiday. When he'd inherited the property, he'd been in the Royal Marines. He'd sold the property to an old family acquaintance who'd wanted to turn it into a bed and breakfast. Ray had given Liam a more than fair price, with the understanding that the doors would always be open when Ray needed a refuge. And after a mission like the one in Peshawar, Ray definitely needed one.

"Sorry, Malcolm. It seems I've been bad company tonight."

"That's all right. It looks like you need a good night's rest, and it's almost time for me to turn in for the night. A little quiet is always nice." With a brief, reassuring smile, Malcolm got out of the driver's seat and circled around to the trunk.

Ray opened the door, got out stiffly, and then stretched his aching muscles, feeling another piece of tension break away. He took his backpack from Malcolm and paid him, saying, "Thanks. I'll give you a call tomorrow night or the next, whenever I head back to the pub." Normally, Ray preferred to walk whenever he was on the island, but he was still feeling too stiff and achy from the mission and all his subsequent travel.

Malcolm's nod felt awkward and unusually reticent, as if he were hiding something. A shiver of suspicion went up Ray's spine, though he pushed it aside. He was overtrained in dealing with combat situations, stressed, and exhausted. He was seeing shadows where there were none. So he just said, "Good night, Malcolm. Say hello to Helen for me."

"Of course. You take care of yourself, Ray," Malcolm answered, heading back to the driver's side while Ray went up the path to the front door.

He knocked, feeling a twinge of guilt at the late hour, even though Helen had promised him she'd phone ahead to ensure he had a room. Liam was getting on in years, and—

And *wasn't* the one who opened the door. Instead of a graying old man with a weathered, cheerful grin, Ray found himself looking down at a petite, unfamiliar woman in a fluffy pink sweater and blue jeans. In the soft porch light, her brown hair looked dark as espresso, matching the huge eyes that went wide as she took in the cuts and abrasions on his face. She was absolutely enchanting.

Who was she? Ray resisted the temptation to crowd her back into the well-lit foyer so he could see her more closely.

Realizing he looked like a thug who'd come out on the wrong end of a bar brawl, Ray put on his best smile and said, "Sorry for the late arrival. Are you Liam's niece?" He had to struggle with his memory for a moment. "Vicky, right?"

"Um. Actually, no. I'm Michelle Cole. Vicky asked

me to look after the place." She didn't step back to invite him inside.

Her New York accent caught him off guard, distracting him from asking why Vicky, not Liam, would be hiring help. "You're—" He cut himself off before he could say something ridiculous, like "American." Instead, he said, "I'm sorry. I've been traveling for days. I'm Ray Powell."

"Traveling," she muttered, her brows drawing together in a frown.

Out in the street, Ray heard the low rumble of a car engine and the squeal of a steering system in need of fluid. Michelle shook her head and leaned to the side, looking past Ray. He turned to look back over his shoulder, and they both watched Malcolm make a U-turn and drive back toward Hugh Town.

Once the car was gone, Michelle took a breath as if steeling herself and looked up at Ray again. Her smile seemed forced, but she politely said, "Come on in. I made up one of the rooms for you."

"Thank you." He followed her inside, noting that she locked the door. Was she the only staff present? That would explain her reticence to let him in. Hell, in her position, he wouldn't let *himself* into the B and B, given the way he looked—not without a police escort.

She picked up a key from the side table near the door to the manager's office. "Let me show you to your room."

Wanting to set her at ease, he said, "No need. I know my way around. Which room is it?"

"Top of the stairs, turn right, go to the end of the hall. It's the big one with a full bath."

To prove that he really was a frequent guest, he said, "The Serica room. Thank you." He held out his hand for the key.

This time, her smile was a bit more genuine. She set the key in his palm and said, "I think there's a first aid kit in the kitchen, if you need. Would you like me to get it for you?"

For one brief moment, he imagined how her hands might feel on him, tending the cuts, abrasions, and bruises that the on-site medic had neglected. A blink— and the memory of her shocked expression at first seeing him—pushed the thought aside. "Thanks, but no. A hot shower and a good night's rest will do more than enough."

"All right. The kitchen opens at"—she hesitated for a single breath—"seven. If you need anything before then, just knock on the office door." She gestured at the door off the foyer, near the foot of the stairs. "Good night, Mr. Powell."

"Good night, Ms. Cole," he answered, bemused at the formality. He started up the stairs, listening as she went into the manager's office and locked the door. Behind the office, he knew, was a small apartment with a bedroom, kitchenette, and private bath. But that was where Liam lived. Why would she go in there? Where was Liam?

Avoiding the creaky fourth stair without conscious thought, Ray dragged his free hand up the railing, feeling a fine layer of dust. Unusual, that. A sniff verified that the air felt closed and musty. The hallway lights were on, but no lights shone under the guest bedroom doorways. His senses were still battlefield-sharp. He stopped at the top step, overlooking the dark sitting room below, and concentrated on listening to the space around him.

The silence was so heavy, he could hear the faint rattle of the water heater refilling. Valhalla's Rest never attracted particularly rowdy guests, but this sort of quiet felt empty. Deserted.

No guests. An unfamiliar attendant who was staying on-site, in Liam's apartment. Dust in the air.

He went to the Serica room and found the door locked—another oddity. Why would Michelle lock the door, especially if the B and B was empty?

He had too many questions and not enough answers. He went into his room, closed the door without bothering to lock it, and set his backpack on the chair by the window. His jacket followed, and he sat on the edge of the bed so he could take off his boots and socks. The effort was exhausting. He stripped to his briefs only because he knew he'd sleep poorly if he wore his jeans for another night.

Thankfully, he'd remembered to take one of his last remaining antibiotic tablets with lunch before taking the boat from Newlyn. He never would have made it to the bathroom for a glass of water. He certainly didn't have the energy to brush his teeth.

He only got up long enough to open the window. Fresh sea air rushed in, displacing the closed-in, musty feeling. That thought brought back the nagging feeling that something was wrong—a mystery whose solution had to do with the empty guest rooms and the pretty American woman who was apparently running the B and B by herself.

Whatever was going on, though, it didn't feel

threatening, which meant he could put it all off until tomorrow. For now, he wanted nothing more than sleep. Even the shower could wait.

———————

Breathe, Michelle told herself, leaning back against the office door. She'd expected some harmless, temporarily homeless local. In her imagination, she'd had a picture of an older man with a small overnight bag, a guest looking to stay just one night until he could call a handyman.

Instead, she'd gotten more than six feet of danger and muscles and fire barely hidden behind blue eyes and a mischievous, crooked smile. Ray Powell was precisely the type of man Michelle avoided at all costs—the exact opposite of every boyfriend she'd ever had. Certainly he was no one she'd ever feel comfortable having as the sole guest in her old B and B, Anchor's Cove. In fact, her self-preservation instincts had nearly made her slam the door in his somewhat battered face.

But he'd been patient with her. He hadn't tried to force his way inside and hadn't expected her to take his bag. And he was obviously hurt, whatever the cause. She hadn't had the heart to refuse.

Almost a foot shorter than his six-foot-one, give or take, she'd felt like a child standing in front of him. Instead of craning her neck back to meet his intense gaze, she'd found herself talking to his broad chest—not that she had objected to the view. His leather jacket had hung open, showing an old T-shirt that had done nothing to hide the beautifully defined muscles underneath, and though his jeans were baggy and worn, she didn't think there was a spare ounce on him anywhere.

Still, she couldn't push aside her memory of the cuts on his face. They looked just days old, with a hint of healing bruises on his cheek and jaw, just faint touches of yellow that almost disappeared in the soft foyer light. His size was imposing enough to make her feel threatened just by standing there, and that was without the evidence that he'd been in some sort of a fight.

Or, she admitted to herself, maybe he'd been in an accident. Just because he felt dangerous—deadly—didn't mean he actually *was*. Besides, he'd been nothing but polite, despite the way she'd stared at him like an idiot.

One night. He needed somewhere to stay for one night. Was that what the woman from the taxi service had said? Michelle couldn't remember.

One night wasn't so bad. She nudged her mind away from thoughts of muscles and wicked eyes and an engaging, lopsided smile, trying to get herself back into management mode. She hadn't actually run a B and B for almost a year, but it wasn't too difficult for her to start putting together her to-do list.

Her guest had looked exhausted, so she doubted he'd be up before eight or nine. She'd wake up early, do her yoga, and then be ready to make him breakfast whenever he got up. If the weather held, maybe she'd pick flowers and set up a dining table on the patio so her solitary guest didn't feel uncomfortable in the big dining room. Then she'd tend to his room and try to discreetly find out how long he needed to stay. She thought it was one night, but she'd actually feel better once she had confirmation of that.

Chapter 2

Saturday, July 6

RAY AWOKE TO A CHILL WIND GUSTING ACROSS HIS bed, driving him deeper into warm blankets. He opened his eyes as he rolled onto his side, expecting to see his cell phone plugged into the charger cable clipped to the nightstand. Instead, he saw a tiny, unfamiliar wicker table and a shaded lamp covered with seashells.

His next breath brought the smell of the ocean, and with it came memory. *Valhalla's Rest.*

He reached out for the lamp, only to freeze as pain shot through his arm, and more of his memory returned. Peshawar. The mission.

As the last sleepy fog faded, all the aches seemed to hit at once. He'd pushed himself hard on this last mission—maybe too hard, but he'd refused to accept the possibility of failure. Not with a child's life at stake.

But he hadn't failed. He and his hostage response team had rescued both mother and child. All the team's hard work and bloodshed had been a small price to pay for the looks on their faces when the woman and child had realized they'd been rescued.

The memory of their desperate smiles helped him ignore his aches long enough for him to remember another smile, this one polite and strained. Michelle

Cole, the bed and breakfast's new night caretaker...
Who was she?

Lounging around in bed wouldn't bring him any
answers. He pushed aside the covers and stretched until
the surgical tape on his biceps pulled at his skin. He'd
pulled out his first set of stitches, so the on-site medic
had backed up the second set with three pieces of tape
that would sting like mad when removed.

The stitches meant half of his usual morning calisthenics were out of the question. Instead, he did sit-ups
and stomach crunches until his blood raced, chasing the
last of the sleep and fatigue out of his system, and then
went for a hot shower. In deference to the card request-
ing that guests conserve water, he stayed in just long
enough to get clean, much as he would have enjoyed just
standing there under the hot water. He'd have to settle
for two ibuprofen and a cup of tea to help relax muscles
that still ached from torturous airplane and train seats,
not to mention almost six hours on the *Penzance Runner*.

Any other day, he wouldn't have shaved until the cuts
on his face had started to heal. Looking in the steamy
mirror, though, he realized just how criminal he looked
with a three-day start on a black beard. It really was no
wonder Michelle had almost slammed the door in his
face. So he shaved with care, trying to remember the
last time he'd intentionally tried to look harmless. Back
in university, probably. The Royal Marines certainly
hadn't taught him that sort of skill, and at Samaritan,
clients expected a senior specialist like him to look
competent, able to handle any situation that could crop
up in the field, and that meant looking as dangerous
as possible.

Getting rid of the stubble helped, but he could do nothing about the cuts and bruises. Wanting to hide the stitched wound on his left biceps, he pulled a lightweight sweater over his T-shirt. Then he found his power adapter, plugged in the cell phone, and left it to charge. No one would call him while he was on vacation—Preston would see to that—so there was no harm in leaving the phone in his room.

When he stepped into the hallway, he was struck once more by the silent, deserted air of Valhalla's Rest. It seemed his suspicions last night had been correct: there were no other guests. No guests, in July? The bed and breakfast should have been packed with visitors. Ray had half expected to end up on an overflow cot in Liam's apartment or the attic.

Feeling uncomfortably like an intruder, Ray made his way into the spacious kitchen, where he stopped. Liam was a good cook, but after he was through, the kitchen looked like it had been hit by a hurricane. Now, not a single thing was out of place. The double sinks were empty of dishes. The cooktop sparkled with polish.

Motion in the yard caught his eye. He went to the glass doors and looked out into the garden. A slender figure stood on one bare foot. The other foot was raised, caught in one hand, leg extended straight into the air. It was a gorgeous feat of balance, a dance captured in a single pose, framed by the cloud-streaked blue sky and rippling grass.

Then the dancer moved, stretching both arms up to the sky, bringing both feet close together. A quarter turn showed Ray the delicate profile of his hostess, Michelle.

Her eyes were closed, lips parted as she breathed deeply, not from the chest but from the belly, like a martial artist. Slowly, she reached high and arched her back; her long brown ponytail brushed at the soft curve of her lower back, drawing Ray's eye down further.

She began another turn toward the patio doors, and Ray ducked back out of sight. He craved the sort of tranquillity that radiated from her, but it wasn't his to take. It wasn't even his place to watch.

—*m*—

The breeze off the ocean was cool and welcome, caressing Michelle's skin to whisk away the heat that surged through her body. This morning, she'd pushed herself, challenging her strength and balance in a way that she hadn't for months, and the exertion had paid off. She felt energized, revitalized.

She picked up her mat and crossed the yard, enjoying the feel of soft grass and cool earth under her bare feet. She ran lightly up the patio steps to the table where she'd left a pitcher of water and her towel. Wanting to avoid a chill, she tossed the towel over her shoulders before she poured herself a glass.

A soft *click*, too quiet to startle her, intruded on her consciousness. As she sipped her water, she looked up and only then felt a jolt of surprise. For one single heartbeat, at the sight of the man standing in the doorway, every instinct in her body urged her to *run*.

Belatedly she recalled her late-night guest, and she replaced her wide-eyed stare with what she hoped was a friendly, professional smile. "Good morning—" She stopped, realizing that he hadn't signed a guest ledger.

That was how she memorized her guests' names: by associating names with handwriting quirks.

Her hesitation must have shown on her face. He stepped out onto the porch, mouth quirked up in a lop-sided smile that turned his blue-gray eyes even lighter. "Ray Powell," he supplied, and Michelle felt her cheeks go warm.

"Hi, Ray. Let me get breakfast started. The, uh, kitchen's a little bare. Are pancakes okay? Did you want coffee?" Then, remembering they were in Great Britain, she added, "Or tea?"

"Tea, please. And pancakes are fine, thank you," he added with a smile.

Tea. Of course, he'd like tea and not her specialty, coffee. Racking her brain to try and remember how Vicky preferred her tea, Michelle led Ray into the spacious kitchen. Compared to the cramped kitchen at her old B and B, it was a chef's dream, with two ovens, a six-burner cooktop, and a spacious refrigerator and freezer.

When she'd first gotten into the hotel business, she'd taken a couple of cooking classes. The rest of her hard-earned skill was self-taught. She was proud of some of her signature recipes, but of course she didn't have the ingredients to cook any of them. She was stuck using a mix, a brand she'd never heard of. She hoped the result wouldn't be too terrible.

Some of the counter space had been turned into a breakfast bar, encouraging visitors to stay and chat. Naturally, Ray did just that, rather than giving Michelle the privacy to compose herself. She was extremely conscious of how much her sports bra and leggings revealed. Though he was too discreet to openly stare, she was certain he'd noticed.

Before the silence could get uncomfortable, Ray spoke up, his deep voice soft and friendly: "Have you worked here long, then?"

Michelle hid a grimace. How much should she tell him? Of all the contingencies she and Vicky had discussed, a surprise guest wasn't one of them. Michelle's instinct was to keep things confidential. She was, after all, only a temporary caretaker for Valhalla's Rest.

"I'm actually a business consultant, not an employee." It was on the tip of her tongue to add that Valhalla's Rest was technically closed, but she didn't want to make him feel bad. *Be nice to the locals*, she reminded herself.

She glanced back to see that Ray was frowning, though he was looking around rather than watching her. He didn't seem *angry*, though—or if he was angry, it wasn't at her. No, his frown looked worried, if anything.

He had to know about Liam, right?

About two thousand people lived on all the little islands combined, with more than half of them right here on St. Mary's. Michelle had the impression that everyone knew each other.

She measured dry mix into a bowl, cracked in two eggs, and then went to the fridge. As she passed Ray, she glanced at him, and their eyes met. Gorgeous eyes, really. And he seemed less disreputable now that he'd shaved and combed his hair, even though a part of her had enjoyed the rough-edged, wild look from last night.

Maybe she would've crossed the street to get away from him, but secretly she would've stared at him as she did.

"Is Liam here?" he asked as she took out the milk.

The question snapped her out of her thoughts. She returned to the bowl, trying to remember where she'd seen measuring cups. "I'm afraid not." Remembering their conversation last night, she added, "Did you need to speak to Vicky?"

"I might at that," he muttered. He glanced aside for a moment, frowning even more. "He's in hospital, isn't he? Liam?"

If Michelle hadn't heard Vicky use that precise expression, she might have thought Ray was from somewhere other than Britain. As it was, she took the time to measure and pour in the milk while trying to find her words.

Finally, she set everything down and turned to the breakfast bar, meeting Ray's eyes. "He's not in the hospital, no. I'm afraid he's passed away. I'm sorry."

A ball of ice lodged in Ray's chest at Michelle's gently spoken words. *Liam, dead?* He was old but tough as the island rock. He'd been the heart and soul of Valhalla's Rest since the day the B and B had opened. Somewhere inside, Ray believed that he'd end up dead before the old man, because Liam was *safe*. Eternal. The guardian of Ray's sanctuary.

"How?" he asked, though a part of him didn't want to know the answer. Liam hadn't been ill the last time Ray had visited, though it had been two years. Nearly three. But he couldn't have met a violent end. St. Mary's was the sort of place where you could leave a bicycle unlocked outside the pub at night and expect it to be returned the next morning, if it went missing at all.

"A heart attack, I think. Vicky didn't say specifically—only that it was very fast." That explained Vicky's involvement. Liam had no wife or children; the B and B must have passed to his niece instead. The thought of anyone other than Liam owning Valhalla's Rest was unsettling.

"I should speak to her," he said, distracted by thoughts of his bank accounts and escalating property values on St. Mary's. His share of Samaritan's profits meant he was more than just comfortably well-off, especially since his debts were minimal. Preston was the one with the fancy house, the boat in Miami, and so on. Ray lived frugally. And while it might clear out his savings, he could afford a substantial purchase here on St. Mary's.

He couldn't let Valhalla's Rest fall into a stranger's hands, could he?

A touch scattered his thoughts like startled birds. He blinked at the long, thin fingers barely resting on the back of his hand. Michelle's nails were cut neatly short, though her mint-green polish was chipped at the edges. Her skin was smooth, unmarred by calluses or scars. Without conscious thought, he started to turn his hand over, wanting to close his fingers around hers—to accept and keep the kindness she offered.

"I'm sorry," she said gently.

Reminding himself she was a stranger, he set his hand back down and gave her a distant, polite smile. "Thank you."

When their eyes met, she slid her fingers away and went back to the mixing bowl. "I can call her later and let her know you'd like to talk," she offered over her shoulder.

What was he going to do with a bed and breakfast—especially one more than three thousand miles away? He didn't even want to commit to a houseplant.

"Please," he said, deciding that it didn't hurt to talk to Liam's niece. If nothing else, he could express his condolences to her.

—◆◆◆—

Michelle didn't even give Vicky the chance to say more than hello before furiously whispering, "What did you get me into?"

Vicky barely hesitated. "Hello to you, too, Chelly. Is something the matter?"

"Yes!" Michelle looked up at the ceiling, listening to the creak as her guest—her gorgeous, dangerous, possibly-not-local guest—walked back to his room. "Who's Ray Powell?"

"What? It's too early for pub trivia."

"This isn't pub trivia, Vicky. This is some VIP guest who knew your uncle but didn't know he was dead, and now he's upstairs, and I have *no idea* what to do with him!" She caught herself as her whisper nearly rose to a shout; she didn't want Ray to overhear.

"Bloody hell. Did you tell him the B and B is closed?"

"As if anyone would listen to me?" Michelle muttered. "I tried. He's here anyway, and now he's asking to speak with you. Who *is* he, Vicky? He looks…" She fell silent, trying to find the words to convey her apprehension without sounding like a coward. Ray was *exactly* Vicky's type. One look, and she would have been all over him.

After a moment, Vicky prompted, "Chelly?"

"He looks *dangerous*. Like he's been in an accident—or a fight. And he's—"

"Shit, shit," Vicky interrupted, her voice strained. "Are you *certain* he knew Uncle Liam?"

A shiver swept through Michelle. "I think so," she answered slowly. "Why?"

Vicky took a deep breath. "Because property on the Isles of Scilly is valuable. Very valuable. The land beneath Valhalla's Rest is worth ten times more than the building itself. There are companies that would love to get their hands on it—ones who wouldn't hesitate to *encourage* me to sell."

It was Michelle's turn to whisper, "Shit." She closed her eyes, rubbing at her temples. "He *does* want to talk to you. As soon as I told him about Liam, he asked about you."

"Did he say anything threatening?"

Michelle swallowed. "No. He's been, well, very polite, actually."

Vicky's sigh was full of relief. "All right, good. Perhaps he's willing to wait a bit. It's the weekend now, so tell him you have no way to get in touch with me. Gives you a bit of breathing room. Try to enjoy yourself."

"Enjoy myself? With *him* here?"

"Michelle," Vicky said soothingly, "it's gorgeous there. If he *is* after the property, he'll be after me, not you. Just do as you think is best, and try to have fun."

Michelle's apprehension over her "guest" disappeared under a rush of suspicion. Vicky had come from money, and after college, she'd gone into finance and prospered, but her current fortune didn't mean she could afford to hold on to an aging bed and breakfast on a tiny island for sentimental reasons. As far as Michelle knew, Vicky hadn't even been close with her uncle. She'd simply been his sole heiress.

So why have Michelle come here to investigate the property and assess what it would take to get it up and running? There was only one possible answer.

"When were you going to make your offer?" Michelle asked sharply, forgetting all about her guest upstairs.

"What? What offer?"

"Don't try to play innocent with me. Ever since I lost Anchor's Cove, you've been trying to talk me into starting up a new B and B—"

"Chelly, you *love* running—"

"So, what, then? This place falls into your lap, and you take the opportunity to ask me here in hopes that I'll fall in love with it? That we can be partners?" Though she knew her anger was running uncharacteristically high, though she knew none of this was Vicky's fault, Michelle couldn't hold back the words that poured out in a rush. "*I don't want a partner!*"

"Chelly, no! I just—I had hoped—" Vicky faltered, her voice full of regret. "You've been adrift for months now, since that whole thing with Dana and Anchor's Cove. If nothing else, this let you escape your mother's house for a little holiday."

Gritting her teeth, Michelle reined in her temper. She inhaled. Exhaled. Centered herself, searching for the peace that had filled her this morning, while she'd done yoga on the windy lawn overlooking the water.

"I'm going out," she said more calmly. "I need groceries anyway, so I have an excuse. Find out who this Ray Powell is and what he's doing here. Text me the minute you know anything. If he's some"—she searched for a word that wasn't too overdramatic—"thug working for a real estate developer, I'm not coming back here without a police escort."

"Of course. Anything you need," Vicky surrendered immediately.

"And if he kills me, I'm haunting you for the rest of your life," Michelle threatened.

Vicky laughed tensely. "You'll be just fine, love. I'm certain this is all just a misunderstanding—some old friend of Uncle Liam's. He, ah, could even be... Well, Uncle Liam never married or even mentioned a special woman."

Michelle thought about how Ray looked at her, polite but definitely interested. "Not only is he half your uncle's age; he's not gay, Vicky. Believe me."

"Well, then," Vicky said, her voice going sly. "If you send me a picture, just so I look up the right person—"

"No. You have enough boyfriends in London. And he *still* might be here to burn down the B and B with me in it, so..." Michelle pushed her chair back from the desk. "Hanging up now. Text me. Or else," she said and went to go find her power adapter. Now she really needed her cell phone charged.

—⁓—

Ray wasn't healed enough to go for a run, but injuries rarely stopped him. He wasn't one to let common sense get in the way, especially not when he needed mindless physical exercise to distract him from thinking about the death of old Liam and the mystery of Michelle Cole.

He changed into running shorts, sneakers, and a faded gray U.S. Army T-shirt he'd stolen from Preston long ago. With his arms and legs bare, Ray looked more like a car accident victim than a private soldier just in from the field. The Peshawar rescue mission had cropped up too quickly for him to change. Though he'd worn a bulletproof vest, he'd otherwise been in civvies—a bloody suit, in fact—instead of proper body armor. He'd survived; his suit was another matter.

Back in Virginia, he would've been running at the Samaritan training grounds with earbuds and music turned low. Here on St. Mary's, he preferred to immerse himself in the sounds of the island: the wind through the trees, the waves on the rocks, even the whisper of passing bicycles and the occasional car. He took his cell phone only out of habit, in case of emergency, and left his room key on the dresser. He'd never bothered to lock his room here, and he saw no reason to start now—especially if he was the only guest.

Sunglasses in hand, he headed back downstairs, only to nearly get run down by Michelle as she came out of the manager's office. Reflexively, he caught her just as the door swung closed, hitting her in the back. Her hands landed on his chest, and he wrapped his arm around her waist to steady her.

She fitted against his body perfectly, soft curves hiding strong muscles that reminded him of the graceful yoga he'd witnessed earlier that morning. She'd freed her hair from its neat ponytail, and it hung loose down her back, damp ends tickling over his forearm. Her breath caught on a gasp, deep brown eyes going wide. The air filled with the scent of vanilla soap.

His arm tightened, holding her snug against his body. "Careful," he warned, ignoring the sting of his stitches.

She blinked up at him, lips parted in surprise. Her fingers twitched against his T-shirt. "Sorry!" she breathed, color rising in her cheeks.

He would have happily held her close, but she shifted uncomfortably, and he released her at once. Dismissing any awkwardness, he said, "I was just going out for a run."

"Oh." She frowned slightly, looking toward the front door. "I've only got the one key."

Smiling encouragingly, he said, "This is St. Mary's. It's safe enough to leave the door unlocked." When she still hesitated, he suggested, "The back door, perhaps?"

After a moment, she said, "There's a barbecue on the patio. I'll put the key in there."

He was tempted to mention that he could pick locks, but that sort of skill was as likely to alarm as it was to impress. "That'd be fine. Thanks." With one last smile, he went out the front door, listening as she promptly locked it behind him.

He headed out to the street, thinking she'd been an unexpected pleasure to have in his arms. It was too bad Michelle didn't seem interested. He pushed her out of his mind—or tried to, at any rate. He had more than enough to worry about. Fortunately, whatever was going on with Valhalla's Rest, he had plenty of time to sort it out.

Michelle bolted the door and let her head thump against the cool wood. She closed her eyes, trying to convince herself that she couldn't still feel Ray's powerful arm locked around her waist. Her fingertips tingled at the memory of his broad, hard chest under her hands. The heat of his body had seared her palms right through his T-shirt, and she'd briefly wondered how he'd react if she shoved the fabric up to touch bare skin.

Tempting as he was, though, he was equally dangerous. The cuts and bruises weren't limited to his face and hands. Under one short sleeve, she'd glimpsed surgical tape—the type of tape meant to help close cuts that were deep enough to require stitches.

What had happened to him?

Last night, her first impression had been that Ray Powell was dangerous—an image backed up by this morning's implied threat of greedy real estate developers. But Michelle trusted her instincts, too, which were telling her that while Ray might be dangerous, he wasn't a threat. At least, not to her.

Still, instincts weren't facts, and she had no reason to trust him right now. Through common sense, she'd always managed the danger that came with running a bed and breakfast, renting rooms to strangers, and there was no reason to change that right now. She needed information, and Vicky was her best source at the moment.

Well, no, she corrected herself. The locals of St. Mary's surely knew about Ray; otherwise, the woman from the taxi service wouldn't have insisted Michelle open Valhalla's Rest for him. But going to them presented two problems: First, as an outsider, they might not tell her anything at all. Worse, they might tell Ray she'd been asking about him. And second, if he *was* dangerous, who was to say the islanders knew the real

Ray Powell? He could easily have deceived them into believing anything he liked. Isolated as they were, there was little chance that they might discover some nefarious secret by accident.

She went out the back door and, feeling just a bit apprehensive, hid the keys in the barbecue. Before finding out Ray was going for a run, she'd decided to skip the taxi and walk to town. From what she'd glimpsed yesterday evening, the walk was along a quiet, peaceful road, with gardens and greenery on both sides. Was that where Ray had gone jogging? He'd set off from the backyard and gone toward the cliff, rather than the front of the property, but that didn't mean he wouldn't eventually return to the road. She'd just have to keep an eye out for him so they didn't unexpectedly cross paths.

Maybe if her instincts were right—if her fears were unfounded—she could ask him to show her the best trails to run. Just because she preferred yoga didn't mean she didn't enjoy jogging as well, especially with a good partner.

Of course, that thought led to imagining other, more engaging activities partnered with Ray.

She shook her head, trying to banish the thoughts that were so unlike her. Vicky had always been the wild one. Both Vicky and Dana, actually. Michelle had been the voice of reason, reining in the worst of their excesses. She'd been the one who made sure they didn't go home with anyone questionable, the one who slipped condoms into purses and drank soda instead of margaritas. While she hadn't ended college a virgin, she'd always preferred long, slow relationships over one-night stands.

A vacation fling had never been in the cards for her. Now, though, she couldn't help but think that sharing this vacation to St. Mary's with someone so handsome might well be a genius idea—assuming Ray Powell was just an innocent visitor and not actually someone sent here to threaten her.

Chapter 3

MUSCLES TINGLING WITH WARMTH AND ENERGY, RAY came to a halt by a stand of bushes at the top of the cliff, where the wind off the sea cooled his skin. He was just past the halfway point of the route he'd chosen, a gently weaving trail that wouldn't tax his injuries. He was still recovering from his mission in Peshawar.

Physically, he was healing nicely. He'd be done with his antibiotics in a couple of days, and he could probably go down to St. Mary's hospital to have the stitches removed. Or he could take them out himself and spare himself a scolding from nurses who'd known him all his life, cowardly as that was.

While he felt good physically, his state of mind was something else entirely. The news of Liam's death had shaken him, as if one of the fundamental props of the universe had been pulled away, leaving the world to slide another inch toward chaos. And finding out about it from a stranger, no matter how pretty or polite, had been jarring.

Then again, although the old man had been practically family—more like an uncle than a lifelong friend—Ray wasn't surprised that he'd received no notice of Liam's death. Stoic and practical, Liam had wanted to die as he'd lived: quietly and without a fuss.

The last time Ray had visited Valhalla's Rest, Liam had bluntly mentioned that he didn't even want to be buried in the small church cemetery on St. Mary's. "Cremation is good enough for me, and my ashes can return to the soil here. I don't need a plaque or a stone for the island to remember me."

But even without Liam's presence, Ray should have been able to find peace. He enjoyed the solitude that St. Mary's offered. Downtime on the quiet island was exactly what he needed after a rough mission. But now, Liam's absence—his death—had upset that tranquillity. And while Ray could find some measure of tranquillity with Michelle Cole, he found himself unwilling to show his interest in her.

Not that she wasn't attractive, because she definitely was. She'd just looked at him so warily last night, as if expecting him to pull a knife on her. And this morning, while she hadn't avoided darting an admiring glance or two his way, she'd made no effort to encourage him.

Besides, something about her spoke of long-term relationships, of love and commitment, not a holiday affair. As enticing as she'd been in his arms, with just the right balance of curves and muscles, shyness and self-confidence, she was definitely *not* his type.

He set his phone to his ear without even consciously realizing he'd dialed. After two rings, Preston's gruff voice answered, "Give me one good reason you're calling me at this hour."

Ray chanced a quick look at his phone. All of England was one time zone, even this far west, off the coast. Ten a.m. here meant it was five a.m. in Virginia. "You lazy bastard. Your alarm's already gone off."

"It's Saturday. The dogs and I are sleeping in."

"Stop trying to lie to me. I haven't known you to sleep in since we met."

Preston's irritated snort didn't quite hide his laugh. "True. So what are you doing calling me at this hour? You're on vacation. And if you tell me you slept in and decided to call me from bed, we're going to have a long talk about personal space and how you've managed to invade mine from three thousand miles away."

Ray laughed, feeling some of his discomfort ease at the familiar banter. "I'm actually standing on a cliff, halfway through my morning run."

"I'm glad to see you're taking the doctor's instructions about rest and recuperation seriously."

"Bugger that." Ray took a deep breath and walked toward an outcropping of rocks. As he sat down, he said, "Liam—the old bloke who ran the B and B here. He's dead."

"Shit. What happened?" Preston asked, all humor gone from his voice.

"Nothing nefarious, as I understand. It was a heart attack or something. No surprise, there. He was in his eighties, after all."

"I'm sorry."

"Thank you," Ray answered automatically. "Anyway, his niece inherited Valhalla's Rest. She's not here herself, so I think she's looking for a property manager. But rather than hiring a local, she's got an American running the place for now."

"An American? Who is he?"

"She," Ray corrected. "Her name's Michelle Cole. She seems"—he hesitated, his mind filling in all manner of inappropriate words: enticing, alluring, tempting—"competent."

"That's good." When Ray didn't respond, Preston asked, "Isn't it?"

"I'm being a stubborn idiot," Ray admitted, more to himself than to Preston. "It's not the same here, without Liam. And if the niece sells…"

With unusual delicacy, Preston said, "That B and B has always been special for you, hasn't it?"

"It was my grandparents' house before I sold it to Liam. I thought of buying it myself." He still was, at least half the time. The rest of the time, he was reminding himself that it'd be a stupid idea to even consider. Just the fact that he was engaging in that sort of mental debate at all was a bad sign. He wasn't indecisive. *Ever*. If he were, he would've been long since dead on the battlefield.

"And?" Preston asked carefully.

Ray forced out a laugh. "I thought about it, but that's all, I promise. I'm as suited to running a hotel as a cat is to ice skating."

Sounding relieved, Preston said, "Worse, probably. After all, cats have good balance and four legs."

"So very helpful."

"Always. So does this mean you're coming back early? The guest room is occupied, if you were thinking of weaseling your way into my house."

Ray hadn't been consciously thinking that at all, though now that Preston mentioned it, the idea sounded brilliant. Preston's house was spacious and full of all the necessary creature comforts, including a pool, a well-stocked kitchen, and two German shepherds who were always up for a game of fetch. "Is that so?"

"Ian and Cecily are down from New York. God help me, I'm having a family barbecue for everyone to meet her." Slyly, Preston added, "I could use you as backup."

"Oh, bloody hell, no. You don't pay me enough to put up with all your family at once."

"You're my damned VP. Give yourself a raise."

Ray grinned. "Thanks, mate, I will. You have fun at your barbecue. Without me," he added and then hung up before Preston could protest.

Much as Ray liked Preston's younger brother, Ian, he had dealt with the extended Fairchild clan precisely once. No force on earth could compel him to repeat that experience.

Still, he was glad he'd called. Talking to Preston had helped clear his mind. Ray wasn't seriously considering quitting Samaritan to run a bed and breakfast on the other side of the Atlantic. He could let Valhalla's Rest go. He'd still have his memories, and there were other, even nicer inns throughout the Isles of Scilly. He could come back at any time and stay somewhere else. Make new memories.

Either way, he didn't have to decide now. He needed to lay to rest the ghosts of the Peshawar mission before doing anything else. With no pressing business back home, he could easily spend a couple of weeks or more here, letting the rest of the world pass him by.

Feeling much more at ease, he tucked away his phone and got down from the rock. He'd run back to the inn for a shower, go to town for a quick lunch, and then spend the rest of the day being indulgently lazy. Even if rest and relaxation brought no answers, at least his medic would approve.

—∿∿—

> No info on Ray Powell. Sorry! The name's too
> common. Send more details when you can.

Michelle read Vicky's text and shifted the reusable grocery bags in her hands with a sigh. How many Ray Powells could there be in the Isles of Scilly? Of course, maybe he *wasn't* from a local family, which meant Vicky would never track him down with any certainty. Vicky worked for an investment firm, not the FBI—or the British equivalent. MI5? Scotland Yard?

The lack of concrete answers was frustrating. If Vicky couldn't get any answers, Michelle would have to find her own. But how? While she could probably go to the tiny local police station and ask them, the idea of acting the part of a skittish woman, afraid to run a business on her own, was unpalatable at best. Besides, technically she wasn't allowed to run a business here in the UK. She had no license, no tax certificate, no insurance. Going to the police to ask about a guest might be more trouble than it was worth.

To make the day even worse, Michelle was so used to having her own car that she'd completely forgotten she'd need to take a taxi back to Valhalla's Rest. Yesterday afternoon, she'd called a taxi from the airport, but she hadn't bothered to save the phone number. Wondering what else could go wrong, she went back into the co-op to ask. When she finally called, she found herself with a forty-five minute wait.

What else can go wrong? She arranged to be picked up at a nearby pub, hefted her grocery bags, and left the co-op again, dragging her feet. This "vacation" idea of Vicky's was turning into a disaster—

Michelle stopped, took a deep breath, and lifted her chin. Negative thinking would only make things worse, not better. She looked around, allowing herself to live in the moment. Only a few white clouds streaked the otherwise sunny sky. The air was filled with the fresh smell of salt and sea. All around her, life moved at a slower pace. It was nothing like Arizona. Nothing like New York.

Some of the tension bled away, and she resumed walking with a lighter step despite the weight of the grocery bags. Positive thinking wasn't a mystical cureall, but the brief moment of reflection had helped to clear her mind. Smiling, she went into the pub, where she ordered a prawn sandwich and took the bartender's recommendation for a pint of ale. And as she enjoyed her surprisingly good lunch, she tried to think—positively— about what to do next.

So far, she had no reason to evict Ray and lock up the B and B. Ray had asked about Liam and Vicky, but that was all. No veiled threats. No prying for more information about the future of Valhalla's Rest. In fact, he'd been the sort of polite, undemanding guest she'd always preferred. The only reasons for caution at all were his physical condition—evidence that seemed, at least, to speak clearly of a fight and not some more innocent accident—and Vicky's speculation about predatory real estate developers.

Conscious that she couldn't decide what to think of Ray, Michelle sighed, paid her bill, and walked out to wait for her taxi. She really did have very good instincts about people—a warning prickle at the back of her neck that would tell her in no uncertain terms to stay away. Every time she'd ignored that instinct, she'd later realized her mistake. Disastrous first dates, tumultuous relationships, even her friendship with Dana—all of them had happened because Michelle had decided to take a chance.

With Ray, though, that warning prickle wasn't *entirely* there. But it also wasn't absent.

Indecision. How she hated it. She wasn't one of those wavering, waffling types who spent an hour picking the day's outfit or was endlessly asking waiters for one more minute to look over the menu. She prided herself on her ability to think on her feet—to gather all the information, to analyze the facts, and then to make a solid, logical decision and stick with it.

Well, she *had* been, up until this past year, but that was only in one matter: her own future. And that had nothing to do with Ray Powell.

She still had no answers by the time the cheerful taxi driver dropped her off at Valhalla's Rest. She started toward the front door, only to remember leaving the keys around back. As she walked around the side lawn, she could feel the beginnings of a headache.

So much for the restful two-week holiday Vicky had promised. Maybe she'd lie down for a little while after she put the groceries away. After all, she hadn't slept well last night.

She found the keys in the barbecue, though the back door was unlocked. The rumbling water heater hinted that Ray was taking a shower and probably wouldn't be down any time soon. She had a reprieve. Time to think. But remembering the view of Ray in his tight T-shirt and running shorts, Michelle couldn't help feeling as disappointed as she was relieved.

She put away the groceries, hoping she'd have enough time to look into the B and B's hospitality policy. Would Ray be expecting her to cook dinner as well as breakfast? She didn't mind—she'd just have to run back to the co-op sooner rather than later—but she would like some forewarning. When cooking for herself, she usually made simple meals; she went all-out only for guests and friends.

Then again, she'd picked up fresh sea bass at the market, and she had an excellent recipe for oven-baked fish in a garlic and white wine sauce. The dish was fast and easy, and she wouldn't have to do any prep work at all. She could cook two servings as easily as one.

What was she thinking? She was doing Ray a favor by allowing him to stay here. She didn't need to impress him with her cooking. But he was a guest, and on vacation or not, she was a professional—apparently a professional who couldn't make up her mind. So much for not wavering and waffling!

Frustrated with her own inability to make a decision about Ray, she washed up the breakfast dishes and straightened up the kitchen until it looked as pristine as it had when she'd arrived yesterday.

That done, she went into the sitting room and threw open the drapes, filling the spacious, high-ceilinged room with light. She also opened every window to let the ocean breeze drive out the musty air. The grand old fireplace would provide welcome warmth in the winter months, but now it was nothing but a dark eyesore. If Valhalla's Rest were hers, she'd probably put a vase in front of the fireplace and fill it with cut flowers from the garden.

She knew it could be hers, though not solely. Her savings and her share of the insurance payout for Anchor's Cove couldn't cover even half the cost of the land and building, but Vicky wouldn't protest. She'd be a silent partner, allowing Michelle to run the B and B as she wished. No arguments over marketing strategy or decorating budget. No fights over vacation planning or division of labor. No chance of shady bookkeeping catching Michelle by surprise.

But Michelle couldn't take that risk again. She *wouldn't*.

She'd ignored her instincts and trusted Dana, only to end up burned—bereft of the bed and breakfast she'd once loved. Friends, she'd learned, should not be business partners, no matter how close the relationship or how trustworthy the person was. And no business was important enough to sacrifice a treasured friendship. In one terrible storm, she'd lost both Dana and Anchor's Cove. She wouldn't risk falling in love with Valhalla's Rest, only to lose both it and Vicky to some unforeseen misfortune. Better to go it alone next time.

Granted, running a B and B with a partner was easier. Alone, Michelle would have no time for sick days, and would have to schedule her days, morning till night, around the schedules of her guests. If she needed to go to the store, she'd have to either trust her guest with keys or hire a service to watch the property.

She could always find a business partner outside her small circle of friends, but how could she trust a stranger with something so important? She was very much a do-it-yourself type. The few times she'd hired help in the kitchen for handling large parties, she'd nearly run herself ragged trying to supervise everyone all at once.

So, she couldn't bring herself to trust a stranger, and she wouldn't risk losing another friendship. That conundrum was the reason she'd been in limbo for the last year, trying to get up the courage to open a business on her own. And to make her decision more complicated, she'd started receiving job offers from major hotel chains, and as much as she loathed the idea of working for a corporation, the money they offered was tempting.

She'd have to decide something, but not now. Over the last year she'd become uncharacteristically good at living in the moment, enjoying life's little gifts—in other words, procrastinating.

Now, she had thirteen days until her vacation was over. Thirteen more days on a picturesque island full of flower fields and palm trees, rocky beaches and endless skies.

As long as nothing else went wrong—as long as Ray proved to be a harmless guest and not a threat—Michelle was determined to enjoy the rest of her time on St. Mary's. She could think about what to do with the rest of her life once she was back in the States.

———※———

Michelle was sitting in the manager's office, reviewing the B and B's ledgers, when she heard the soft sound of footsteps coming down the stairs. Ray had turned off the shower some time ago. She guessed he'd napped or stayed upstairs to read in privacy, since there wasn't a single television in the entire building other than the one in the manager's apartment. Now, she wondered if he was going out again or if he'd need something from her.

Well, he knew where the manager's office was. She turned her attention back to the ancient computer. Valhalla's Rest was in decent financial shape, though she already had an entire page of recommendations for Vicky. Full insurance coverage, while expensive, was mandatory, as the ultimate fate of Anchor's Cove had proved. An investment of a few thousand dollars—or pounds, she supposed—to modernize crucial systems, like plumbing and heating, would help keep subsequent costs down. Placards in every bathroom reminded guests to conserve water, but on-demand water heating systems and low-flow fixtures could help with that as well. Were there conservation incentives offered by the government to help offset the cost of high-efficiency appliances? She'd have to look into that, once she figured out where on the island to find decent Internet access.

Of course, the other side of the coin was direct income from guests. She wouldn't be able to do a full analysis of room rates until she dug into the bookings history and found a way to compare the popularity of other hotels on the islands, but she could at least take some notes. She found the seasonal rates table in the database and picked up her pen when inspiration struck. She needed a way to narrow down Ray Powell's identity, and it was right there, staring her in the face.

Trying to act casual, she got up from the desk and opened the door. This time, she looked before walking out of the office, though a tiny corner of her mind admitted she wouldn't mind another accidental collision.

Ray had already made it to the bottom of the stairs

and out into the sitting room. At the soft creak of the office door, he turned back to smile at her. He'd changed into dark jeans and a blue polo shirt the precise shade of his eyes, and Michelle couldn't help but stare. Cleaned up and presentable, he'd turn heads just walking down the street, despite the remnants of cuts and bruises on his face. His black hair was growing out of a severe military-style cut, and she couldn't help wondering what it would feel like to comb her fingers through the strands.

"Good afternoon, Ms. Cole." His polite greeting snapped her out of her daze.

"Mr. Powell," she said, wondering if the formality was a reprimand. Had he caught her staring?

"Please, call me Ray," he invited, walking toward her.

"Thanks, Ray. Call me Michelle," she said, feeling an odd sense of daring at the small intimacy. She put on a professional smile and continued, "Sorry to interrupt. Do you have a minute?"

He stopped right at the edge of her personal space, close but not threatening, and smiled down at her, asking, "What can I do for you?"

The list that popped into her mind was entirely unprofessional and wildly inappropriate if he was a criminal. Even if he wasn't, in fact. She deliberately turned away, gesturing toward the office door to hide her blush, and said, "Your registration—I forgot to ask you to fill it out last night."

"Ah, right. Sorry about that." When she looked back at him, he gave her a sly smile, adding, "If the authorities come to investigate the books, I won't say a word. I'll hold them off while you run out the back door."

Charmed despite her apprehension about him, she smiled. "Thanks, but we're on an island. Running from the law seems sort of pointless."

"There are boats," he said, blue eyes sparkling with humor. "You could take up piracy."

She couldn't help but laugh at that, thinking that if he was a criminal, he was at least an *interesting* one. "Good point. I'll keep that in mind."

She led him into the office and found it easier to catch her breath with the expanse of the old desk separating them. The management software wasn't what she'd used back at Anchor's Cove, but she'd familiarized herself with it enough to quickly open a new guest form. "If I could have your ID, please?"

Still smiling good-naturedly, Ray gave her a curious look. "What for?" he asked, though he shifted in his seat so he could get at his jeans pocket.

Alarm flickered through her, banishing some of her amusement. Was he suspicious or just caught by surprise? Wasn't it policy in England to get a photo ID for a hotel room? She had no idea. The last time she'd visited, she'd stayed with Vicky's family.

As calmly as she could manage, she said, "To fill out your registration form." She quickly checked the monitor and confirmed that all the expected fields were there: name, address, telephone number, credit card information.

"I imagine I'm already in the system," Ray guessed as he took out his wallet. "Though maybe not. Liam and I had an understanding." He slid out an ID card and a credit card, and then put both down on the desk.

An understanding. That sounded ominous. "Oh?

What was it?" she asked, trying to sound casual instead of apprehensive.

"It's not important," Ray answered dismissively.

Michelle disagreed, though she didn't push him to explain. Had Liam been involved with something underhanded? St. Mary's wasn't exactly a bustling port of commerce, but it was a sad rule that where there were people, there were criminals of some kind. What sort of "understanding" could there have been between an old man running a bed and breakfast and…whoever Ray Powell was?

Instead, she silently picked up the license. To her surprise it was American, not British, with an apartment in Virginia listed as the address. She propped the license against the keyboard and started to type. As soon as she entered his last name, the rest of his information filled in automatically, including mobile and work phone numbers. Only his home number was left blank, but she wasn't surprised. Landlines were going the way of the dinosaur, these days.

The fact that he was a frequent guest, though, was comforting. A hired thug sent to intimidate Vicky into selling the property wouldn't have stayed here before, right?

Still, she typed his driver's license number into the notes field, just in case Vicky could use it, and then switched to the financial tab. She had no idea how to price his visit, so she quickly searched for the most discounted rates already entered into the computer. "I'll ring this up as off-season, if that's all right?" she proposed.

Without even asking what the off-season rate was, he

answered, "Whatever you think is appropriate. I don't want to be any inconvenience."

Her business instinct told her she should have negotiated, but she reminded herself that her job here wasn't to bring in a profit. Instead, she asked, "How long were you planning to stay?"

"I *usually* stay a couple of weeks," he said, frowning. "I don't want to impose. I can try to find rooms elsewhere."

Should she encourage him to go or keep him close in hopes of learning more? With each passing hour, he seemed less threatening. Less of a danger to her, at least.

Impulsively, she said, "That's all right. I'll put you down for, say, ten days?" That would give her time to learn more about him and a day to clean up and square everything away, leaving Valhalla's Rest in Vicky's hands. Smiling, she told Ray, "If you change your mind, no harm done."

His answering smile, crooked and charming, chipped away a bit more of her apprehension. "Thank you. If this is to be my last time…" He paused, looking around the office. "I appreciate it."

As she entered his credit card information into the computer, she asked, "Have you been coming here long, then?"

"You could say that, yes. I don't mean to be any trouble." His expression turned thoughtful. "Liam and I used to have dinner whenever I'd come for a visit. Any chance you'd like to continue the tradition?"

"That's kind of you, but there's no need," she answered thoughtlessly, a professional reaction that had become ingrained habit by now. As a single woman running Anchor's Cove, she'd had to gently and not-so-gently turn away quite a few advances over the years.

But she'd never regretted it—not until Ray wished her a good evening and excused himself from the office.

The door swung quietly shut. Sighing, she picked up her cell phone and texted Ray's driver's license information to Vicky. Then she went back to digging through the finances, content to hide in the office for the time being. Cowardly as it felt, she'd go make herself dinner after Ray left.

Chapter 4

Sunday, July 7

THE EARLY MORNING SKY WAS PALE, STEELY BLUE, A gorgeous contrast to the rich, deep color of the sea. Michelle stared at the white-tipped waves as she slowly bent forward, arms outstretched. Her balance tipped, and she turned the fall into a controlled descent until her palms were flat on her yoga mat. Beneath the mat, the springy grass gave way, cushioning her hands and feet. Exhaling slowly, she lifted her right leg until it was perfectly straight, forming a line from her nape to her heel.

Breathing through the stretch, she held the pose and tried not to think beyond the moment. With her eyes closed, she could let her problems melt away for a few precious, peaceful minutes. Now that she'd warmed up, the cool morning air was energizing. Bracing. She could understand why Ray had gone out for a morning run yesterday despite his injuries.

And she could all too clearly recall how handsome he'd looked in a T-shirt and shorts. That first night, he'd looked like a dangerous, down-and-out thug in his baggy, worn jeans and leather jacket. Who would have guessed he was hiding such a gorgeous body underneath?

The wicked, enticing mental image burned through her tranquillity like hot sunlight through mist. She took a deep, focusing breath and prepared to switch legs, only to have her already-fraying concentration shatter under the sound of a harsh guitar riff followed by fast, powerful drumming.

It was the theme song from *Buffy the Vampire Slayer*—the TV show that had kept Michelle, Vicky, and Dana sane through college. Michelle had programmed it as Vicky's ringtone.

Worried, Michelle pushed upright and ran for the patio, remembering belatedly that her guest's open window wasn't too far from the table where she'd left the cell phone. Vicky *never* called at this hour, especially not on a weekend. She cherished being able to sleep in.

Michelle snatched up the phone, silenced the ringing, and fumbled it to her ear. "Hello?"

"Good morning, Chelly!" Vicky sang out.

"What are you doing up at this hour?" Michelle asked suspiciously. Vicky sounded unusually cheerful for a night owl. Normally, she was downright grumpy until about ten, and then only if she'd had her morning coffee. Without caffeine, she could barely communicate at all.

"Did you *not* want to hear what I found out?" Vicky countered innocently. "I know your unhealthy obsession with morning yoga, and I specifically set my alarm so I could call you at this ungodly hour. But, if you'd rather I go back to bed, I can—"

"No!" Michelle glanced up at Ray's open window. Pinning the phone to her ear with one shoulder, she poured herself a glass of water and said more softly, "Tell me. What did you find?"

"Well, I had a lovely evening last night. This bloke I'm dating, Owen, got us tickets for this underground restaurant in an old watchtower—"

"Vicky," Michelle said in a quiet, warning tone.

The answering laugh was bright, though a bit sleepy. "All right! I was able to locate *your* Ray Powell."

"*My—*" Michelle cut herself off. With a last glance at Ray's window, she picked up her glass and headed back onto the lawn.

"*Mmm-hmm*," Vicky purred. "If he's not yours, then I'll bloody well take him. He's gorgeous! Why didn't you mention that little fact, Chelly?"

For one brief instant, jealousy spiked through Michelle. That was all she needed—Vicky getting interested enough in Ray to come out to St. Mary's to "check up on the property" or something. "I'm more concerned with the 'dangerous' part," Michelle pointed out, trying to keep Vicky focused.

"Understandable, that. As it turns out, he's the vice president of a private military contracting company, one Samaritan International Security, based in Virginia."

"Private military contracting…" That sounded ominous, though not *as* ominous as the criminal background she'd imagined.

"According to the website, they do both private work and government contracting. Bodyguards and drivers for diplomats, security for sites—including in war zones. They do training, too, for security guards and private soldiers."

"So the real estate thing is just a false alarm?"

"I doubt he's involved in anything like that. Even for the type of money we're talking about, land developers wouldn't hire a bloody executive from an American paramilitary corporation to play strong-arm. Not unless they had some sort of hold on him." Vicky paused. "Though obviously he's British. His biography listed him as former Royal Marines. So there could be *some* connection."

Michelle let out a sigh as she sank down onto the garden bench in front of the small, untended bed of flowers and the palm trees that edged the cliff. Ten feet down, a thin strip of white sand and dark rocks slipped below the ocean waves. "So I *do* or *don't* have to worry?"

"I don't *think* so," Vicky said cautiously.

"That's not a 'no.'"

"It's also not a 'yes.'" Vicky's tone turned sympathetic. "Look, Chelly. I shouldn't have mentioned the real estate thing at all. I know how you worry."

"Worry!" Michelle glared out at the water, wondering how *she* had gotten into this position. Vicky was the one who attracted trouble the way a flower attracted bees—and she always came out of it smelling like roses. "It's not *worry*. It's common sense. Not exactly your strong suit," she added acidly.

Knife-sharp silence followed, thick with resentment.

Letting out a breath, Michelle stammered, "I'm sorry, Vicky. He's just... With him showing up like that, all cut up and bruised... Talk about intimidating."

Vicky's answer was a frosty silence. Guilt twisted through Michelle. Her best friend didn't deserve her anger. This whole mess had happened because Vicky had been trying to *help*, not to cause the sort of trouble that had made their college road trip years so exciting. Vicky had wanted to shake Michelle out of her yearlong gloom with this trip and the temptation of Valhalla's Rest.

While Michelle was still trying to think of how best to explain, her phone buzzed with an incoming text. Curious, she took the phone from her ear and watched as an image downloaded.

Her eyes widened. The picture was the back view of a black-haired, tanned soldier climbing a rope over a wooden wall, the type of thing found on military obstacle courses. The olive drab tank top and camouflage pants did nothing to hide gorgeous muscles and tanned skin streaked with mud. The soldier had turned to look over his shoulder and down, and he was laughing at someone or something below him.

Heart skipping, Michelle swiped the screen to zoom in on his face. All she could see was one bright blue eye, the line of a strong jaw, a hint of his nose, but that was all she needed to recognize her guest. Her stomach gave a little flip at the brightness of his smile. The picture hadn't been taken too long ago; except for the cuts on his face, he looked almost the same.

Uncomfortably warm despite the cool breeze, she put the phone back to her ear. "Yeah," she said a little roughly. "That's him."

"*Mmm-hmm*," Vicky agreed. "Not exactly Kenny Simmons, is he?"

Michelle winced at the memory of the self-centered, overemotional artist she'd dated in her freshman year. Kenny's "nice" side had been superficial at best. Underneath, he'd been a real bastard. Fortunately, he was too lazy to be truly malicious.

"Well, no," she admitted, "but—"

"Or Brent Wallace. Or Frank what's-his-name. Or that bloke from the coffee shop down the road from our flat, sophomore year," Vicky continued relentlessly, plunging into the list of Michelle's exes. Every one of them had been pulled from the same mold—scholarly, artistic, and introverted. Charitably, Michelle had thought of them as sensitive and introspective; Vicky's kindest words for them were "weedy" and "spineless."

"All right, all right!" Michelle cut in, slouching down on the bench. "So Ray is the exact opposite of everyone I ever dated. So what?"

"So"—Vicky drew out the word in a singsong drawl—"you're on holiday, Chelly, and your Ray Powell is *not* the enemy. Perhaps it's fate's way of telling you to live a little."

Heat bloomed in her cheeks. "Vicky, I don't *do* that sort—"

"Isn't this *exactly* what you were always on about, with your yoga and universal consciousness and karma? God knows after dating *those* types all your life, you're about due for some tall, strong, gorgeous karma to come your way."

"That's not how it works," Michelle muttered.

Vicky ignored her. "Look, I don't think you need to worry about him at all. So enjoy your holiday, enjoy the view, and don't fret about this real estate thing at all. And if it doesn't work out long term with your bloke—"

"He's *not* mine!"

"—at least you'll have good memories."

Michelle sighed, closing her eyes. "You're not helping, Vicky."

"I should hope you don't need my help with *this*. Just have a bit of fun, all right?"

Knowing Vicky wouldn't relent, Michelle lied. "I'll give it some thought."

"That's my girl. Have a *fantastic* time, Chelly," Vicky continued. She was still laughing when she disconnected.

Michelle dropped the phone in her lap and looked up at the sky, exasperated. Vicky hadn't changed one bit since college. She was still impossible, still trying to tempt Michelle into her version of "fun."

But the news of Ray's perfectly legitimate, legal profession—even if it sounded hazardous and controversial—did help Michelle feel better about sharing an otherwise deserted bed and breakfast with her unexpected guest. And while she absolutely would *not* take Vicky's unsolicited advice, she was now free to relax and have a little fun. *By herself*.

As she got up, her phone buzzed with another incoming text. Eyes narrowed suspiciously, she watched the message download, then tapped it to open the picture.

It was a close-up view of camouflage trousers and a band of bare, tanned skin above a green web belt. The fabric was stretched taut over a tight, muscular backside. One leg was bent up, boot scraping on a wooden wall; the other was extended, ready to swing up and over. The sight was every bit as gorgeous as the view from the cliffside flower bed—in a very different way.

She didn't even need to see Ray's face to recognize him. And now, the image of his tight, perfect ass was going to be seared into her brain for the rest of the day.

"Not helping, Vicky," she complained under her breath, wondering if she'd be able to concentrate on her yoga at all with that sort of distraction, or if she should just give up and go make coffee.

A harsh blare of unfamiliar music shattered Ray's comfortable dream of a small, lithe, dark-haired beauty. The music went silent too late for him to recapture the images that faded from his mind. He sighed, threw off the covers, and sat up on the edge of the bed, stretching. His arm twinged, but the rest of his bruises seemed to have finally healed, and he was breathing and moving generally without pain.

He smirked at that. He'd told the medic that his ribs were just bruised, not broken. Bloody know-it-all doctors.

Curious about the music, he looked out the back window. Michelle's yoga mat was laid out on the grass, though she was sitting on one of the benches overlooking the ocean. When she turned, he saw she had a phone to her ear. That must have been what he'd heard—a custom ringtone.

After his morning calisthenics and a quick stop in the bathroom, Ray put on jeans, a T-shirt, and sneakers. He wanted to run the perimeter of the island, an eleven-mile trail that would require something substantial for breakfast. If his hostess couldn't provide, he hoped to coax her into a quick walk to Hugh Town to visit one of the cafés.

Downstairs, he went to the kitchen, took his morning antibiotic, and then set about making tea. If Liam had been around, Ray wouldn't have hesitated to cook something for himself. Now, though, he didn't want to intrude, which was an uncomfortable thought. Valhalla's Rest had been *his* long before Michelle had ever set foot on the grounds.

And that was uncharitable. She was supposed to be here, and even if he'd had a reservation, it would have been canceled. She'd been gracious in allowing him to stay. There was no call for him to be unkind in return. He'd give Michelle a little while to finish her call before he asked about breakfast.

Ten minutes later, tea in hand, he sat down at the far end of the breakfast bar, where he could enjoy the breeze through the open doors. As he waited for the tea to cool, he idly picked through the tourist brochures in a little stand off to one side. He hadn't played tourist in Scilly for years, if he ever really had. Oh, he'd done some family excursions to see the seals and taken a walking tour of some ruins, but Scilly wasn't a tourist destination for him. It was a home away from home.

What changes had he missed over the years? He knew the old secret places, off the tourist trails, but there was so much more to experience. In a way, he was as new to the islands as his hostess.

They could discover the islands together, he thought as he sipped his tea. In fact, the idea of seeing the islands anew through Michelle's eyes was surprisingly appealing.

Only then did he realize that he felt...better, actually. Just days ago, he'd been under fire, a heartbeat from death. Usually, it took weeks for him to shake off the alertness, the twitchy edge of wariness that would have him jumping at every little noise, but it had eased seemingly overnight.

He couldn't attribute it solely to Valhalla's Rest. He *always* came here after a bad mission, because this place—the land, the building, the island itself—was his sanctuary. Was it his hostess's influence? They'd barely interacted beyond a few polite words and their accidental collision. In the past, he'd tried to find solace in the arms of other women, but no level of intimacy had ever smoothed out his mission-rough edges. Not like this. And certainly not without any intimacy at all.

He was still trying to puzzle it out when Michelle came into the kitchen, yoga mat rolled under one arm. "Oh. Good morning," she said, flashing him a quick smile. As she turned away, she shook her ponytail so her face was hidden behind the fall of her hair, but not before he caught sight of color rising in her cheeks.

What had caused her to blush so appealingly? Had he been staring? She was attractive enough to catch any man's eye, especially in her body-hugging yoga clothes. Her high ponytail hung halfway down her back, and he was struck by the urge to tug off the elastic and run his fingers through the dark, wavy strands.

Now he was staring. Quickly, he turned his attention back to his tea, watching her surreptitiously instead. "Good morning," he said as casually as he could manage. "The water's still hot, if you want a cup of tea."

"Thanks. I'll make coffee after I shower," she said, heading for the laundry room at the back of the kitchen. "Or did you want breakfast now?"

"Actually, I can cook breakfast, if you'd like. Or there are some good cafés in town I can show you. Just as friends," he added before she could shoot down the idea as a date. As enticing as she was, he'd enjoy her company as a friend, too. Even a deliberately quiet vacation could turn lonely. "If you're on holiday, you need to see more of the island than the garden and the co-op."

Michelle turned back, giving him a thoughtful look. She bit her lower lip, showing a hint of white teeth. Then she straightened as though unconsciously bracing herself and said, "All right. I'd like that. Thirty minutes?"

Just enough time for him to shower and shave. "Thirty minutes," he agreed.

—⁓—

Michelle was pleasantly surprised to find Ray was a polite, quiet walking companion. He was content to guide her down the paths and over gentle hills without rushing to their destination or filling the silence with chatter.

Was he always so reserved, or was it their surroundings? The island's peace seemed to encourage quiet introspection.

Of course, with nothing to distract her, she was all too aware of his presence at her side. Her head didn't even come up to his shoulder. Every time she glanced his way, she had a perfect view of a solidly muscled arm, lightly shadowed with hair that she itched to touch. Around his wrist was a fading tan line, perhaps from a watch. He was bruised and cut, though most of his wounds had healed to white lines and patches of faded yellow. And high up on his biceps was that surgical tape.

As they came into sight of Hugh Town, the island's main community, curiosity finally got the better of her. She looked up at him, silent for a moment, enjoying his handsome profile. He'd shaved while she'd been showering. With the tiny cuts on his face healing to thin lines, he looked much more respectable than he had two nights ago.

Before he could catch her staring, she turned away and asked, "What happened to your arm?"

He looked down, dark brows drawn together in a slight frown. "A work injury. It looks worse than it is," he added, frown disappearing as he gave her an easy, friendly smile.

Michelle had never been very accomplished at lying. Self-consciously, trying to sound as if she didn't already know the answer, she asked, "What do you do?"

"I run a consulting company back in Virginia." He glanced at his arm again; one corner of his mouth quirked up in a wry smile. "Security consulting, mostly government and high-profile clients."

"How did you end up in Virginia?"

He laughed softly, a deep sound that sent shivers across her skin. "My business partner and I were both military. He was U.S. Army, and I was Royal Marines. He started Samaritan a year before I got out."

Put that way, it all sounded so innocuous. More to the point, it matched precisely with what Vicky had discovered in her Internet search. As another bit of her reservations fell away, she asked, "Samaritan?"

His crooked grin appeared, and a rush of warmth swept through her. "It's a bit of a joke on me. He'd planned on luring me to the colonies to help, so he named the company Samaritan International Security, or SIS."

"That's…" She trailed off, trying and failing to guess at the meaning.

"Secret Intelligence Service? More commonly known as MI6, from all the spy movies."

"I suppose it worked, since you ended up in 'the colonies,'" she teased.

He leaned in a bit closer and added, in a conspiratorial whisper, "Don't let him hear you say that. I held out until he offered me the vice presidency instead of just head of field operations, but secretly I've always had a thing for espionage."

She laughed, looking him deliberately up and down. "Yes, because you're so subtle and unnoticeable."

"Well, perhaps not, but you've yet to see me in a proper tuxedo."

No, but she could imagine it with perfect clarity. Her face went hot, and she looked out toward the sea. After taking a few seconds to compose herself, she turned back, asking, "Do you like it there? In Virginia?"

"Everything but the mosquitoes." His blue eyes lit up with amusement. "Clever of you Americans, building your capital on a malarial swamp."

She laughed, remembering Vicky saying much the same thing. "And yet, you Brits *still* kept trying to take it back," she teased.

This time, his laugh was loud and rich, his smile so bright that it stole her breath. She grinned and looked toward the scenery without really seeing it, her mind filled instead with thoughts of blue eyes and a powerful body and a charming, crooked smile.

"What about you?" he asked, steering her toward a nearby corner when they reached the paved road. "What do you do, other than not-run a deserted bed and breakfast?"

Her smile faded as Anchor's Cove flashed through her memory. "That's about it, actually," she admitted, embarrassed at how boring her life had become. "Vicky and I went to college together. I had a B and B for a little while, out on Long Island, so she asked me to come take a look at Valhalla's Rest for her."

"As a business consultant."

She opened her mouth to elaborate—to tell him about Vicky's plan for her to fall in love with Valhalla's Rest and accept Vicky as a silent partner—but she held her tongue. She had no desire to even think about Dana and Anchor's Cove, much less to admit to her fear of going into business with her last remaining close friend, and if she started telling the whole story, she might not be able to stop.

Instead, she said, "It's a beautiful location. And the island is absolutely charming. You said you're a frequent guest?"

"Every couple of years, yes." He smiled again, though it was less bright, not quite touching his eyes. "If I don't leave the country, Preston—that's my business partner—he tends to find emergencies to call me back to the office. If I take a holiday here, I can ignore his calls and blame poor reception."

"True," she agreed, wondering how to bring that smile back. "Did you grow up here?"

"In a way." His smile stayed fixed as he glanced at her, then turned his attention back to their surroundings. "My family came here for summer holidays. It's where I learned to fish and sail. I even did a bit of gig racing before I went off with the Marines."

"Gig racing?" she asked, thinking she'd misheard.

"Rowboats, used for competitive racing. The club should still be out on Wednesday and Friday nights. It's the big sport here on the islands."

"Rowing," she said delightedly. "We had rowing

teams at Brown University, I think. I was never really involved in sports."

"Oh? What did you do, then?"

"Road trips. We'd hit the road on Friday after class and not come back till Sunday night—sometimes Monday morning. I saw every roadside diner and tourist trap in the Northeast. And during breaks, we'd take longer trips. Including through DC, all the way down to Florida."

"I can't arrange much in the way of road trips here. There are more footpaths than roads on the islands, if you don't mind rambling," he said, giving her another sly, playful smile.

Michelle couldn't hide the laugh that escaped. "Rambling?"

"Walking. I couldn't help but notice you do yoga, so I'm certain you could manage a walk or two around the island, hmm?" he challenged.

She hesitated for only a second before she nodded. "All right. I suppose I can't sit in the manager's office all day."

"That's the spirit. We'll give you a good holiday yet." Eyes alight, he nodded ahead, saying, "But we're done with that for now. Here's the café."

He opened the café door for her, and she paused in mid-step, hit with the delicious smell of a bakery in full swing. Her stomach let out an undignified growl. "Oh, that smells wonderful," she said quickly, trying to cover the sound.

Ray touched her arm lightly, saying, "Here, let's take a table by the window. Good thing we're morning people. The tourists won't descend in force for another hour." He pulled a chair away from the table for her.

Charmed by the courtesy, she sat and asked, "I don't qualify as a tourist, then?"

He sat down opposite her and leaned in close, lowering his voice to ask, "Would you rather see the tourist attractions or the secrets of the islands?"

Her gut gave a little flip at his sly smile. The bistro-style table was small enough that their knees touched. All she had to do was lean forward, and their lips would also touch. The thought made her heart race.

Karma, she thought, and laughter bubbled up inside her. She was always cautious, never taking risks. She was the sensible, practical one.

But she didn't have to be that way. Not all the time. Did she?

Greatly daring, she leaned forward an inch or two, just enough to draw a feeling of intimacy and conspiracy around their table. "Show me the secrets," she challenged softly.

His pleased smile sent tingles flooding through her body. "My pleasure."

Chapter 5

TWO HOURS LATER, AFTER HE HAD RETURNED TO Valhalla's Rest alone, Ray started on his run. An old running partner of his had once told him the hardest part of a long run was that first step. Most of the time, it was true, but not here on St. Mary's. Here, the island trails beckoned to him, easing him forward until he finally hit his running stride, leaving behind all the lingering aches of the Peshawar mission and the thought of Liam's death.

The path ahead curved, gently easing back down toward the beach. To either side, shrubbery encroached on the dirt. Leaves brushed against Ray's calves, and purple flowers filled the air with perfume. And though he needed this run, a part of him regretted choosing it over a more gentle walk with Michelle.

Tomorrow, he told himself as he hit the beachside trail. Tomorrow, if she was amenable, they could spend the whole day walking the coastal path, stopping at scenic overlooks and quiet beaches. Hadn't one of the cafés advertised picnic lunch baskets for tourists to take on their explorations?

The thought made him slow to a halt. *Picnic lunches?* What the hell was he thinking?

Needing a moment to catch his thoughts and regain

his composure, he uncapped his water bottle and drank, feeling the sun on his face. The wind from the sea kept the July air from being stifling and humid. The perfect climate was one of the things he loved about Scilly in the summertime.

Even if Michelle wasn't up for the sort of endurance run he enjoyed, she seemed the outdoorsy type. She'd like the coastal path. Why that mattered so much, he didn't know. He'd known her for two days—two days out of the two weeks they would both be here. And after those two weeks, they'd go back to the States—Ray to Virginia, his company, and his missions, and Michelle to...wherever she lived. They might never see each other again.

Friendly as she was, she'd been reticent about giving away too much personal information. Brown University. Road trips with her friends. Her own bed and breakfast, which she no longer had. That was all he knew about her. He didn't know her age, if she was in a relationship, or what she now did with her life.

But she was interested in him, he reminded himself as the path curved away from the beach again. The path turned harder, with less sand and more packed earth, and he picked up the pace. There was no mistaking her open, encouraging demeanor for anything but flirtation. Something had changed yesterday's professional reserve into today's warmth. *What?*

His next exhale was a frustrated huff. He tried to focus on once more losing himself in his run, but his thoughts kept returning to Michelle. Sitting across the little table from her, he'd barely been able to keep from reaching for her hand or touching her hair. He'd been so caught up in her presence that the morning was a blur. She'd asked questions about St. Mary's and the other islands, and he'd be damned if he could remember a single one. Even her voice, light and high, with just a hint of a New York accent, had him utterly captivated.

Two weeks was more than enough time for seduction and loving and then parting. There was absolutely nothing wrong with a holiday affair. It was, in fact, *convenient*. No expectations. No commitment. No complaints about Ray's long hours or unexpected missions when he sometimes lost contact with HQ for days or weeks at a time.

That thought made him set his jaw and increase his speed, as if physical exertion could help bring him back to his senses. He didn't want a relationship. He'd never give up his career or his company. His friendship with Preston—his dedication to Preston's ambitions—had been forged in blood and fire, and no woman was worth losing that.

—⁓—

A neat, almost perfect grid of boats filled the gentle arc of the harbor, with more small boats pulled up onto the beach. Michelle had no great talent with photography, but she couldn't resist using her phone to try and capture the postcard-perfect scene. Even the blurry result couldn't dampen her spirits. She'd had too much fun this morning on her impromptu breakfast date.

Could she call it a "date," though? It had felt more like a date than most others she'd been on. Of course, unlike most of her self-absorbed ex-boyfriends, Ray had actually paid attention to her. He'd been so engaging, so *easy* to talk to, that she'd been hard-pressed not to just spill the details of her life story.

He was proof not to judge a book by its cover. Ray Powell was gorgeous, yes, but equally charming and polite. He was no stereotypical hot, self-absorbed, shallow jock. And no matter how dangerous he looked, she'd come to trust him. When he'd left her to go on his run around the island, she hadn't hesitated to relinquish the keys to Valhalla's Rest.

She could still feel his hand against hers, warm and strong. Simple words— *"They'll be in the barbecue when you return"* —had never been spoken in such an inviting tone before. At least not to her.

She was tempted to call Vicky, but she decided to wait. She wanted to keep this moment solely *hers*. She had no idea what would happen next with Ray, but if she so much as hinted how she was feeling, Vicky would pick apart every possibility and analyze everything to death. Already, Michelle knew that the thought of a two-week whirlwind romance in the unlikely paradise of St. Mary's island had lit Vicky's imagination on fire. The pictures she'd found of Ray would only fan the flames. And her enthusiastic suggestions might well overwhelm Michelle's spark of interest.

Instead of calling, she went back to the B and B alone, reveling in the possibilities that she had never thought would open up for her. She lived in Arizona for now, but she'd always loved the East Coast. She'd always intended to return there one day, whether to New York or somewhere else. No matter where she settled, Virginia was centrally located, just a couple of days' drive away.

Just like yesterday, she found the keys in the barbecue, though this time the back door was locked. She felt a stab of disappointment, though Ray had warned her that he wouldn't be back from his run for a couple of hours. The coastal trail was eleven miles, farther than she'd ever consider jogging, at least without training up to it. But she could walk those eleven miles easily, especially with good company to help pass the time— assuming he wanted her company, of course.

Her lips curved up in a slow, interested smile as she considered Ray's physical condition. She couldn't remember the last time she'd seen a man in such good shape. And she'd never found one who was equally interested in her.

But for the moment, at least, theirs was still a professional relationship, no matter how that might change in the future. And she had a B and B to run, sort of. She left her windbreaker in the manager's office, found the master room key, and went upstairs, to the oddly named Serica room. All the rooms had strange names, in fact: Serica, Father Thames, Jane Owen, and so on. She'd have to ask Ray about that.

She was surprised to find he'd left the door unlocked. Tucking the master key back into her pocket, she went in, hoping Ray hadn't made too much of a mess. Of course, he'd arrived with only the clothes on his back and one backpack. There wasn't much for him to scatter around.

And he hadn't. His open backpack was on the corner armchair, and the blankets had been rumpled and then tossed back from one side of the bed. Otherwise, the room was as neat as a pin.

Pleased, she straightened out the bedding and neatly tucked away the top sheet before she rearranged the duvet and pillows. The window closest to the bed was still open; Ray apparently liked the fresh air and light just as much as she did. She went to the other window, spread the drapes wide, and pushed the window open, filling the room with fresh air and light.

She checked the bathroom and saw Ray had hung his towels over the curtain rod, rather than leaving them on the floor for her to launder. All she had to do was wipe down the sink and mirror, check the trash can and toilet paper, and she was done.

His neatness was one more point in his favor. Messes reminded her too much of living with her mother, who'd come to depend on a maid to clean up after her.

Ray wasn't her type. She'd always gravitated toward intellectuals and artists, men who'd spend Saturday night with a good book or watching a classic movie. She'd never even considered dating a soldier—not even an ex-soldier.

Not until now.

Ray had finally pushed his run until he found his quiet zone, that place where the world slipped away, leaving him exhilarated and at peace. The future—Michelle, the bed and breakfast, everything—could wait.

At least until Valhalla's Rest came into view.

Once, its white walls and slate roof had brought him a sense of safety and tranquillity, reminding him of childhood summer holidays. Now, his imagination was filled with warm brown eyes and hair the color of rich espresso and soft pink lips curved up in a welcoming smile. The enticing mental image shattered his relaxation, and the fatigue of his run hit like a truck.

What a bloody complicated mess this "holiday" had become.

He bent over, bracing his hands on his knees, and took a couple of deep breaths. He concentrated on counting his heartbeat. Only when it had slowed a bit did he straighten up and finish the last of his water.

More slowly, he walked through a gap in the hedges, automatically scanning the backyard for any hint of Michelle. He wanted to see her, but he was also uncertain about seeing her, as if her unexpected presence here had been as disruptive, for better or for worse, as Liam's death. He was still drawn to her, a moth to her flame. How close did he dare get before he was burned?

He crossed the springy side lawn to reach the patio, where the keys weren't in the barbecue; the back door was unlocked. He paused in the kitchen long enough to refill his water bottle, then headed through the dining room. He needed a shower and a change of clothes, assuming he had any that were clean.

He made it one step into the sitting room before he stopped, staring at one of the sofas by the cold fireplace. Michelle was sleeping there, head pillowed on a folded quilt, feet up on the other arm. Sunlight streamed through the window, picking out amber highlights in her deep brown hair. Ray's lips twitched up into a smile when he saw her bright blue socks had snowmen on them, of all things. In the middle of summer.

For a few silent, peaceful seconds, he watched her sleep. His fingers itched to brush her hair back from her face. He hadn't noticed how tense she'd been earlier. Now, she was relaxed. The faint worry lines had smoothed from her face. Her lips had parted slightly, and he caught himself staring at the soft curve of her mouth.

Bloody creep, he scolded himself, tearing his gaze from her. He made his quiet way across the room before realizing she probably wouldn't thank him for sneaking about unexpectedly. She clearly hadn't expected any guests, and if she was the type to awaken disoriented, he'd startle her.

Just as silently, he retraced his steps into the kitchen, where he opened the back door, only to close it more loudly. At the sink, he ran the water for a few seconds, topping off his water bottle. Then, not knowing if she was a heavy sleeper, he took the ice tray out of the freezer and gave it a sharp crack to make even more noise. He let a few pieces fall into the bottle and then screwed the cap back into place.

This time, when he walked through the dining room, he saw her sitting up, running one hand through her hair to brush it out of her eyes. When she saw him, she smiled, warm and inviting.

"Ray?" she asked, her voice soft with sleep.

He'd meant to keep his distance. To head upstairs for a shower. To put her out of his mind. If he couldn't have her for a brief holiday fling, he didn't want her at all, for fear of becoming completely ensnared.

He'd always been strong-willed—stubborn, people would say. Now, though, all it took was a smile and quiet word to shatter his careful plans.

Instead of climbing the stairs, he went into the sitting room, and the only reason he kept his distance was that he really did want to shower before getting too close to her.

"Sorry if I woke you," he said as he sat down across the coffee table from her.

"No, it's fine. I just meant to close my eyes for a few minutes..." She laughed, looking down at herself. She subtly stretched, rolling her shoulders. Momentary tension in her jaw betrayed her effort to hide a yawn. "There's something about this island that encourages laziness."

Ray smiled encouragingly, wondering when she'd last allowed herself to truly relax. Already, she was going tense again, as if her awakening meant she had to take up some heavy burden once more. Gently, he reminded her, "It wouldn't be much of a holiday otherwise."

"Says the man who just ran eleven miles for fun," she teased.

He grinned, thinking of the views from the cliffs and the empty beaches he'd passed on his run. Even at the height of the season, most tourists were off taking the boats to the other islands in a fervor to see everything Scilly had to offer. Despite St. Mary's being Scilly's largest island and the transportation hub, many of the beaches were deserted. Private.

"Come with me tomorrow," he invited, forgetting all about his plan to stay away from her. "Not a run— we'll walk."

He saw the way her eyes lit up, as if she'd been hoping for just such an invitation, even though she politely said, "If you're in training for a marathon or something, I don't want to interfere."

"Not at all. I run to keep a step ahead of the puppies, not for fun. Or, well, not just for fun."

"Puppies?"

He shook his head. "Our new recruits. Most are fresh out of the military and determined to prove themselves. If we don't put them in their place, they might do something reckless on a job, and there's no room for error in the field."

Her smile faded; she tilted her head thoughtfully and curled up against the arm of the couch. "It sounds dangerous."

Ray took a sip of his water, thinking fast. Since his earliest days with the Royal Marines, he'd used his profession to his advantage. Some women, he'd learned, were attracted to the thrill of danger, though Michelle didn't seem to be that type. He didn't want to impress her; he wanted to *protect* her, to keep her separate from the harsh reality of war, but he also didn't want to deceive her.

"It is," he said simply. "We do everything we can to minimize the risks, but we operate in some of the most dangerous places in the world. It's our job to take risks."

Her eyes flicked to his arm, one brow raised questioningly.

He heard her unspoken words and nodded in response. "It was worth it," he answered quietly, bracing for her demand to know more. If they did have that conversation, she might not like what she learned, but she'd be strong enough to hopefully understand.

But instead of asking for ugly details that had no place on this holiday, she smiled again and let the subject drop. "Did you have plans for dinner? I could cook," she offered.

"No plans at all," he said, pleasure warming him at the offer—and at the lack of condemnation for his chosen career. His work tended to be polarizing; people either found it too exciting for his comfort or too violent for their own. "We could go out, if you'd prefer. There's no need to trouble yourself."

"It's no trouble. I like cooking." Her eyes narrowed playfully as she added, "Given what you had for breakfast, I assume you're not vegan or gluten-sensitive."

He couldn't quite hide a flinch. "Not even close." It took him a moment to remember she'd ordered waffles for breakfast. "You're not, are you?"

"Absolutely not."

He let his grin turn challenging. "Well, if you could match my grandmother's recipe for roast beef and Yorkshire pudding, I'd rob the bloody Royal Treasury to pay you."

Her laugh filled the sitting room with delight. "I've never met a recipe I couldn't beat."

"Then I'll find it for you, and we'll go shopping for the ingredients tomorrow or the day after. We'll see if you can out-cook my grandmother."

"No disrespect to your grandmother, but..." She grinned wickedly. "You're on."

⁓

That night, dinner proved to be delicate baked sea bass on a bed of sautéed spinach and wild rice. Ray knew he was missing intricacies to the flavor, but it was all he could do to not tear through his first helping and go for seconds. Possibly thirds.

To slow himself down, he sipped white wine between

bites, though he said nothing until he'd cleared his plate. "This is fantastic."

Michelle glowed and immediately lifted another piece of fish out of the serving dish. "Thank you. After so many years in the Hamptons, fish are a specialty."

"It's perfect," he said truthfully. "And growing up here means I'm an expert, so you can't even argue." That got him a laugh and a flush of color in her cheeks.

She'd almost finished her own serving, so Ray didn't feel like an ogre for digging in once more. He'd never liked dinners with women who picked at a small salad and insisted they weren't hungry, as if hoping to impress him with their talents for self-deprivation. Privately, he suspected they gorged themselves before or after the meal, ridiculous as the thought was.

"Speaking of 'here,'" she said thoughtfully, lifting a forkful of rice, "is there a meaning to the names of the rooms upstairs?"

The question caught him by surprise, though in retrospect, it shouldn't have. She probably hadn't planned her trip to Scilly as a tourist. "We'll have to go to the Abbey Gardens before the holiday is over. The rooms are all named for ships—shipwrecks, actually. The Abbey Garden on Tresco Island has a museum of figureheads. It's called the Valhalla collection."

"Ah, that makes sense. I suspected there was a theme to it." She picked up the bottle of wine and gave him a questioning look.

With a nod of thanks, he held out his glass for her to refill. "I suppose Liam had to choose between shipwrecks, flowers, or birds. You've seen the flower fields here?"

She topped off her own glass and hinted, "I wouldn't mind seeing more."

"Tomorrow," he promised.

"And the birds?"

"Scilly is on the path for their migration. You can see birdwatchers out and about all the time. I've never been interested, myself, I'll admit."

She smiled. "Birds aren't really my thing, either. Though feel free to make up the names of any birds we do see. I won't know if you're cheating."

He laughed, delighted with her sense of humor. "I'll keep it in mind," he teased. "So what's it like in the Hamptons? I've never been there before."

Her smile faded a touch. "Touristy in the summer, deserted in the winter, kind of like here, I suppose, though without the palm trees. It's built up, too—a lot of luxury properties." She shrugged, dragging the tines of her fork through her fish. "The beach is nice."

Mentally kicking himself, he quickly changed the subject, hoping not to lose the cheerful mood completely. "I've only been to Manhattan and upstate New York, and then only briefly. And I've never been west of the Mississippi."

"I've been staying in Arizona lately." Her lips curved up in a wry smile. "Two words: brown and hot."

Images of the Peshawar mission flickered through Ray's consciousness. He sipped his wine and took a breath of cool island air blowing in through the open windows. "Then we're definitely walking the coastal path tomorrow. You're probably craving green plants and blue water."

She laughed and lifted her glass in agreement. "How did you guess?"

"My work takes me to the desert all too often."

"Oh." Her smile shifted, sympathy showing in her expression. "You mean…"

"Pakistan, last time. Not the nice parts." He left out any mention of the not-entirely-legal crossing into Afghanistan, the two days they'd spent in Jalalabad, and the tense, terrifying trip back. They'd survived. That was all that mattered.

"Are you…" She set down her glass and gestured at Ray's arm. "Was that where that happened?"

He nodded, giving her a reassuring smile. "It really is just a scratch. Our field medics tend to overdo it to keep our insurance rates down, preventing secondary infections and the like."

She let out a disbelieving huff and broke off a piece of her fish. "And you never ignore your injuries so you can keep doing…whatever," she challenged, gesturing with her fork before she took a bite.

Ray watched her eyes fall closed as she savored the taste of the fish. Her tongue darted out to catch a drop of the white wine and garlic sauce on her bottom lip. He quickly looked down at his plate before she could catch him staring.

"The mission comes first. It always has. But," he continued, holding up a finger when she went to speak, "I take care of myself well enough between jobs. I'm here, aren't I?"

"Yes. And you go on eleven-mile runs for fun," she accused, eyes sparkling.

"You just wait until tomorrow. You'll see why," he countered slyly. "But tonight…"

She tipped her head, smile turning curious. "Tonight?"

"Tonight, I'd like to show you one of the island's secrets. It's right out back."

She stared at him, and he knew she was most likely reviewing what she'd seen of the property out back. It was admittedly beautiful, with a lawn sweeping right to the flower beds by the cliff, a neglected vegetable garden, and trees acting as a windbreak. Of course, he wasn't thinking of any of those things, so he held her gaze knowingly and let her thoughts run wild with speculation.

"All right," she finally said. She picked up her glass and took a sip, asking, "Won't it be cold?"

"Possibly, so wear a warm jacket," he said innocently, knowing she probably thought he'd chosen some romantic, isolated spot to seduce her.

He was right. Her brows twitched up, and she blinked. "All right," she repeated, this time more thoughtfully. "Surprise me."

Chapter 6

Sunday, July 7

AFTER DINNER, RAY INSISTED ON HELPING WITH THE dishes before he went upstairs to get ready. Michelle went into the manager's apartment, where she changed into a warm sweater and walking shoes. Then she brushed out her hair and spent some time to tame it into a neat ponytail.

What could Ray possibly have planned?

She studied her reflection in the mirror as she touched up her lip gloss, telling herself it was protection against the wind rather than an attempt to bolster her self-confidence. She always felt plain without a hint of color on her lips—certainly too plain to catch the eye of someone like Ray Powell.

Somehow, though, she *had* caught his eye. Maybe it was lack of competition, she admitted as she leaned closer to the mirror to see if her eyeliner had smudged. Was Ray settling for her? Did he think she was an easy target, conveniently sharing the same roof? She didn't think so, but when it came to men, her instincts weren't infallible. Not by a long shot.

Back in college, no one had bothered to look twice at plain, boring Michelle, once Vicky and Dana had shown up. *But they're not here*, a voice whispered in the back of her head. A flutter of excitement shot through her. Just because there was no one to compete with her didn't mean she couldn't take advantage of the clear playing field.

The thought of having Ray all to herself was...well, *appealing* didn't seem like a strong enough word for it.

She gave her reflection an encouraging nod and then headed into the main room to find her jacket. It was a little light, but with the sweater, she hoped she'd be warm enough. And if not, there was always Ray to provide a sheltering arm and a little shared body warmth, right?

Still, there was no point in *being* an easy target, whether he thought she was or not. She could enjoy his company, even bask in his attention, and make sure things progressed no faster than *she* wanted.

She zipped up her jacket and went to meet Ray in the kitchen, where he'd turned off all the lights except the one closest to the dining room doorway. He'd put on his leather jacket, though he left it open over the polo shirt he'd worn at dinner.

"Ready?" he asked.

"As ready as I can be," she answered. Her heart skipped a beat at the way he smiled at her—as if she truly was worth smiling at. "What's the plan?"

He walked toward her with slow, easy steps, his smile friendly, and held out his hand. "Close your eyes."

Her breath caught as the night's possibilities turned even more intimate than she'd imagined. "Sorry, what?"

"It's a secret, remember?"

Every instinct urged her to get more information about his plans for her—to coax, to ask, even to demand, if necessary—but she reminded herself that not everything in life had to be planned. Not everything had to be safe and certain.

She set her hand in his, shivering as strong fingers closed gently around hers. His hand was rough with calluses; his skin burned against her, through her, until the shiver turned into a flush of warmth that reached deep inside.

Closing her eyes was a relief, a retreat into darkness. She felt self-conscious, but at least the darkness offered a measure of privacy, as if hiding her eyes helped to hide her thoughts.

A gentle touch got her moving. He guided her around the breakfast bar and then warned, "Mind your step," as he led her out onto the patio. "Reach out. The handrail is to your right."

She groped in the darkness until her fingers touched the wooden railing. Her other hand tightened on his. Together, they walked slowly down the steps and into the grass. Her footing was uncertain. She pressed closer to his side, and he slowed down, allowing her to set their pace.

The night was silent except for the soft sigh of the wind and the song of crickets all around them. The grass underfoot was too soft for her to hear their footsteps. Disoriented by the darkness, she quickly lost track of time as well as direction.

"Where—"

"*Shh*," he interrupted gently, giving her hand a reassuring squeeze. "Not far now."

Not far for him, perhaps, but to her, it felt as if they walked forever. Surely they'd gone beyond the boundaries of the property. She wanted to open her eyes, but she felt compelled to play by the rules. Even like this, she trusted him.

Underfoot, the sound of grass changed. The ground sloped gently upward. She racked her brain to orient herself, but she hadn't explored the area around the B and B thoroughly enough to know where they were.

This time, her shiver was edged with fear. He must have felt it; he squeezed her hand again and said, "Almost there."

"Almost *where*?" she hinted.

His answering laugh was low and wicked, lighting fires in her imagination. Even the threat of darkness and danger seemed more thrilling than ominous.

By the time they reached level ground again, she was a touch breathless and dying of curiosity. He stopped and said, "Sit down. There's a blanket right in front of you. Eyes closed, still. No cheating."

She huffed in mock frustration and lowered herself to a careful crouch. When she reached out, she felt a thick blanket spread over the grass. When had he put it there? What did he have planned?

"A dessert picnic?" she guessed nervously, warily trying to feel for any plates or glasses. When she didn't encounter any, her stomach gave another anxious, excited little flip.

He laughed. "Sorry, no. We can get a picnic lunch tomorrow, if you like." She heard him moving beside her and felt the tug of the blanket under her hands. "Lie down, on your back."

Suspicion flared, freezing her in place, but underneath it, her heart raced. She could imagine how it would feel to lie back on the cool grass, the ocean breeze sliding over her skin, as Ray leaned close over her, touching her, kissing…

Yes or no?

She swallowed, pushing aside her nervousness, and eased herself down to the blanket, making the decision in silence. She wanted Ray. Whether this was a one-night stand, a vacation fling, or something more, she was attracted to him.

Attracted. She nearly laughed at the thought. That was putting it mildly.

She rolled over onto her back and listened to his movements, trying to place his exact position. Her skin tingled with awareness, as if the air between them crackled with energy.

"Ray," slipped out, though she hadn't realized she'd drawn breath to speak.

"Honorable intentions, I promise," Ray answered softly.

Disappointment struck, but only a little. Sexual or not, the night still felt intimate, a secret for just the two of them to share. She was grateful for the darkness that hid her blush. Lying on her back, she found herself very self-conscious of how exposed her body was. She had to fight to keep her eyes closed.

Beside her, she heard Ray move once more. She suspected he was lying down beside her. Though they were no longer touching, she imagined she could feel the warmth of his body even through their jackets.

After he'd gone still, he said, "Open your eyes, Michelle."

Taking a deep breath, she braced for darkness, thinking it would take time for her vision to adjust. Then she opened her eyes.

She gasped at the sight of the infinite night sky

stretching all around her, full of more stars than she'd ever imagined. A thick swath of them striped the night with silver from horizon to horizon, as far as she could see. Without even a hint of moonlight as competition, the stars glowed brightly against the velvet sky. She turned her head just slightly, and the world seemed to tilt and twist around her as, in her peripheral vision, more stars burst into view.

"Oh," she breathed, captivated. She'd seen pictures of the night sky like this, free of the light pollution from cities, but photos couldn't do this sight justice, and she'd never actually witnessed it for herself. Even at her mother's house, Phoenix was too close, too bright for her to see more than a handful of stars by comparison.

Ray made a quiet, affirmative sound but didn't speak. Not that she could blame him. She had no words that could possibly express how she felt.

He'd thought of this. For *her*. Out of countless ways he could have tried to seduce her, he chose this instead. Not a romantic dessert at one of the island restaurants, not cuddling on a bench looking out at the night-dark sea, but *this*.

It was so perfect, so romantic, it stole her breath. He wasn't touching her, pulling her close to cuddle and take advantage of the ambiance. This was his gift to her, not a scheme to seduce her.

She stared up at the sky until the ground seemed to tremble beneath her body. Vertigo hit suddenly, as if she were moments from flying off the earth and falling into the darkness between the stars. She closed her eyes tightly and licked her lips, tasting her lip gloss. Her fingers clenched. Fabric bunched around her left hand, but she felt solid, hard heat beneath her right.

Tentatively, she twitched her fingers and felt hot skin. Soft hair. Hard muscle.

When had she grabbed Ray's arm?

She told herself to let go, but the most she could do was slide her hand down, following the contour of Ray's wrist to his hand. She still felt an irrational fear of falling up into the depthless sky, foolish as it was.

But he didn't laugh at her. Given how she'd clenched his arm in desperation, he had to know she'd been surprised and disoriented. Slowly, he turned his hand over, fingers spread. She exhaled, feeling both steadier and dizzier, and allowed her fingers to lace with his.

The stars were still there, but the infinite night was no longer threatening. Her hand rested atop Ray's, supported by his gentle strength, anchoring her without holding her back.

She smiled and breathed deeply, calmly, and curled her fingers around Ray's. This, she thought as she stared up at the sky, was much better than seduction.

Growing up, the low hilltop had been Ray's favorite place to escape the family and watch the stars. It was right off the walking trail that cut through the property, but the path was hidden unless you knew what to look for. When he'd rushed out to set up the blanket, he'd nearly missed the turnoff; he would have, without the flashlight that was safely tucked away in his pocket.

He'd decided to bring her here on a whim. Much as he loved the waters around the island, the night sky—the cloudless night sky, when the moon was dark—was what he loved the most here on St. Mary's. And as far as he was concerned, this spot, this hilltop, was the best place for stargazing anywhere on the island.

Even as a teenager, when he'd gone on dates with tourists or locals, he'd never shown anyone this secret hilltop. He'd never wanted to sprawl under the sky with a beautiful woman and *not* take advantage of the opportunity for seduction. How many nights had he spent on the beaches and hills of Scilly ignoring the stars completely in favor of a promising date?

Tonight, a part of him thought he should do just that. He should roll over and touch her jaw to turn her face toward him. He should lean in to kiss her—softly at first, and then with growing heat, until she was gasping beneath him.

Two weeks. The thought was preying on him, a deadline that ticked closer with every breath. So why wasn't he moving things along?

Her hand was small and warm, her fingers perfectly formed, her skin as soft as silk. Her grip on him was neither limp nor clenching tight. She was strong, for someone so slender, so small.

He held her hand with care, very much aware of his own strength, guiltily thinking he should have warned her about the vertigo of staring up at the night sky unprepared. It still affected him, though he'd been ready for it, and his moment of disorientation had passed unnoticed.

But they both remained silent, joined only by their hands and their focus on the stars overhead. Ray rubbed his thumb over her skin, keeping his touch light and undemanding. He felt a shiver pass through her arm. She still didn't try to pull away.

A little thrill of excitement passed through him. Slow seduction had never been his style, but he was already enthralled with the idea of taking his time with her.

In fact, he had no interest in coaxing Michelle into his bed tonight—or if he did, it was lost beyond the greater reward of building something more, as if this night were simply the foundation to what they could have together.

The thought was jarring.

Ray stared up at the sky, fighting his own sense of vertigo, not from the hypnotic pull of the stars but from something far more fundamental inside himself. He didn't *need* that sort of foundation on which to build a relationship, because he didn't *want* a relationship. Did he?

And if he did, surely it wouldn't be with a woman who was essentially a stranger, no matter how her smile filled him with warmth or how perfectly she fit against him or how clever she was in conversation.

He bit back a sigh at his own foolishness. Apparently, that was precisely his intent.

He had less than two weeks to get to know her. If it came to nothing, he'd still have had his two-week holiday. And if it didn't, he'd have her, too.

———

"You're getting cold."

Ray's soft words didn't shatter the silence on the hilltop so much as ease Michelle out of her relaxed state of bliss. She blinked away from the stars and turned her head. Though her eyes had adjusted to the darkness, she could barely see him, even inches away.

"I'm fine," she lied, fingers pressing against his hand. In truth, their joined hands were the only point of warmth in her whole body. She couldn't bear the thought of breaking the night's tenuous spell—of releasing Ray's hand and losing this gentle intimacy.

He laughed quietly, squeezing her fingers in return. "You're shivering."

"It's a little chilly," she admitted. Instead of answering, he turned away and spread his fingers as if to let go. She clenched his hand, asking, "What? Where are you going?"

He stopped trying to pull away, though he didn't settle back down beside her. "I just want to give you the blanket," he said, as if it should have been obvious.

Her sudden blush drove away the chill in her face, all the way to the tip of her nose. "It's not *that* cold."

He moved away without releasing her hand. "Chivalry is part of my heritage. Indulge me?"

Laughing, she relented and allowed him to tug the blanket into place over her body. He finally did let go of her hand, only to move opposite where the blanket's fold so he could take her other hand without pulling her arm from beneath the fabric. Then he lay back down in the grass, squeezed her hand, and asked, "Better?"

Warmed all the way to her toes—and not by the blanket—she nodded and grinned up at the stars. "Thank you."

Cozy and content, Michelle tried to lose herself in the beauty of the stars, but Ray's presence tugged at her thoughts. He made no demands for conversation or attention, but the feel of his hand and the weight of the blanket combined to turn Michelle's thoughts solely to him.

Conscious that he was lying unprotected on the cold earth, she finally rolled onto her side to face him. "We should go back."

His silhouette shifted as he turned toward her. "If you'd like."

"We can come back tomorrow," she suggested, pushing the blanket aside so she could sit up.

He rose with her, catching the blanket without releasing her hand. "After dinner?" he suggested as they worked together to fold the blanket into a manageable bundle. "There's a restaurant overlooking the harbor. I thought you might like the view." He let go of her so he could tuck the blanket under his arm.

"Mmm, I can't wait."

After a click, a circle of red light appeared on the grass, turning the leaves black. The light was muted enough that it didn't sting her eyes. "Here, take the torch," he offered.

She took the cold metal flashlight and swept the light around the area. The hill was smaller than she'd suspected, with low shrubbery around the perimeter. "The light, the blanket... You really did plan this out, didn't you?"

"Shouldn't I have done?" He sounded surprised.

"No. I mean, yes." She shook her head, remembering disastrous outings with friends and dates—running out of gas in the middle of nowhere, closed venues, and even bad weather that could've been predicted with a simple Internet search. Eventually, Michelle had taken all the planning responsibility for herself. She believed firmly in contingency planning.

"Thanks for clearing that up," Ray teased.

Michelle laughed and swung the flashlight around, trying to find the path off the hilltop. With her free hand, she reached tentatively for Ray; when he clasped his fingers around hers, a little thrill went through her body. "I'm always the one doing the planning. Whether it's menus or budgeting or putting together tour packages…"

"Supplies and logistics, mission planning, visa and travel arrangements," he said, giving her a gentle tug in the right direction.

Squeezing his hand, she started walking, keeping the light where it could benefit them both. "Maybe," she teased, "but could you plan a winery tour for twelve dear old ladies at their fortieth high school reunion without having it end in drunk and disorderly arrests *en masse*?"

His laugh was loud and rich. "I wouldn't dare try. I'll leave that to the experts."

With the aid of the flashlight, they made it to the B and B grounds without incident. Their eyes had adjusted to the darkness, and the single light burning between the kitchen and dining room filled the patio doorway with a soft, welcoming glow.

But as they approached the patio stairs, Michelle slowed her steps. She wanted to preserve the night, to capture the fragile closeness she felt with Ray, to hold it tight against whatever tomorrow might bring.

She was, in fact, tempted to invite him to her room— or to go with him to his room, given the narrow single bed in the manager's apartment. She could almost hear

Vicky's voice urging her to seize the moment, to let her hair down. To live a little.

That wasn't her way, but she could…adapt. With a little smile, she stopped two steps up the stairs and turned. With Ray still on the grass, they were nearly the same height. She smiled at him and slipped the flashlight into his jacket pocket, but then her courage faltered. She couldn't just lean into his arms and steal a kiss.

"Thank you for tonight," she said, inching forward to the very edge of the step, hoping he'd read her intent and meet her halfway.

He put one foot on the bottom step and draped the blanket over the stairway railing. "Thank you for trusting me to surprise you," he said, lifting his now-free hand to her face.

The touch stole her breath, sparking heat across her cold skin. She closed her eyes and tipped her head, pressing against his fingers.

And then she felt his lips on hers, deceptively soft and undemanding, though she felt the strength coiled behind that gentle touch. Her lips parted on a sharp inhale that he stole, the heat of their breath mixing, captive between them. His hand slid back through strands that had fallen free of her ponytail, cupping her nape. Shivers raced through her body, and she lifted up on her toes to lean even closer, bracing her free hand on his chest. His jacket was like ice under her palm, but the leather was soft, pliant, barely hiding the powerful chest underneath.

He chased her gasp with his tongue, a soft swipe across her bottom lip as if he were tasting her. Vertigo hit more powerfully than it had under the infinite stars.

She slid her hand up over his shoulder to hold his nape, seeking his strength, his steadiness.

Keeping his fingers entwined with hers, he dropped his other hand from her hair. His arm wrapped around her body, forearm fitted against the curve of her back. She sighed into the kiss, inviting him deeper. He didn't refuse.

Their tongues touched for a single heartbeat. Parted. Touched again. He drew back and tipped his head the other way as he pulled her close against his chest, her toes now barely touching the edge of the stair. She held tightly, trusting his strength more than her own sense of balance, and gave in to the kiss with a sense of greedy indulgence she'd never before felt.

The raw power of him was a drug to her senses. There was no hesitation in him, no wavering in his intent. Everything she offered, he claimed.

Only when she pulled back, dazed, did he ease his hold on her body. He settled her back down onto the step, fingers trailing beneath the hem of her jacket to her hip before falling away. His eyes, so brilliantly blue in sunlight, had turned dark with desire, fixed on her so keenly that she shivered.

Predator, a little voice whispered, reminding her that she was playing with fire. Had *she* really been the one to ask for his breath-stealing, toe-curling kiss? She wouldn't trade it for the world, but how much more did she dare ask for?

Tonight, nothing. She needed space to think, to regain more than her physical footing. Her equilibrium was shattered. Had she ever been so aroused—so *inspired*—by a single kiss?

Their hands were still joined, her right in his left. She looked down and relaxed her fingers; he took the hint and released her hand. The night's wind stole the warmth from her skin, chilling her to the bones.

When she looked back up, their gazes met. The predator was still there, lurking in his eyes, in the way one corner of his mouth was lifted. All she had to do was to step forward, even just to lean forward, and she knew he'd have her in his arms. And this time, he wouldn't let her go.

"Good night," she said, her voice ragged.

His lips curved into a smile too subtle to be called sly, but she suspected he could read every one of her thoughts. That he knew precisely what effect he'd had on her.

"Sleep well," he said, his voice dropped down into a low growl that fanned the flames beneath her skin to new heights.

Before her composure could break, she turned and walked up two steps, across the patio, and into the kitchen. She made it all the way to the dining room doorway before a shudder hit, and she broke into a run that didn't stop until she was safely alone in the manager's apartment, with two doors between her and temptation.

Chapter 7

RAY AWOKE LATE, HIS EYES GRITTY, MUSCLES ACHING, after a night plagued with visions and dreams of Michelle. The Serica room was in the back corner of the guest wing, over the manager's apartment. Unless Liam had redecorated before his death or Michelle had moved the furniture, her bed was directly beneath where Ray slept.

What did she wear to bed? Was she bundled warmly in a nightgown or pajamas? Did she prefer a silky camisole? An adorably oversized T-shirt? Or nothing at all?

That thought was its own special sort of torture, and he couldn't help but wonder what happened to the idea that virtue brought rewards. He'd certainly been virtuous enough last night when he'd let her go with nothing more than a kiss.

Nothing more than a kiss, he thought, lips curving up in a wicked smile. The kiss had blazed through them both, threatening to incinerate Ray's self-control, if not hers as well, judging by how she'd clung to him. That kiss had been more intense—more consuming—than most of the one-night stands in his past. One-night stands that had, until now, always been more than enough to satisfy him.

His smile faded at the realization of just how much

more he wanted from her. He didn't just want to taste her body. He wanted to study her, to learn everything that made her gasp and tremble and sigh in contentment. He wanted to take her apart, to drive her out of her own mind and so deep into her own body that she couldn't think—only feel.

More than that, though, he wanted to know *everything* about her. Polite, superficial conversation or witty flirtation wasn't enough. As much as he wanted to know her body, he wanted to know everything else about her—to know her past and present, her plans for life, even her favorite dessert. And he wanted to share even more with her, just as they'd shared the stars last night.

That realization was more than a little terrifying. He didn't commit. He *liked* his way of life. He liked being able to go where he wanted without having to report to anyone but Preston or his scheduling secretary. He liked having the freedom to move out of his apartment if he got bored or accidentally set the kitchen on fire—and he definitely preferred to be yelled at by an angry building superintendent than an angry girlfriend. He'd had enough of the latter in his past.

Should he cling to his freedom or gamble on Michelle?

Fortunately, years of experience helped him to remember that he shouldn't go making decisions on little sleep and no caffeine. He got out of bed, dropped to the floor, and was so distracted by thoughts of Michelle that he made it through three push-ups before the pain of his stitches reminded him he was a bloody idiot. Gritting his teeth against the sharp pain, he sat up and looked closely at the wound. Thankfully, the surgical tape had kept the stitches from pulling through his skin.

Instead of pressing his luck with more push-ups, he turned onto his back and folded his hands behind his head. Stomach crunches, sit-ups, and squats did nothing to help put thoughts of Michelle out of his mind, but he felt more awake after he was done.

A shower drove away the last of his sleepiness, especially since he didn't wait for the water heater to kick in. He swallowed his last antibiotic tablet and then picked up his cell phone. Out of habit, he'd brought it with him into the bathroom. He used a corner of his towel to wipe the screen dry, then opened his private email account. Almost no one had that address, so it loaded quickly, despite the poor local connection.

He opened a new message to Preston, using both his work and personal email addresses:

Done with antibiotics. Tell Doc I'm fine. Had a great date last night. Enjoy the Monday morning budget meeting.

Grinning, he sent it and then put his phone on the counter to let it sync with the mail server. He wiped condensation off the mirror and leaned in close, studying his face. The last of the cuts had healed to thin lines that would soon disappear. He considered shaving, but he was feeling too damned lazy this morning. Besides, he was on holiday.

Being on holiday was no excuse for living like a vagabond, though. He went back into the bedroom, dropped the phone on his dresser, and went to his backpack.

The last of his clean clothes were still shoved down

at the bottom of the pack, along with his ruined dress shoes, a pair of black wool socks, and perhaps the strangest post-mission souvenir he'd ever had. He put the dress shoes on the floor, nudged them under the bed, and then refolded his clean clothes and put them in a drawer. He dumped everything else onto his bed and then shook the backpack out over the trash can. Sand, gum wrappers, and tufts of fur from Preston's two German shepherds fell out.

Then he grimaced at the mess. If Michelle caught him living like this, she might well throw him out of Valhalla's Rest altogether.

It was time to at least pretend to be a civilized adult, he decided. He dressed as neatly as he could, shoved his dirty clothes into the backpack, and ran a comb through his hair before heading downstairs. He'd ask about doing laundry, but not until tomorrow. Today, he looked forward to getting to know Michelle.

Michelle trapped the phone between her ear and the pillow, listening to it ring, and bundled herself down into her warm nest of blankets. As soon as she heard an answering click, she said, "Good morning, Vicky."

"Well, aren't you just cheerful?" Vicky sounded stressed, though not tired. It was just before eight in the morning, which meant she'd already had one cup of tea and two shots of espresso, if her old habits still held true. "You *are* cheerful. Why?"

Grinning foolishly, Michelle said, "No reason. I think you can stop looking."

"Looking. Looking at—" Vicky cut off. "*Oh*. Well,

then, have we had some new revelation about your gorgeous Mr. Powell?"

"*We* have decided that he's a perfectly nice hotel guest, and *we* don't think he's associated with any real estate agency or land speculator or criminal enterprise at all," Michelle declared. She nearly burst out giggling before she caught herself, horrified at the thought. She didn't *giggle*. Not in college, not in high school, probably not since the fourth-grade school play, when she'd been costumed as a floppy-eared dog and had to chase her teacher while barking as loud as she could.

"I see," Vicky declared, voice thick with suspicion. "Is he there with you now? *Ray, darling! Are you there?*" she shouted.

Michelle jerked her head away from the phone. "Vicky!"

"You didn't throw the poor lad out of bed after you were finished with him, did you? That's not done, Chelly."

Michelle sighed and dropped her head back onto the phone. "Have I told you what a horrible person you are lately?"

"No, but you did so frequently in college, you've got extras banked." Vicky laughed, this time free of teasing. "Are you enjoying your holiday? *Really* enjoying it?"

Last night, Michelle had slept better than she had in months—better than she had since her last night in Anchor's Cove, in fact. She'd dreamed of stars and the powerful strength of Ray's body and the sweetly romantic, scorching hot kiss. "Yes. I am," she answered simply.

"Good. Then I can stop worrying about you and get back to planning my meeting later today."

Michelle smirked. "I think I can handle this all by myself. Good luck with your meeting."

"And good luck with your—*ahem*—handling."

As Vicky hung up, Michelle rolled her eyes and turned onto her back. She grinned up at the ceiling, listening to the pipes rattle. She'd awakened to the creak of Ray's bed only a few feet straight above where she slept. As she'd stared up at the ceiling, she'd tried to use sound to determine what he was doing, but her brain had stalled with the realization that she hadn't seen any pajamas in his room. Not even sweats. So either he slept in his boxer briefs or...

She grinned wickedly, wondering what sort of shopping she could find on the islands. She hadn't been expecting company when she'd packed an oversized T-shirt and leggings as sleepwear. Maybe she could find something less dumpy if she went into town by herself.

But Ray had wanted to walk the island today—an idea that sounded surprisingly fun. Her original plan had been to spend today and tomorrow going into the B and B's books in depth, but as much as she enjoyed imposing order on chaos, she'd be perfectly happy to spend the day with Ray instead.

Valhalla's Rest had two substantial water heaters, so she took her time and indulged in a long, leisurely hot shower. She'd packed minimal makeup; mascara and sheer peach lip gloss would do for today. If they went out tonight, she could touch up to match whatever outfit she chose for the evening.

At least she had a decent wardrobe here. After losing almost everything but the clothes on her back at Anchor's Cove, her mother had insisted on spending a solid week shopping. They'd gone from the boutiques of Sedona to the designer shops at Biltmore Fashion Park and then down to Tucson, and Michelle had found herself with more clothes than she'd owned in the last five years. Her mother had encouraged—bullied, really—her into breaking free of her usual casual-conservative style, and she now had a wardrobe full of bold, stylish clothes.

"Thanks, Mom," she whispered as she turned in front of the mirror, regarding her printed bronze and brown T-shirt. It perfectly matched her distressed leather shorts. She'd bring along an olive green jacket in case it got windy and a wide-brimmed hat. Her mother had bought her a Coach wristlet, the perfect size for her lip gloss, phone, and credit card.

She debated wearing cute flats, but her sensible side won out. She put on sneakers, then picked up her windbreaker and left the office with a spring in her step.

She found Ray in the kitchen, looking unfairly gorgeous in a silky-soft V-neck T-shirt that made her fingers itch to pet his chest. She dragged her gaze down, only to have her eyes lock onto blue jeans that fit him like a second skin, worn in all the right places. With effort, she looked back up into his eyes, and she blushed at his sly, crooked smile.

"Good morning," he said with a hint of laughter in his voice.

"Morning," she answered as cheerfully as she could manage. She looked away, trying to find anything to distract her. The electric kettle was rattling softly on the counter beside a mug with a tea bag already in it.

"I hope you don't mind, but I started water for tea."

"No problem," she said, trying to suppress a thrill of

anticipation as she walked over to the kettle, close to where Ray was lounging against the counter. After last night, would he want a good morning kiss? Would it be quick and sweet, or another sudden brushfire?

Hiding a grin, she started to make coffee, thinking either would be just fine with her. They weren't on a schedule. If they spent half the morning making out in the kitchen—or maybe *more*—she certainly wouldn't complain.

He stayed where he was, just outside of arm's reach, but the intensity of his gaze burned her skin. "If you can hold off on breakfast or just eat something light, I have an idea for brunch. It'll only add a couple of miles to our walk, but I think you'll enjoy it."

The way he said it—the way he looked at her, his blue eyes full of wicked humor—made her wonder if "brunch" had anything to do with food at all.

Heart pounding, she smiled and closed the distance between them. Without looking away from her eyes, he lifted his hand and rested it on her hip. The warm touch was already comfortable. Familiar.

"I'd like that," she said, and tipped her face up in invitation.

He accepted, leaning down to give her the slow, sweet kiss she'd imagined. She closed her eyes and shivered in delight at the touch of his lips, the soft brush of his tongue against hers. His heart beat strong and fast beneath her palm.

When the kiss broke, she stepped away and met his smile with her own. She couldn't remember the last time she'd been this content with the world, and she nearly burst out laughing out of sheer happiness. "Is toast all right?" she offered, turning back to the coffeepot. Brunch or not, she'd still need one cup.

"Toast sounds perfect," he answered with a quiet laugh that made her grin even more.

—⁓—

Old Town was a small collection of homes and shops clustered by the airport. Ray brought Michelle to a café there, where they picked up scones and freshly baked sausage-and-bacon pasties. "Trust me, you'll enjoy it," he assured her, seeing her skeptical frown.

"What exactly *is* a pasty?" she asked, watching as he put everything into the canvas shopping bag he'd brought from the B and B. Anticipating being gone most of the day, he'd packed a couple of water bottles.

"Sausage, bacon, eggs, and tomatoes in pastry dough. And it's proper thick bacon, too—none of those thin strips we get in the colonies," he teased.

Just as he'd intended, she laughed, bright and unfettered. "All right. I trust you," she said, taking his arm in hers.

"I won't steer you wrong," he promised. As they started walking again, heading north on Old Town Lane, he pointed with the hand holding the grocery bag. "The airport is just over there. The coastal trail goes back behind the runway. When a plane comes in, there's a light to warn hikers to duck or stand clear."

With an exaggerated shudder, she said, "I think we can skip that part."

"I'd planned on that," he admitted. "Actually, we're going to divert off the coastal trail for part of the way. There's something else I want to show you."

"Oh? What's that?" she asked, smiling as she took in the scenery with open interest.

They passed a few other early morning pedestrians who nodded in greeting and smiled specifically at Michelle. Ray couldn't help but do the same. His gaze dipped to her long, lightly tanned legs before meeting her eyes. In the morning sunlight, with the wind tugging at her long, dark hair, she looked especially beautiful.

Instead of answering her question, Ray asked, "You're not allergic to flowers, are you? I should have asked. The island's full of them, if you hadn't noticed."

"It *is* a little late for that," she teased, shifting to walk a bit closer. Her shoulder bumped into his arm just below his stitches. "But no, no allergies. No allergies, no illnesses, not even sick days to get me out of school. My mother would say it's her good influence."

"Oh? How's that?"

"She's a health food nut. Whatever the latest fad is, she's all over it. Organic food, macrobiotics, gluten-free, you name it—whether there's scientific evidence or not."

Ray squeezed her hand. "And what do you think is behind your good health?"

"Cheeseburgers." Her eyes sparkled. "Pizza. Every sort of junk food you can imagine. I spent my allowance buying lunch off the other kids at school. And it got worse in college, until I took up yoga."

"I'm afraid I don't have quite the same clean record of health," he said, nodding toward his injured arm.

"I don't think rushing off into a war zone counts, except maybe toward your sanity."

"Or lack?"

She gave him a sly smile. "I didn't want to say it, but…"

He laughed and stopped to tug her into a quick kiss, ignoring the fact that they were on a public street. To his delight, she wrapped her arms around his waist and returned the kiss without hesitation.

When it ended, he released her reluctantly. Instead of taking her hand, he put his arm around her shoulders, wanting—needing—to feel her body against his. As they started walking again, she snuggled as close as she could without tripping.

"If it's any comfort, as vice president, I only go in the field to troubleshoot major issues. The rest of the on-the-ground action is left for our team leaders to supervise."

She hummed thoughtfully, hooking her fingers in his belt loop. "All right. You get a couple of points for that, I suppose," she conceded. "What's it like, though, going into that sort of danger?"

He took a deep breath instead of answering immediately. The only people who truly understood had already been there and experienced it for themselves. He'd eventually started to brush off the questions, but Michelle deserved something closer to an honest answer.

"If we do our jobs and the mission goes perfectly, it's actually boring. A lot of time spent standing around trying to stay alert, hour after hour, day after day." He shrugged. "Of course, nothing ever goes perfectly. That's when it gets exhilarating and terrifying all at once."

She nodded, arm tightening around his waist for a moment. "What *exactly* do you do, though?"

"Whatever's necessary." He shrugged again, explaining, "Mostly, we provide security—small teams guarding high-profile targets or residences in high-risk areas. Sort of like the American Secret Service does for the president."

She tipped her head back and looked up at him. He braced for the inevitable questions about what happened when missions went wrong, but she just smiled and turned to look at the scenery instead. He hid a sigh of relief and focused on the present: the green trees and hedges, the fields of flowers, the fresh air blowing in off the sea.

The beautiful woman holding him close.

In comfortable silence, they walked up the road toward the center of the island. When they reached a stand of pines, Ray dropped his arm to take hold of her hand again and led her onto a neat walking trail that plunged into the trees.

"You know, I never imagined pine trees and palm trees growing in the same place until I went to Arizona," she said thoughtfully.

"You're seeing the island at a perfect time. It does get cold, and the storms can be fierce," he warned. He liked the idea of a storm rolling in over the next couple of weeks. Nothing too devastating. Just enough wind and rain to chill the air and encourage a lazy day on the couch by the fire. Or maybe on the rug, with some throw pillows and a good bottle of wine. Thoughtfully, he said, "We should visit the other islands over the next few days, if the weather stays clear. There's a winery on St. Martin's."

"I'd like that. And the…wherever it was that all the rooms are named for?"

"Tresco Abbey Gardens. Oh, and there are prehistoric ruins. And colonies of seals—"

"Hang on," she interrupted, grin flashing bright as she

looked up at him. "This is my vacation, and you're supposed to be healing up, aren't you?" She looked pointedly
at his stitched arm. "How is playing tourist at all restful?"

"Everything's restful here. That's the point of coming
here instead of somewhere more crowded," he countered, squeezing her hand. Then, as they reached his
destination, he grinned and pointed ahead, shopping bag
rustling. "See?"

—◦◦◦—

Michelle's arguments against overexerting themselves
by playing tourist all vanished as the path opened up into
a shadowed paradise. It was a garden gone wild, with
calf-high grass and flowers carpeting the small field,
surrounded by rich green hedges and trees that gave an
illusion of privacy beneath the brilliant blue sky.

A gap in the trees drew her gaze to another field, and
her hand slipped free of Ray's. She crossed the grass
and went to investigate what proved to be a series of
sun-dappled gardens, each more beautiful than the last.
Feeling like an intruder in another world, she picked her
way carefully across a field of bluebells until she found
a path that led to a brown wooden garden bench.

"What is this place?" she asked, turning to smile
at Ray.

His grin was proud, pleased at her delight. "Crake
Dew," he said—or something like it.

She frowned, though her smile remained.
"Sorry, what?"

He laughed and reclaimed her hand, giving her a tug
toward the bench. "C-a-r-r-e-g D-h-u," he spelled. "It's
Welsh. No idea what it means, but that's where we are.

It's a community garden. In fact, it's open for anyone to help out. There are gardening tools somewhere around here, if you're interested in doing a bit of digging." They sat down on the bench, where Ray started arranging their breakfast between them.

Michelle set down her purse and hat. "I never learned much about gardening," she admitted, taking one of the breakfast pasties. It was wrapped in wax paper and still warm. Her stomach growled at the delicious smells rising from the wax paper. "Anchor's Cove had a landscaper."

Michelle bit off a corner off her pasty. The dough flaked and dissolved on her tongue, buttery and rich. The filling was hearty, with just enough pepper to excite her taste buds. She couldn't hide an appreciative "Mmm."

"Good, then?" he asked.

She swallowed and paused just long enough to say, "Delicious," before taking another bigger bite.

Ray opened one of the water bottles and offered it to her. "Anchor's Cove. That was your old B and B, right?"

Here it comes, she thought, accepting the bottle with a nod. Swallowing her food, she took a long drink, thinking that this probably was as good a time as any to have this particular talk.

As he opened the other bottle, he asked, "What happened to it?"

She took another bite and let herself enjoy the taste for a moment so she could gather her thoughts. "It was leveled in the hurricane that tore up the coast last year. We thought about rebuilding," she said, neatly folding a napkin around the pasty. "Dana and I—we ran Anchor's Cove together. We'd been best friends since college.

After the hurricane, I had to go through all the old financials on paper."

"You found something," he guessed quietly.

She nodded, focusing on the flowers surrounding them. "I mostly dealt with the guests, the marketing, that sort of thing. Dana was the accountant. There were... discrepancies. She tried to call it accounting errors, but finally she admitted to needing money for an emergency. Only when I dug deeper, I found out it had been going on for years."

He didn't demand to know if she'd taken legal action. He didn't tell her she'd been an idiot to trust her finances to someone else. He didn't do as so many other men would have and try to *fix* the problem.

"I'm sorry. That must have been difficult," was all he said.

Relieved by his calm demeanor, she smiled. "At least she had kept up the insurance payments. We were completely covered, so the storm didn't wipe us out. Before I found the files, we'd talked about rebuilding. Afterward..." She shook her head.

He rested his arm across the back of the seat and rubbed her shoulder. "What do *you* want to do?"

After a moment's consideration, she said, "Vicky wants me to take over Valhalla's Rest, but I don't think I could. I trust Vicky, and I know she's not Dana, but..." She shook her head, leaning closer to Ray, pressing into his touch. "You said your partner is a friend, right? Doesn't that worry you?"

Ray shook his head without hesitation. "I trust Preston with my life. The business is just money. Some things are more important."

Chapter 8

Monday, July 8

THE DAY'S WARMTH FADED SLOWLY AS RAY AND Michelle walked down the coastal trail, heading toward the harbor. Wanting to linger, to capture the beauty of the moment, Michelle slowed and finished off the last of her water as she looked to the west, where clouds streaked all the way to the horizon.

The scene reminded her of yesterday's attempt to photograph the harbor. "How good are you at taking pictures?"

"Sorry?" he asked, folding the now-empty grocery bag. He tucked it into the pocket of his jacket.

"I'm terrible at it," she admitted. "I have whole photo albums full of blurry, off-center pictures of roadside attractions up and down the East Coast."

He wrapped his arm around her shoulders, holding her comfortably close. "I'm not bad, though it's been some time since I've taken photos outside work, and those are usually site surveillance."

"That sounds ominous."

"Not as such. When we're on protection detail, we scout the areas we expect to visit ahead of time to assess potential threats."

"How is that not ominous?"

"It's a matter of safety—both for our clients and our

teams." He leaned down and kissed the top of her head. "It'd be nice to take pictures for a less 'ominous' reason."

Michelle unzipped her wristlet and took out her phone. She opened the camera app, then offered the phone to Ray. "Would you mind?"

He took the phone and stepped away. "Back up."

"Oh. No, not me. I don't—"

"Go on."

Michelle never liked being in pictures, but the hopeful look in Ray's eyes convinced her. Just this once couldn't hurt, and the picture would be on her phone. There was no danger of Vicky uploading it to Facebook or something. Self-consciously, she stepped back and tried to smile as Ray snapped a half-dozen pictures in quick succession.

Finally she broke her pose and reached for her phone, amused by his enthusiasm. "Isn't that a little excessive?"

He shrugged, turning to look over her shoulder as she opened the gallery to review the pictures. "Habit. You have to take a lot of pictures to guarantee getting something useful."

She tipped her head, looking thoughtfully up at him. "You like your habits, don't you?"

One black brow shot up. "Sorry?"

"Routine." She locked her phone and tucked it back into her wristlet. "You're a creature of habit."

"Except on holiday," he countered.

"Except for your daily jogging."

"And your yoga?"

"I like routine, too." She looked back at the harbor, trying to remember the last time she'd had such a fun, relaxing day. "Thank you for today," she said sincerely.

The walk around the gorgeous island had helped her to relax, but more than that, talking about Dana had lifted a weight from Michelle's shoulders.

"It was my pleasure," Ray answered, resting his hand on the small of her back. "Tresco tomorrow, for the gardens, or St. Martin's for the vineyard?"

"Surprise me again," she challenged with a soft laugh.

"I'm rather enjoying surprising you." His deep, quiet tone sent a shiver of delight through Michelle.

"Do you have any more surprises in store for tonight?"

"Just one more—for tonight," he said mischievously. "We skipped lunch in favor of tea. Are you hungry again?"

"If I say I'm starving, it's only because you've had me walking all day," she said, faking a prim, proper attitude. "It's entirely your fault."

With a satisfied grin, he said, "Then my plan worked. This way."

She took his arm and allowed him to lead her away from the coast and up to a broad flagstone path, broken here and there with stairs, toward a beautiful stone building. Michelle slowed at a trash can and threw away her water bottle. "I'd ask where we're going, but knowing you…"

"I'll just say 'It's a surprise,' *hmm*?" he asked, continuing up the path.

Michelle nodded, taking off her sunglasses. She hung them on the neckline of her shirt. "Exactly."

"You've been enjoying my surprises so far, haven't you?" he asked, voice pitched seductively low.

She felt her cheeks go hot, even though their day had been entirely innocent. Or maybe it was the unspoken promise in his tone, a promise that tonight's surprises might not be innocent at all.

"Yes," she said softly.

For a moment, his wicked smile flashed to life, as if he could read her thoughts. But then it eased into something more open and casual. He stopped walking and said, "For now, turn around."

Curious, Michelle turned, then gasped at the breathtaking view. To the west, the sun was inching down to the horizon, painting the wispy clouds with fire, and the sea was darkening to rich sapphire. A thin promontory of land jutted out into the bay; beyond it, boats were making their serene way into the harbor.

"Oh, that's gorgeous," she breathed. She looked back up the slope, to where waiters were lighting glass lanterns. The white building at the crest of the hill was full of windows, with a huge patio where workers were taking down umbrellas over small tables. There were more tables set precariously along the slope below the patio, most with just one bench facing out toward the water. "Where are we? What is this place?"

"It's a flower farm. See the greenhouse?" Ray pointed back down the slope, to the foot of the hill, where a long, narrow greenhouse had been hidden behind a small outbuilding. "The restaurant is up top. Would you prefer to sit inside or outside? It does get nippy in the evenings," he warned.

Nippy, she thought, finding his British-isms almost as charming as his concern for her comfort. "Inside, I think," she said agreeably. "If I'd known we were going out to dinner, I would've worn something nicer. I thought we'd be going back to the B and B to change first."

He cupped her face between his palms and leaned down to give her a brief, gentle kiss. "If it's not too forward of me to say, you're beautiful exactly as you are," he said softly.

Her cheeks burned, and a lump rose in her throat at his sincerity. His crooked smile was warm with pleasure; his blue eyes roved over her face, as intimate as a caress. At that moment, she really could believe he meant it—that he really did find her beautiful.

"Thank you," she managed to whisper.

He smiled and playfully kissed the tip of her nose, breaking the solemn moment. "Dinner—and this time, we'll have dessert," he said, offering his arm once more. When she took it, he resumed walking up the slope. "And if you're still keen to dare my grandmother's recipe, the co-op is open until ten. We can stop there for ingredients on the way back to Valhalla's Rest."

"Oh, I'm keen," she said, suppressing a laugh at the phrasing. "In fact, if you've got a favorite dessert recipe, I can give that a try, too. I've baked more than a few wedding cakes in my day, you know."

"How'd they turn out?"

"Three successful angel food cakes, one not so successful lemon cake, and one emergency re-iced sheet cake from the grocery store, resulting in four happy brides and one lactose intolerant maid of honor who really should have known better." She shuddered at the memory and looked sidelong at Ray. "No allergies?"

"None at all, I promise.

—◆—

Ray didn't recognize the hostess on duty, but he was able to secure them a good table by the window all the same. The night was still young, and most tourists wanted to sit outside and enjoy the evening breeze before the air grew too chilly, leaving the dining room half empty.

He seated Michelle where she'd have an unobstructed view of the harbor, and as she stared at the scenery, he in turn studied her. She'd touched up her lip gloss through the day, and her lashes held a hint of mascara, but those were the only cosmetics she wore. She'd worn her hat most of the day. Only a hint of sunlight had colored her skin, darkening the bridge of her nose and her cheeks. The candle on the table added a touch of gold to her skin. In the sunlight, her brown eyes showed flecks of mahogany and amber; now, they were like pools of shadow, deep and warm.

She looked unexpectedly away from the window and caught him staring. A shy smile played at her lips. She turned her gaze down at the menu, asking, "So, what's good?"

"Any of the seafood specials will be excellent," Ray said, scanning his menu—or, more accurately, using it to hide how intently he'd been staring. "Or the lamb cutlets. You might like those, if you've only ever had them in the colonies."

Laughing, she set the menu back down. "If that's how you're going to be, let's add my *colonial* lamb chops to the menu later this week. I'll have you convinced that *colonial* cooking is superior to anything you…you *monarchists* can come up with."

Grinning at her spirit, he abandoned his menu to take

hold of her hands. "Oh, will you, now? If I let you have free rein, I might well end up getting fat by the end of this holiday."

"Like that's going to happen, with these eleven-mile hikes of yours?" she scoffed, fingers tightening around his. "I guess that habit goes back to your army days, hmm?"

"The Royal Marines, yes." He grinned and leaned close, lowering his voice. "Confidentially, I never much liked exercise growing up. I was always weedy and tall, one of the last picked in school sports, until I was seventeen."

"Uh-huh," she scoffed. "As if I believe that?"

"I was!" he protested, amused. "It wasn't until I turned seventeen that I shot up another three inches and finally put on some decent weight."

"So, you decided to take physical fitness to the extreme and join the military?"

"Well, no. I'd always wanted to be a Royal Marine." He shrugged thoughtfully, remembering how young and naive he'd been. "I started training to pass the fitness test when I was thirteen. I knew I wanted to go straight into officer training."

"Somehow, that doesn't surprise me," she said, rubbing her thumbs against the backs of his hands. "But why the Royal Marines?"

"Because I love the water. The Royal Marines are the Royal Navy's infantry," he said, glossing over the specifics. Words like "commando" and "assault group" had no place at this quiet, romantic dinner.

But before he could change the subject to something more appropriate, she asked, "What did you do while you were in the service? Or are you not allowed to talk about that?"

Accustomed to deflecting such questions, Ray shrugged and answered, "Just the usual sort of thing you'd expect. A lot of travel, though I rarely got to play at being a tourist. It wasn't particularly interesting."

"Of course not. Not to you, at any rate," she said, nudging her foot against his shin.

He smiled. "All right, I really did enjoy it," he admitted, gently squeezing her hands. "But Preston offered an interesting opportunity, and I thought it was time for a change." Privately, he laughed at his own choice of wording. *Interesting* was hardly the word for the operation that had brought Preston Fairchild to his attention. *Chaos*, maybe, or *insanity*.

"No regrets? I always heard that Marines—at least, U.S. Marines—are Marines for life."

Their young waitress saved him from having to answer. Releasing Michelle's hands, he leaned back and picked up the menu, gesturing for Michelle to order first. She flashed him a smile and told the waitress, "The lamb cutlets, please, since they come highly recommended."

When they both turned to him, he gave the menu one last glance and said, "Catch of the day, please." The sirloin was tempting, but fresh fish was one of his favorite parts of visiting Scilly.

"Did you want a starter?"

"I think we should save room for dessert. Unless you want one?" Ray asked Michelle.

She shook her head. "Dessert, definitely."

"And to drink?" the waitress asked.

Ray turned back to Michelle. "Why don't you choose? You're an expert with wines, aren't you?"

"Mmm, maybe a gifted amateur," she said coyly as she turned to the back of the menu, quickly examining the wine list. "A white zinfandel, I think," she said thoughtfully and then conferred briefly with the waitress before they settled on a choice.

As the waitress walked off, giving them one last smile, Michelle turned back to Ray. "So, you were saying? Regrets?"

He wanted to change the subject, but for the life of him, he had no idea how to do so gracefully or subtly. "No regrets," he finally told her. "Not for joining, nor for leaving." It wasn't the complete truth, but it was close enough.

"You like what you do now just as much?"

"In some ways, more." He leaned back, looking out at the quiet harbor. "Most of our work is security or rescue work. Even our patrols are strictly defensive." Peshawar came to mind, and he resisted the urge to rub at his stitches. He wasn't ready to discuss hostage rescue. Not yet.

"That sounds safer than going into combat," she said thoughtfully.

He nodded, not mentioning that a lot of their work was in or near active engagements, and the rest was in areas considered high risk for both American and British travelers. "We try to get all the intel we need without worrying about what the higher-ups might be hiding from us or what the politicians are doing back home."

She wrinkled her nose, saying, "I hate politics. I try to steer clear of them."

"Unfortunately, politics are everywhere," he said grimly. "Samaritan's jobs are split between private contracts, primarily acting as bodyguards to the rich and reckless, and government work escorting diplomats, assets, and persons of interest whose work takes them to dangerous locations. Fortunately, though, Preston handles ninety percent of the politics, since we operate out of the States. The other ten percent, I can usually clear up with a phone call to London, where I still have a contact or two." He shook his head, realizing he'd said more than he'd intended. "With Samaritan, Preston and I can make all of the decisions, and we can turn down missions if we feel they're too risky or politically dangerous. The ability to say 'no' is probably the best part of being a civilian."

He caught her staring at him, her head tilted thoughtfully. Quietly, she said, "Then, while you were in the Royal Marines, was there a mission that went... One you couldn't refuse?"

He took a deep breath as he carefully chose his words. "Something like that, but it wasn't my mission. It was Preston's. I just came in at the end, to help clean up. That's how he and I met."

This time, she was the one who reached across the table to take his hand. "What happened?" she asked in a low, worried tone.

He smiled reassuringly and squeezed her hand. "Preston was trying to rescue someone. My team was the closest, so we were sent in as backup, but it was too late. We barely got Preston and his troops out."

"But not whoever he was trying to rescue?" she asked gently.

Ray shook his head, remembering the dust of the desert, the stifling heat in his lungs, the weight of his body armor. When he'd tried to pull Preston to safety, Preston had drawn a gun on him. After failing to talk Preston out of his grief-fueled rage, Ray had ordered his men to leave without him, so he could stay and give Preston a fighting chance at survival.

Until that moment, Ray had never understood just how powerful—how *terrible*—love could be.

"No, I'm afraid not," he said softly. "She died."

"I'm sorry," Michelle said softly.

"I never knew her. Preston..." Ray took a deep breath, letting the smell of the sea and the smoke of the nearby candle drive away his memories. "Preston was going to ask her to marry him."

The lamb chops were excellent, as promised—almost as satisfying as Ray's company. The more they talked, the more curious she became, though she didn't want to push for answers, especially after the shadow of Preston's tragedy had passed over them, momentarily darkening the night. After all, she wouldn't reveal Vicky's secrets, so she'd give Ray and Preston the same courtesy.

Instead, she allowed Ray to guide the conversation to happier subjects, mostly about Michelle herself. He asked about her experiences at Brown and the sometimes disastrous road trips with Vicky and Dana. He was surprisingly good at listening, and she found herself opening up to him in ways she never had before, with other boyfriends.

But never once did the conversation turn toward the

future, hers or his. And once she became aware of it, she became self-conscious about trying to steer the conversation that way. Every question she considered asking sounded awkward or obvious in her mind.

When the waitress came to clear their plates and ask about dessert, Michelle was ready to go home—or to go to the co-op to pick up the ingredients for Ray's grandmother's recipe, though without having the recipe in hand, she'd probably have to come back for anything Ray forgot to mention.

Michelle opened her mouth to refuse dessert, but Ray grinned at the waitress and asked, "What crumbles do you have?"

"Blueberry or… I think there should be some strawberry and almond left," she said cheerfully. "Would you like me to check?"

He held up a hand and turned to Michelle. "Is blueberry all right?"

So much for getting back to Valhalla's Rest. She smiled politely and said, "Oh, no. I couldn't eat another bite."

His smile faded, and he offered, "We could get it in a takeaway box, for tomorrow."

She'd hoped he'd take the hint that she wanted to leave, but he was so polite about it, she couldn't resist. "That's all right. I'll try a little bit of yours, if you don't mind."

"Blueberry, two forks, please," he told the waitress at once. "And coffee. Two?" When Michelle nodded, figuring she might as well, he confirmed, "Two."

"I'll have that for you right away," the waitress said cheerfully, carrying away their dinner dishes.

"You're a bad influence," Michelle accused, no

longer irritated. That charming smile of his was far too
disarming. "Now who's trying to get who fat?"

"We'll walk it off," he said with a shrug. "Besides,
look at you. You're just a little wren."

She stiffened and forced a smile as she turned to look
out at the harbor. *Plain brown bird*, she thought wryly.
Maybe he was settling after all.

———

This was why Ray didn't do relationships. One minute,
they were having a lovely dinner, and the next, Michelle
just…shut down. She'd tried a bite of the dessert and
pronounced it tasty, had a couple of sips of coffee, and
then politely insisted, with American stubbornness, on
paying her half of the bill.

As they walked down into Hugh Town, every instinct
screamed for Ray to call Michelle a taxi and send her
back to Valhalla's Rest alone. A pint or two would help
him relax, at least, and giving her some time alone might
settle whatever had turned the mood sour.

"Do you remember all the ingredients?"

Ray shot Michelle a baffled look. "Sorry?"

She didn't look back up at him; she didn't even smile.
"Your grandmother's recipe."

Bloody hell. Ray nodded, turning to head for the co-op.
"Beef roast, eggs, milk, flour…" He trailed off, trying
to remember if there was anything else. The recipe was
uncomplicated, which was the frustrating part; he was
no expert cook, but he'd always felt he should've been
able to handle something with a half-dozen ingredients.

"That's it?" She frowned up at him.

"Salt and pepper," he guessed. "Oh, and lard or oil.

Not butter." He remembered that part quite clearly, though he had no idea why butter wouldn't work.

"Should be easy enough," she said thoughtfully.

"Did you want me to pick up everything?" he offered, seeing an escape route. He could go to the co-op for their groceries and then stop by a pub for an hour or two. He'd get back to Valhalla's Rest long after Michelle had gone to bed, saving them both from an awkward, uncomfortable evening. "After all the walking we did, you must be tired."

Her steps quickened. "I'm fine," she said evenly, though it felt like a lie.

Even British reserve and courtesy had its limits—that or Preston's brash ways had been a bad influence. Ray stopped, took a deep breath, and then asked, "Have I done something? Offended you in some way?"

"No," she said—another obvious lie—and started to walk down the street again.

Ray stared after her but didn't follow. Not yet. It would be so easy to smooth this all over, to try and charm her into smiling again, or maybe to just keep away until she was over whatever dark mood had struck. The peace between them had to last less than two weeks now, if that. He could always just leave early. Go back home to Virginia. Or maybe go south to Florida and take out the boat. Spend the rest of his vacation on the water. *Alone*.

Two weeks. An easy holiday fling. No emotional entanglements. No lasting commitment. Two weeks of fun, and no regrets afterward. That was what he'd hoped for, wasn't it?

Bloody hell, he thought and then went after her. "Michelle? Michelle!"

Her steps slowed. She turned just enough for him to see the corner of one eye. She didn't say anything.

"Michelle, wait," he protested, the whole time wondering *why*. An in-depth, emotional discussion of any sort was the exact opposite of what he wanted, but he couldn't bear the thought of letting her walk off like this. Whatever had happened to bring this cold distance between them, he needed to know. To fix it.

She sighed and finally stopped. "Maybe I'm tired," she admitted, looking up at him.

He couldn't accept the excuse. He wanted to touch her, to take her hands, to pull her into his arms, but he felt as if he didn't have that right anymore. "What happened, Michelle? What did I do?"

With another quiet sigh, she said, "It's nothing. Really."

"Michelle." She was carrying her hat in one hand, wristlet dangling; he took the other hand, clasping it gently between both of his. "Please. Tell me."

"I don't... I don't do this," she finally admitted, avoiding his eyes. She kept her gaze fixed on their joined hands and made no effort to pull away.

He knew right away what she was talking about: she was no more the type to have a quick holiday affair than he was likely to get into a long-term relationship. Instead of saying so, he tried to lighten the moment by asking, "Go grocery shopping?"

She huffed out a laugh and shifted her weight. "Ray..." She shook her head. "No. I just... I know I'm not your type, that's all."

Bloody hell, he thought again, and for just one moment, all he wanted was to walk away. But he was already in too deep, already too interested—perhaps even *infatuated*—to abandon any chance at having something more with Michelle.

As sincerely as he could manage, he asked, "I'm here with you now, aren't I?"

But instead of accepting that as truth, she shot him a narrow-eyed look. Her hand went tense in his before she pulled away. "Yeah. Yeah, you are," she muttered.

"That's…a problem?" he asked, baffled. What had he missed? "Michelle—"

"It's nothing." She shook her head, tossing her hair back. "Let's just go to the co-op before it closes."

She was offering him a way out, but he didn't want to take it. "Michelle, please," he said, holding out his hand. "What's wrong?"

She looked away, fussing with her purse. Her exhale sounded frustrated. "Nothing. Look, why don't you go to the co-op? I've…got a headache."

Again, she was lying to him. Worse, she was using the oldest excuse in the book, just so she could get away from him.

Why?

"Fine," he said, though he was feeling anything *but* fine. "I'll get you a taxi."

"No." She shook her head again, looking away. "I'll walk. The night air—it's nice."

"I'll come—"

"No, Ray," she interrupted more sharply. She pushed her hair back behind her ear, purse swinging from her wrist, and shifted another step away from him. "Thank you for dinner. Have a good night."

Chapter 9

Monday, July 8

THOUGH IT HAD BEEN TWO YEARS SINCE RAY HAD SET foot in this particular pub, as soon as he walked in, the bartender grinned and called, "Evening, Ray! What'll it be tonight?"

Ray smiled at the reminder that this familiarity, this friendliness, was why he loved St. Mary's, no matter who was in charge back at Valhalla's Rest. "A pint of Guinness, Kincaid, if you would?"

"Sure thing, mate." He picked up a glass and walked down the bar to the taps. "You all right?"

"Good question," Ray muttered. "Come to think of it, can I get a shot of whiskey first?"

Kincaid set the glass down and immediately turned to pour a shot of the house whiskey. "Things that rough?"

"A woman," Ray said grimly.

"Sorry to hear that," Kincaid said sympathetically, handing over the shot. Ray downed it without tasting it, set down the glass with a nod of thanks, and continued to the far end of the bar.

How the *hell* had everything turned so sour, so quickly? Had he done something to upset her? He must have. But then why sit and brood on it until she'd just exploded out of nowhere?

When Kincaid brought the pint over, Ray passed him

a credit card; he hadn't thought to stop at an ATM. "Buy yourself one as well," he invited, the customary way to offer a tip here in the UK. Kincaid nodded and went to run the card, giving Ray his privacy.

Ray took out his phone and spun it on the bar, wishing he were back home in Virginia. At a time like this, he'd drag Preston out to a bar or to company headquarters, where they'd hit the shooting range or the boxing ring. He wouldn't have to resort to a bloody phone call to work things through.

But it was that or get falling-down drunk, which was no solution at all—not when he'd end up back at Valhalla's Rest, where Michelle might well be waiting to start round two with him. Grimacing, he opened a new text to Preston:

Women are too bloody complicated.

He sent it and picked up his pint, thinking that he really would need to limit himself to just the one, or two at the most. There probably wasn't a single open hotel room on any of the islands. Besides, he didn't *want* to go anywhere else. He wanted to be with Michelle. Or, well, the not-so-irrational version of Michelle he'd spent the day with.

Right on cue, the phone rang. Ray picked it up. "Yeah."

"What'd you do this time?" Preston asked.

"Me? Nothing!"

"Well, there's your problem," Preston said with a laugh. "That's the sort of attitude that *makes* women complicated."

Ray sighed and took a drink. "It's idiocy, mate."

"So why bother trying?"

"Because I'm a bloody idiot, obviously."

"Well, then."

Ray laughed softly. "Right. So, is your family still there?"

"Are you thinking of cutting your vacation short?"

Ray's gut churned at the very thought. "I don't know. It might be safer," he answered, trying to sound casual.

"Uh-huh. Well, they're here until next Sunday, so you're shit out of luck. Though actually, Amelia's here on leave. She'd *love* to see you, after that incident with you pushing her in the pool."

"The barbecue caught fire. I was *helping*."

"Women hate that sort of 'help,' Ray. And now she's a fighter pilot. She can shoot you from a hundred miles away."

"Lovely," Ray muttered. He took another drink. "Let's not introduce her to Michelle."

"So, Michelle," Preston said, drawing out her name. "Just how badly did you piss her off?"

"Hell if I know." Ray set the glass down and shook his head. "I thought we were having a nice dinner, but then it all went wrong during dessert."

Preston took a deep breath. "What exactly did you say?"

"I told you—"

"No, you summarized," Preston interrupted calmly. "I've heard you recite battlefield communications word-for-word two weeks after the fact. Now you can't remember what happened at dinner?"

"I don't even know why I bloody care," he went on.

"It's not like I know her. And ten or eleven days from now, that's it. I'll never see her again."

"So why are you on the phone with me?"

"Because you're my best friend. Who else am I supposed to call? Your sister?"

"Not now that she has an F-16, no."

"Well, then." Ray took another drink, feeling some of the tension leave his muscles. Talking to Preston wasn't bringing him any closer to figuring out what happened, but at least he felt a little less off-balance about it all.

"What are you going to do now?"

Ray rubbed at the back of his neck, feeling the stretch of his stitches. Going to the hospital to have them removed would give him something to do tomorrow. Something to get out of Valhalla's Rest and avoid any awkward morning-after confrontations. He really had no idea how he was going to face her.

"I'm a bloody coward," he muttered.

Preston laughed softly. "If there's one thing you're *not*, it's a coward, Ray."

"Then why am I thinking of ways to avoid her?"

"Maybe because you don't want to?"

"How does that make *any* sense?" Ray demanded.

"Because you don't want to make things worse."

Ray sucked in a breath, feeling the truth in Preston's words hit home. "Sod off, bastard."

"I guess I'm right."

"Fine. Yes, you're right." Ray took another drink, hating just how right Preston was. He wanted nothing more than to *fix* things; that was what he did. Only he had no idea where to even begin.

Well, he did, but that thought was as unconscionable as surrender on the field.

"I'm not going to go apologizing to her," he declared.

"Did I say you should?"

"You were probably thinking it," Ray accused.

Preston laughed. "So, you *do* like her."

Ray frowned. "What?"

"Hear me out," Preston said, amused. "Apologizing is probably the fastest way to fix this mess. It's an easy way out. You say you're sorry, everything's fine, and you can get into her pants."

"Preston," Ray said in a low, warning tone.

"I know you, Ray. You're proud, but you're not stupid. If you were wrong, you'd apologize in a heartbeat. But if you don't think you're wrong, you'll stand your ground while everything burns around you."

"How is this at all helping?"

"Because, if you're *not* going to apologize, it means you don't want to lie to her. And *that* tells me that she's important to you."

Ray took the phone from his ear and stared incredulously at it for a few seconds. Then he set it back to his ear and demanded, "How the *hell* do you come up with these things?"

"I've been dealing with your shit for how many years?"

Ray sighed. "Fine. I'm finishing my pint, then heading back to Valhalla's Rest."

Preston laughed. "Just try not to make things worse. Maybe things will blow over by tomorrow morning."

"And maybe pigs will fly," Ray muttered. He disconnected the call before Preston could answer.

The damned thing was, Preston was right. An apology, deserved or not, would probably smooth things over nicely. Then they could get back on track with a quiet, fun holiday together, and then they'd go their separate ways. Who was "right" or "wrong" wouldn't matter at all.

And really, in a way, it *didn't* matter. Unintentionally or not, he'd hurt her feelings. That she'd done the same to him didn't matter at all. No, what mattered was that he didn't like the thought of her hurting—of her sitting at the B and B, sulking. Or, worse, crying.

As he finished his pint, Kincaid returned, sympathetic smile fixed in place. "Another one, mate?"

"Thanks, but no," Ray said, rising from his seat at the bar. "I need to get back to Valhalla's Rest."

"Cheers, mate. And good luck with your woman."

My woman, Ray thought, chest tightening. He just didn't know if it was with apprehension or pleasure at the thought of Michelle being his.

Stupid, stupid, stupid. The mental litany haunted Michelle all the way back to Valhalla's Rest. She'd burned off her irritation in a quick burst of walking, leaving her breathless. Her aching feet reminded her that she'd walked eleven miles today, if not more, with all their detours, and once she'd slowed down, her mind had started replaying their conversation.

She let herself into Valhalla's Rest and breathed out a shaky sigh of relief that she'd made it to the privacy of the manager's office without incident. Not that she was afraid for her safety. She just couldn't bear the thought that Ray might have taken a shortcut and beat her here, and that she'd have to face him again.

How could she have let things go so far? She'd just been so *angry*. No, not angry. Scared.

Today had been perfect—the sort of day that had never happened to her, only to other women. *To Vicky and Dana*, a jealous voice whispered. Jealous but sadly accurate. Michelle never went on romantic getaway dates. A weekend in New York City to see a Broadway play. A sailboat cruise around Boston harbor. A candlelit dinner at a winery. No, Michelle's dates had always been more standard fare: dinner and a movie, chatting at a coffee shop, that sort of thing.

And then... And then Ray had made one offhand comment—*you're just a little wren*—that had eaten through Michelle like drops of acid. She'd tried to tell herself that he had no idea that was how she thought of herself, as a plain brown bird, unremarkable and ordinary, but the hurt never went away. It just grew inside her, five little words that tore open years of self-doubt and uncertainty, until she'd felt justified in walking away from him.

Stupid idiot, she scolded herself again.

Maybe the walk home had cleared her head, but it hadn't brought her any insight on how to fix the mess she'd caused. Maybe Ray really had wanted to be with her before, but it was impossible to imagine he'd feel the same way now.

She hesitated before turning to lock the front door. Ray's assertion that it was safe on the island was a comfort, but Michelle was still aware that this wasn't her property to risk. Instead, she went into the kitchen and unlocked the back door. After the last few days, surely Ray would think to check the patio, rather than knocking on the front door.

Then again…she *really* didn't want to see him before she was ready. She turned on the patio light and hurried back to the foyer, where she unlocked the front door.

There. Now she wouldn't have to deal with him at all until breakfast. If she stayed in bed late enough, she might not even have to see him then.

She went into the manager's office and locked the door behind herself. Stomach churning, she took two steps across the dark room and banged her hip bone right into the corner of the old wooden desk. She yelped in pain and rubbed at her hip, viciously thinking Vicky would interpret this as "karma," too. Karmic revenge for Michelle's being an insecure idiot.

More carefully, she crossed the office and went through her apartment into the bathroom. The bright light made her blink, eyes stinging. She unzipped her shorts and pulled them down enough to look at her hip, where a tiny dark spot had already formed. Tomorrow, she'd have a nice bruise to remind her of tonight's idiocy. Toeing off her shoes, she shoved her shorts down and dropped them on the counter.

Tomorrow. How was she going to face Ray tomorrow?

She dumped the contents of her purse on the counter and picked up her phone. She'd barely touched it at all today, so she had plenty of battery life. She dialed and put the phone to her ear as she walked back out into the apartment, turning on lights as she went. "Please, be home," she whispered as the call rang through.

Then she heard a click, and Vicky said, "Chelly! Why are you calling me instead of shagging—"

Wincing, Michelle interrupted, "Because I'm an idiot."

Vicky paused. Gently, she asked, "What happened, love?"

Michelle sank down into the armchair and curled up, bracing her feet on the edge of the cushion. "He called me a bird."

"*Er...* That's not an insult, you know. It's no worse than your American 'chick' or 'dude,'" Vicky explained.

"A wren," Michelle clarified, rolling her eyes.

"A... I'm sorry, Chelly. What on earth are you talking about?"

"He called me a wren," Michelle muttered, feeling even more like an idiot now that she was explaining it to a third party. "A little wren."

"That's...unusual. Charming, I suppose," Vicky said uncertainly.

Michelle sighed. "Or it's my signal to completely overreact." She laughed, trying and failing to find even a hint of humor in this mess.

"What happened?" Vicky asked gently.

"We had a great day. We walked around the island. He showed me these hidden gardens and private beaches and this café—"

"Sounds romantic," Vicky interrupted, which Michelle knew was another word for *boring*. Vicky's idea of romance tended more toward flashy nightclubs and trendy bars than anywhere you could have a quiet conversation.

"It was," Michelle insisted. "And then we had this candlelit dinner overlooking the harbor, and he wanted dessert, but he wasn't talking, so I said no—"

"Wait, wait. He wasn't talking? About what?"

"About himself!" Michelle took a deep breath. "He kept getting evasive every time I asked anything about his future."

"Oh, Chelly..."

Michelle's eyes narrowed. She curled and flexed her toes, feeling the ache of eleven miles starting to set in. "I know that tone of voice."

"Chelly, love, don't you see?"

"Obviously I don't, or I wouldn't be in this mess."

Vicky sighed. "This bloke—this *complete stranger*—takes you out for a romantically tedious day-long date, and that very night, over an equally romantic dinner, you start trying to discuss the future."

"I—" Understanding struck, and Michelle's jaw dropped. "No! That's not what I meant!"

"No, but that's probably what he heard. Men don't understand how women think, Chelly. If I know you, your questions were probably precise and logical, hmm? And he got more and more evasive and close-mouthed in response?"

"Well, yes," Michelle admitted, angry at herself all over again.

"So he's feeling trapped, you're feeling insecure, and then he makes this silly remark—probably one *he* thought would be a compliment—and..." She trailed off significantly.

"A half hour later, I left him in the middle of the street and went back to the B and B, alone." Michelle dropped one leg to restlessly kick her heel against the leg of the armchair. "So, what do I do now?"

"Tonight? Nothing. Unless you're hoping for a passionate, borderline angry shag."

"No!"

Vicky laughed. "Then nothing. And tomorrow, *he'll* apologize before you can say a single word."

Grudgingly, she admitted, "He didn't do anything." The last thing she wanted was for Vicky to take her side and turn entirely against Ray.

"So? He's a man, and you're a much better catch than you seem to think you are. Trust me. Take a nice, long bath and go straight to bed."

"Thanks so much for the help, Vicky."

Vicky laughed. "Good girl. So go have some fun alone and think about how much more fun you can have tomorrow."

"Uh-huh. Good night, Vicky."

"Good night, love. And trust me. It'll all work itself out by morning."

Despite his resolve to find a way to peacefully settle matters with Michelle, Ray made no rush to return to Valhalla's Rest. Instead, he went down to the harbor, watched the boats rocking gently at the mooring buoys, and tried to think of what he really wanted out of all of this.

Truthfully, a peaceful holiday was the least of his concerns. Already, he'd shaken off the remnants of violence from the Peshawar mission. And somewhere over the last day or two, he'd realized that he wasn't about to deplete his savings account and buy Valhalla's Rest from Liam's niece. He could let that part of his past slip away just as peacefully, but not without Michelle. Her fresh eyes had shown him a St. Mary's he'd forgotten, one not rooted in the walls of his grandparents' old house. He could stay somewhere new, next time he came to the islands. Hopefully with her.

He took the coastal trail back to Valhalla's Rest, expecting to find the keys left in the barbecue for him. Or perhaps she'd left the door unlocked. The master key opened not only the exterior doors but the manager's office and apartment as well. After tonight's argument, she'd probably want a locked door for her own peace of mind, though he hoped she knew he'd never try to intrude on her privacy.

Then again, she'd already made her share of irrational accusations tonight. The thought that he was *settling* for her still lodged in his gut like a stone. He'd enjoyed every moment spent in her company, and every compliment he'd offered her had been genuine. Did she really think so low of him that she'd accuse him, however indirectly, of *lying to her*, just to get laid?

He stopped in the back garden and took a deep breath, trying to hold back his lingering irritation.

She'd left the porch light on for him, a courtesy he didn't expect. He let himself in, locked the door, and turned off the light, wondering how he should be feeling about her mixed message.

Cautiously optimistic, he finally decided. After all, she could have locked all the doors and left him in darkness.

Or was her minimum courtesy an attempt to avoid rousing his temper? Hell, when he went into the foyer, he saw she'd left the front door unlocked as well. Covering her bases? Or trying to make him feel welcome to return?

He gave up thinking about it. He wasn't Sherlock Holmes, able to deduce a person's innermost thoughts in a single glance at unremarkable evidence.

Instead, he stared at the office door, wondering if he should knock. Was it better to try and make amends now, with their wounds still fresh, or to leave her in peace for the night?

He turned away from the door only when he remembered that the only light in the back garden had come from the porch. The manager's apartment windows were dark. The eleven-mile walk, even at a leisurely pace followed by a heated emotional conflict had probably exhausted her. He was certainly dead on his feet.

Quietly, avoiding the creaky fourth step, he made his way upstairs. As was his habit, he had left the door to his room unlocked. He let himself in and glanced around to make certain there were no unexpected surprises—no sign of Michelle waiting for him either naked in his bed or hiding in the corner with an ax.

Laughing tiredly at the thought, he went right into the bathroom to take a quick shower. Hopefully, he'd fall asleep quickly and stay asleep, so he could look at the problem with fresh eyes in the morning.

—⁓—

Michelle stared up at the ceiling, barely breathing, focusing on listening to Ray move about the B and B. The soft click of the patio doors locking had nearly startled the heart out of her chest. As Ray had walked to the foyer, Michelle's heart had lodged in her throat. When he locked the front door, she swallowed, half expecting him to knock or call her name.

But then he went up the stairs and down the hall to the Serica room. His door opened. Closed. The pipes rattled as he started the shower.

She let out a sigh and closed her eyes, telling herself that she was just being sensible, keeping track of where he was. He was her guest. Her responsibility. And honestly, she'd been afraid that he wouldn't come back at all.

Only when the pipes had gone silent and she'd heard Ray's mattress creak as he got into bed did she realize that she hadn't been *afraid*.

Just three days ago, the sight of Ray had her on edge. She'd spent Saturday in knots, worried about his potential violent side. But even after their fight earlier this evening, she trusted him.

How things had changed.

The thought that she trusted him with her safety brought the uncomfortable realization that she really did trust his motives—and his words, too. He'd called her beautiful, and whether she agreed or not, she believed that he'd spoken honestly.

She knew nothing about him. The facts—his employment, hints of his past—were all secondary to her real curiosity. Who was he? For a relationship to thrive, she truly believed that both partners needed to share the same dreams and goals. Friendship was just as important as the dizzying flush of new love. *More* important, even.

Not that she could speak from experience, she admitted silently. Michelle's longest relationship had lasted four and a half months solely because they'd both done more studying than dating. She hadn't even uttered the *L* word since high school, once she'd figured out that a heartbreaking teenage crush had very little to do with the sort of love that could last.

Even her mother was hardly an example of stability in a relationship. Michelle's father had died too young for her to remember him. Once Michelle had hit her teens, her mother had ventured tentatively into society—and then taken it by storm. She'd had three whirlwind marriages ending in two divorces and one annulment after a weekend in Vegas, of all things.

So who was Ray Powell? What did he want from life? Where did he see himself in ten years? Twenty? Did he want a family and children? Did he want a relationship at all?

Two weeks wasn't very long to find out everything. But it was long enough for her to determine if she *wanted* to find out more.

Guilt spurred her out of bed and onto her aching feet. The room was cold, and she shivered in her T-shirt and sweats, but she didn't return to the warmth of her blankets. She crossed the room, socks slipping on the polished wood floor, and unlocked both office doors. She looked up the long staircase, wondering if she should go knock on his door. Talk to him. Apologize for walking out on him so abruptly.

No. Not yet. Tomorrow.

Instead, she padded silently to the kitchen, where she got herself a glass of water, then went to the back door.

Looking out, she couldn't see even the silhouette of trees and plants along the backyard cliff. All she saw were the glorious stars, reminding her of how perfect last night had been.

Why had she let herself get so upset tonight? Ray had

no idea why she'd taken offense at his words. Surely he hadn't spoken out of malice. Why hadn't she given Ray the benefit of the doubt? She'd been so quick to make assumptions...

She finished the water and made her way back to the office.

Tomorrow, she'd talk to him about it. She'd find a way to explain her feelings without sounding like an idiot. She didn't want to ruin the rest of their holiday.

The resolution made her feel better. Now, she just had to figure out exactly what to say.

Chapter 10

THE NEXT MORNING, MICHELLE FELT AS THOUGH SHE'D been hit by a low-speed car. Between the lingering guilt at how she'd treated Ray and the aches from her long walk, she'd slept poorly. Not even a hot shower could wake her fully, and no force on earth could compel her to do yoga. Even the thought of standing in the kitchen to cook breakfast was unpleasant, but a far better alternative than walking to town.

Caught up in her misery, she put on a sweatshirt, jeans, and her thickest, softest socks before she went out into the sitting room. She wasn't quite limping, but that was out of sheer pride and stubbornness. Maybe she'd take a couple of aspirin, much as she hated taking painkillers. First, she'd make a cup of coffee and toast, and then go sit on the bench overlooking the water. Give nature a chance to help her feel better.

But fate was conspiring against her. As soon as she made it to the kitchen, she spotted Ray sitting on the patio. Despite the morning chill, he wore a T-shirt and no jacket. He had the left sleeve rolled up a couple of inches so he could examine his left arm. Michelle could just barely see the ends of the surgical tape.

She had the ridiculous impulse to creep away and hide in the office, but she restrained herself. Eventually, d have to face up to the aftermath of last night. etter to get it over with, like a visit to the dentist.

Instead, she went to the back door. At the first creak of the hinges, Ray pulled down his sleeve and turned to look at her.

When their eyes met, Michelle's calm, cool greeting lodged in her throat.

Ray pushed his chair back from the table and rose. "Good morning, Michelle."

She found her voice and even managed a faint smile. "Good morning."

He lifted a finger and gestured to the chair beside him. "Care to join me?"

She wanted to go back inside and start a pot of coffee, but that would be rude. Instead, she sat down, looking around to avoid his gaze. As he sat down, he moved his half-empty mug of tea out of the way. He had nothing else on the table—not even his phone. He wasn't a smartphone addict like so many other people were these days. In fact, he hadn't checked his phone once yesterday. As far as she knew, it had remained in his pocket even when she'd gone to the bathroom.

It was a nice change from boyfriends—and, yes, even friends—who couldn't go two minutes without checking for new messages or playing games. One more point in Ray's favor.

"About yesterday—"

"Look, I want—"

Their eyes met as they both went silent.

"I'm sorry," he said.

She shook her head. "Go ahead."

"No, please," he insisted.

She let out a tense little laugh and looked down at the table. "No, no, that's okay. You first."

Thankfully, he saved her from having to figure out how to start. He nodded and said, "I'm sorry about what happened last night."

Michelle exhaled. The knot of tension lodged in her chest started to unwind. "No, it's—"

"Please, let me finish." When she nodded, he continued, "I don't...get *involved* when I'm here on holiday. Most of my holidays here, I've spent alone, in fact. I come here when I need to unwind after a mission that's gone wrong. You've seen enough of the island to know that no one comes here for the"—he laughed softly—"the exciting nightlife or the lively pub scene. If not for you, I'd spend a fortnight or so alone, as I always did before." He extended his hands to her, palms turned up in invitation. "I'm very glad this visit turned out differently."

A little more of her tension eased. She laughed nervously and put her hands in his. "All right."

He curled his fingers around her hands, holding back his strength. He was always so gentle with her—so considerate—that it warmed her all the way to her toes.

"Last night, you said you're not my type," he continued, a hint of his charming, crooked smile showing, "but even if this were London instead of St. Mary's, I'd still choose to be with you."

This time, Michelle's laugh was relieved. She squeezed Ray's hands tightly, elated that last night hadn't ruined everything between them. "Thank you."

Ray felt as if he'd crossed a war zone and finally made it to his safe house. He was tempted to leave it there, to smooth over the last rough patches with a kiss, but those lingering questions would nag at him.

"Michelle," he said gently, "can you tell me what I said to make you think I didn't want to be with you?"

She looked back down and pulled one hand free so she could tuck a strand of hair behind her ear. "It's stupid."

He suspected that "it's stupid" translated to "I don't want to talk about it," but he really did need to know. Hoping to coax her into opening up to him, he touched her cheek and said, "We're on holiday. We're allowed to be stupid. It might even be a rule."

She laughed, keeping her head ducked, face hidden. "You called me a wren."

He waited for more, but when she fell silent, he asked, "Is that…bad somehow?"

She squeezed his hand and shrugged. "You wouldn't get it."

"Well, no, not if you won't help me understand."

"Vicky and Dana. They were always the pretty ones. They were the ones who got all the attention." She wrinkled her nose. "Two birds of paradise and a plain brown sparrow. Or a wren."

Finally understanding, Ray said thoughtfully, "I think I mentioned before, I've never paid much mind to birds."

With a surprised twitch, Michelle lifted her head and gave him a puzzled look. "You did, yes."

He smiled at her. "But unless you live in a hobbit hole, you're going to learn *something* about them. Pigeons, if nothing else. And wrens. Do you know what's extraordinary about wrens?"

She raised a brow skeptically. "That they're almost as common as sparrows?" she guessed.

"Their song," he said, giving her a gently scolding frown. "These tiny brown birds, absolutely unremarkable—easily mistaken for sparrows—have the most beautiful song you've ever heard. I used to listen to them sing on summer afternoons. Their calls are fast and light, like they're chattering a mile a minute, and when they all talk to one another, it's deafening."

She looked down, hiding her face again. "So you're saying I talk too much?" she challenged playfully.

He laughed. "Or not enough," he corrected, cupping his hand below her chin to tip her face toward his. "I want," he told her firmly, "to be with you. No questions, no doubts. Understand?"

She smiled and gave a little nod. "Yes," she said softly.

And before she could say anything else, he leaned in and kissed her, allowing the kiss to linger, slow and gentle, for only a moment before he licked at her lip. She surrendered beautifully, sliding to the edge of her seat, and parted her lips to touch her tongue to his. Her hands moved to grip his forearms, pulling him closer.

Heat shot through Ray, entirely inappropriate for a quiet morning after they'd barely settled their argument, but he couldn't bring himself to care about anything but the woman in his arms. He'd come so close to losing her... The kiss turned coaxing, demanding, teasing her into a hot, breathless slide of tongue and lips, bodies molded together for one endless, perfect moment.

When the kiss ended, fires banked but not extinguished, Michelle sat back. Her hands slid back down his arms so she could lace their fingers together. With her face flushed, eyes wide and dark as night, she was no pretty little wren at all but a temptress who threatened his self-control.

He wanted her. He wanted her tonight, in his arms, in his bed. But he couldn't. To push for more than soft touches and heated kisses might well prove, in some convoluted way, exactly what she'd feared: that she was conveniently available and nothing more.

Patience, he told himself. He smiled at her and glanced at his mug of cooling tea to deliberately break the mood. "Shall we go into Hugh Town again for breakfast?"

"Oh, no," she said with a light, genuine laugh. "I'm not walking anywhere. My feet are killing me."

The perfect solution came to him. Standing up, he grinned and said, "You stay there. Let me handle breakfast."

She shook her head and quickly rose. "No, that's all right."

"Sit," he scolded. "How many scoops to make your coffee?"

A hint of apprehension came into her eyes. "Four. But—"

"Please," he interrupted. "Let me do this for you."

She surrendered, settling back into her chair. "All right. Thank you."

He still wanted her. More to the point, she still wanted him, *and* he still wanted her. Last night's hiccup was over and done with. Now she could close her eyes, sit in the sunshine, and enjoy the morning breeze off the water, free from her worry that she'd managed to scare him off last night. Now they could move on to whatever the future held...

Which apparently started with the smoke alarm?

At the first beep, panic shot through Michelle. Forgetting all about her aching feet, she jumped up and rushed into the kitchen, leaving the door open. Smoke billowed up from a cast iron pan on the cooktop.

Ray was already grabbing for it, a dish towel wrapped around his hand. "It's fine, it's fine," he said, yanking the pan off the burner. He turned and glanced around as if searching for somewhere to put it. He had a mixing bowl on one counter, a loaf of bread on the cutting board, and the open bottle of milk on another counter next to his cell phone. A fresh mug stood waiting beside the coffeepot, where the coffee looked suspiciously dark—black instead of rich brown. Or that could have just been the smoke.

He finally put the frying pan in the sink. Drops of water hissed and sputtered. "That's the bacon done for," he said apologetically.

Wincing, Michelle hurried around the breakfast bar and turned off the burner before anything could fall on it and catch fire. "Why don't you let me do this?"

"I *can* cook, you know," he protested. "I just..."

"Windows?" she prompted, seizing the excuse to get him to the other side of the breakfast bar, where he could do far less damage. The incessant beeping cut into Michelle's skull like nails on a chalkboard. She glanced at the frying pan, wondering if any of the bacon could be salvaged, but most of it had been turned to charcoal.

"Sorry." He went around and started pushing open all the windows. Raising his voice, he said, "I was just looking something up and lost track of time."

Resisting the urge to cover her ears, Michelle glanced at the smartphone, where he'd opened a recipe site. "French toast?" she asked, trying not to sound incredulous. *Everyone* knew how to make French toast. She'd learned to make French toast when she was ten.

"Better than plain scrambled eggs," he said defensively.

So he'd been trying to impress her. Despite all the noise and the mess, she started to laugh.

After pushing open the last of the windows, he sat down at the breakfast bar. "I'm something of an expert at bachelor cooking, I'm afraid. Nothing fancy, like you manage."

Charmed by the effort, if not the result, she smiled and said, "Why don't I take it from here?"

Much to her relief, he didn't insist on trying again—and, even better, the smoke alarm finally stopped beeping. "If you'd like," he said. "I did make the coffee, though. And I cracked the eggs without getting any shells in."

A little warily, she glanced into the bowl. Six eggs, no visible shells. She smiled encouragingly at him. "Thanks. And how many scoops for the coffee?" she asked casually as she went for the milk.

"Four, like you said."

She poured milk into the bowl without measuring. "Four…heaping scoops?" she guessed, meeting his eyes.

He frowned. "Too much?"

She glanced back at the night-black pot. "Probably."

"Maybe from now on you should handle the cooking?" he suggested. "I'll provide recommendations to local restaurants instead, hmm?"

She nodded. "Let's do that," she agreed and went to see if there was any vanilla in the cupboards.

———

After breakfast, Michelle excused herself, saying she had work to do on the books, but instead Ray heard the water heater rumbling as she filled the bath. He relaxed just long enough to digest before going out for a run. He took a shorter route than the coastal path, a route that ended in Hugh Town, where he considered going to the hospital to see to his stitches. Instead, thinking of Michelle, he went to the deli to get cold cuts, cheeses, and a fresh loaf of bread. He wouldn't inflict his bachelor cooking habits on her, but he could at least assemble sandwiches without incident.

They ate lunch on the cliffside bench in companionable silence. After finishing the last bite of her sandwich, Michelle said, "You've redeemed yourself for what you did to the bacon."

"And the coffee?" he hinted slyly.

"Oh, no. You'll be paying for that one for *ages*," she threatened, eyes bright with silent laughter. "So, where did you want to start? It's a little late to go off the island, I'm guessing, but we still have half the day."

"Why don't we take it easy today?" he suggested casually, not wanting to let her know that he'd noticed how gingerly she'd been walking earlier. Perhaps eleven miles had been too far for an introduction to walking on the Isles.

She wrinkled her nose, squinting out at the sea. "There's nothing to do here," she said thoughtfully, gesturing back at Valhalla's Rest. "Not unless you want to start another kitchen fire."

"What happened to redemption?" he challenged. As she laughed, he grinned and said, "There's a draughts board in the sitting room. It's an antique, but Liam always meant it to be used, not preserved."

"Draughts—you mean checkers?"

He let out an exaggerated sigh and stood, gathering up their plates. "Colonial barbarian. We call it draughts in civilization."

"Oh, fine," she said, getting up with only the slightest twitch of pain. "But it's been at least fifteen or twenty years since I've played, so don't expect me to remember the rules."

"We'll just make up replacements for any that you've forgotten," he said, following her back to the house.

As they entered the kitchen, she smirked and took the plates out of his hands. "You go set up. I'll clean up. Want another bottle of water?"

"Please." He went to the full bay window at the front of the sitting room, where the antique draughts board sat between two chairs. The squares of light and dark wood were faded from the sun, and the edges of the board were chipped and dented.

The pieces were in a drawer underneath, a mismatched set from two different boards. He sorted out the best twelve of each color, red and white, and was laying them in the lighter squares when Michelle joined him.

"Antique, huh?" she asked, setting the two water bottles on coasters conveniently left on the windowsill for players. Old rings stained into the paint showed not every guest had been so thoughtful.

"Well, it's old, in any case," he admitted. "Red or white? White moves first."

She tipped her head and gave him a thoughtful look. "White," she said, taking a seat on that side of the board. As he sat down, she smiled and moved one of her pieces. "We never did go shopping last night, you know," she said casually, watching Ray move a red piece.

"I can go later, if you'd like."

"Or *we* can go. I need to go grocery shopping anyway. Dinner, then co-op?" she proposed.

Ray nearly mentioned that he'd bought enough sandwich meat and cheese to last them for some time. *Bachelor cooking*, he reminded himself, and nodded instead. "All right. Care to pick where we go?"

"How about the winner picks?" she challenged.

He grinned, determined to win so that he could at least demand they take a taxi instead of walking. "You're on."

—∿∿—

"You're certain you didn't cheat?" Ray accused, looking at Michelle sidelong as she took hold of his hand.

Still smirking at her victory, she said, "Positive. Besides, even if I'd cheated the first game, I gave you best two out of three, and you *still* lost." She turned to lock the back door and then started down the patio.

"The second game was because of your colonial rules. I've never heard of a double-king before."

"Really?" she asked innocently. "I'm positive I read about it somewhere."

He stared down at her, mouth quirked in a crooked smile. "*Cheaters' Guide to Draughts*," he suggested.

She laughed and tugged him out onto the lawn, heading for the path that led to the stargazing hill. Farther along, it met up with the coast path, which was their fastest route to Hugh Town. "The American edition is *Cheaters' Guide to Checkers*."

He coughed—it sounded suspiciously like a laugh—and let go of her hand to put his arm around her shoulders and pull her close. "You're certain you don't want to take a taxi?"

"I'm *fine*, really," she said with a hint of exasperation. "I'm not going to break from a little walking."

"No, not at all. But you're depriving Malcolm of all sorts of gossip," Ray said innocently.

"Malcolm?"

"The usual evening cabbie."

"Ah. Well, Malcolm can get his gossip off the TV. I'd rather keep you to myself."

Ray gave her a startled look that melted into a smile. "Agreed."

She was still grinning when they reached Hugh Town. The lingering shadow of last night was finally gone, leaving her free to think ahead to tonight. Tomorrow. The rest of her vacation. And maybe even more than that, though she wasn't going to rush into anything. No, she'd take her time and enjoy each day as it came.

Speaking of which... "So what are we doing tomorrow?" she asked as they walked down to the harbor. It was late in the afternoon, and boats were coming in, weaving between the neat grid of mooring buoys to find their places for the night.

"Piper's Hole," Ray said thoughtfully.

She tipped her head down to look at him over the rim of her sunglasses. "Excuse me?"

He laughed and hugged her close, looking out toward the setting sun. "It's a cave on the far side of the island. Legend has it that it connects to another cave of the same name on Tresco."

After four years of college road trips to cheesy tourist traps, she could sniff out an urban legend from a mile away. "There's more to it than an underwater cave, I take it?"

He nodded. "According to the stories, somewhere between the islands, the cave leaves this world—and time. You can go in one cave a child and come out the other ancient, as if decades or longer had passed."

"Uh-huh. I suppose you locals have proved this scientifically?"

Ray grinned. "I can take you there, if you like. We can explore by candlelight. It's traditional."

"Candlelit exploration of a cave to another world where we'll get old. Sounds very romantic," Michelle said, struggling not to laugh.

"We'll wait and go to the one on Tresco, maybe when we go to the garden there. That one's much larger. It's an old smuggler's hideout." His arm tightened around her shoulders, and he added more quietly, "It's also meant to be explored by candlelight."

"An old cave *and* smugglers. That's the second time you've hinted at taking up piracy."

He gave her a curious look. Then he laughed, saying, "Royal Marines. I'm fully qualified to steal a boat on your behalf."

Turning away from the harbor, she said, "I'll think about it. I'd have to do up a business plan, risk analysis, look into taxes—"

"For piracy?" he scoffed. "Steal the treasure; shoot the tax collectors. What else is there to plan?"

She laughed and looked around to get her bearings. She thought she remembered a nearby pub where they could pass the time until dinner. As she started in that direction, she said, "Insurance. Retirement planning. Staffing requirements, pay scale, investments, initial stock offerings."

He slowed, looking down at her. "You really are mad, aren't you?"

Too happy to even fake taking offense, she asked, "Is that a good thing or a bad thing?"

Laughing, he pulled her into his arms and kissed her. Answer enough.

———ᴡ———

They bought tickets for the inter-island boat to Tresco at a stationery store. Well, Ray did, insisting on paying for them himself. Michelle had won the argument over paying her share for last night's dinner, so she let it pass and went to browse the displays of postcards, magnets, and other trinkets.

"Find something you like?" Ray asked as he walked up behind where she'd crouched in front of a spinning wire rack of spoons.

"What is it with you people and puffins?" She looked up at him and offered him a spoon.

Before Ray could answer, the shopkeeper called, "It's the tail end of breeding season for them. There's a boat tour of the uninhabited islands, if you like. You might be able to see them this week. They usually leave around mid-July."

Suppressing a laugh, Michelle looked up at Ray, who was grinning down at her, eyes bright. "Want to go see some puffins?" she asked him.

"Only if you're certain you won't get seasick."

"I drove eighteen hours straight in a VW minivan with bad suspension after living on chili cheese dogs at a music fair for an entire weekend." She smirked and stood up, reclaiming the hideous puffin spoon. "I'll get these tickets. And after I *prove* I don't get seasick," she said, tapping his chest with the spoon, "you can buy me dinner. After *both* trips."

She left him laughing by the display of trinkets and spent a few minutes looking over the cruise options. There were more than she'd expected—tours to see seals or birds, trips with guided walking tours to see archaeological sites, even dinner cruises to restaurants on other islands. She was tempted to try them all, but she didn't want to lock in their schedule.

In the end, she bought tickets for the bird-watching tour of two uninhabited islands and the spoon, which she had gift wrapped. She tucked the spoon and tickets away as she met up with Ray at the door to the shop, which he held for her.

"The spoon?" he asked curiously.

"For Vicky. When she moved to London, she got an interior decorator to do her apartment. This is exactly the type of thing she'd *never* have in there."

Slowly, Ray's lips curved up in a wicked smile. "But coming from you…"

"She won't be able to throw it out. She'll *have to* put it on display." Michelle laughed.

"And here I thought you were the *nice* one," he said, laughing.

Trying not to laugh herself, she asked, "Does that mean you don't like me after all?"

He stopped and tugged her hand, pulling her into her arms. "It's genius," he approved, leaning down for another kiss that left her tingling.

She was still grinning as they walked around the corner to the pub she remembered. "Are we—" she began before a high, familiar laugh shattered her tranquillity, freezing her in mid-step.

No.

"Michelle? What's wrong?"

She heard the tension in Ray's voice and wanted to set him at ease, but she couldn't. Not yet. It was impossible, but she had to know…

Moving faster, she went to the corner, following the sound of laughter as it faded into rapid speech. With an *American* accent.

"This isn't happening," she muttered as she rounded the corner.

And there she stopped and stared at a café where two young waiters were laughing with a woman seated at an outdoor table, her back turned to Michelle.

"Michelle?" Ray put a hand on the small of her back, standing protectively close.

Before Michelle could even think of an answer, the woman turned. She tipped down her sunglasses, favored Michelle with a glowing smile, and waved. "Darling! There you are!"

Michelle let out a defeated sigh and stepped forward, away from Ray's comforting touch. As she was enveloped in a cloud of Narciso Rodriguez perfume, she smiled faintly and said, "Hi, Mom."

Chapter 11

MICHELLE'S MOTHER.

Of all the bloody things to have happen, this might not have been the worst, but it was definitely on the list. No, it *wasn't* on the list, because Ray had never even imagined that it could happen at all. Didn't Michelle's mother live in Arizona? She should have been halfway across the world—not thirty miles off the coast of Cornwall on an island most Americans had never even heard of.

Ray watched in disbelief as the woman swept Michelle into an embrace. "I've been trying to call you!" the woman scolded. She had a faint hint of Western drawl to her accent, a contrast to Michelle's East Coast nasality.

"What are you doing here, Mom? You were going to an auction," Michelle said, stepping back the moment she was released. "In San Francisco."

"Oh, I can go to auctions any time," the woman said dismissively. She waved a hand, rings flashing in the late afternoon sunlight. "As soon as I got back from Sedona, I did some digging on the Internet. And the *instant* I saw the pictures of this gorgeous island, I knew I had to come for a visit."

Just when things were finally going right... Ray tried

to push aside his disappointment, to find some way to gracefully accept this new change in plans he shouldn't have had to begin with. Twenty-four hours ago, he and Michelle had been finishing a wonderful, spontaneous walk through St. Mary's. And then...

And then the fight, a tense night of troubled sleep, their talk this morning. And *just* as things had turned bright once more, lightning struck in the form of Michelle's tall, fashionably extravagant mother.

Michelle's shoulders slumped just enough for Ray to pick up on her disappointment. That was something, at least, unfair as it was to take comfort that she shared his unhappiness at this turn of events. This was her mother, and if Michelle wasn't overjoyed at her arrival, she wasn't calling the constables to have her carted away. They seemed to get along well enough.

Michelle turned around and smiled, saying, "Mom, this is Ray Powell. We met...here." She faltered, giving Ray a slightly desperate look. "Ray, this is my mother, Eleanor Cole."

"A pleasure to meet you, ma'am," he said, extending his hand with a polite smile.

The woman pulled off her sunglasses and took his hand between both of hers. Her nails were the same shade of mint green as Michelle's, without the chips. Where Michelle was dressed for comfort, her mother was dressed for style in black, tan, and cream. Her dark eyebrows hinted that her sleek blond hair wasn't natural, and Ray couldn't help contrasting her meticulous cosmetics to Michelle's natural beauty.

Under the surface, though, their mother-daughter relationship was obvious. They had the same deep brown eyes, the same high cheekbones, oval faces, and gently pointed chins. Ray had heard the clichés of mothers who looked more like older sisters, but he'd never seen it until now.

In turn, the woman looked him over just slowly enough for the moment to be awkward. Even after spending years in America, Ray was still British to his very soul. It was one thing to have Michelle regard him with such interest; her mother was something else entirely.

He could imagine Preston's voice over his radio earpiece, ordering, "*Hostile contact. Abort.*"

But British reserve was very different from cowardice. Preston probably would have withdrawn from the field, politely allowing Michelle private time with her mother—and removing himself from her presence—but Ray saw no reason to alienate either woman. He wasn't looking for a one-night stand anymore.

Was he?

"We were going to the pub for a quick drink before dinner," he said smoothly. "Would you care to join us?"

"You could ask me anything with that accent, and I might just say yes. Please, call me Eleanor."

"Mom," Michelle said with a sigh.

Eleanor released Ray's hand and spun away. "Let me just get my purse. The taxi driver is holding my luggage—Malcolm, such a nice man," she said, bustling back to the table. "Everyone here's so polite."

Malcolm, Ray thought with a grimace. He could just imagine the gossip.

Michelle crowded Ray back a couple of steps, whispering, "I'm *so* sorry. This—I never even imagined she'd come here! She's so…so *impulsive*."

"It's all right," Ray assured her, keeping a steady smile as he looked over her shoulder at Eleanor, who was chatting with her waiter again. "Shall we go back to last night's restaurant?" he suggested. "Your mother might appreciate the view."

With a quiet groan, Michelle asked, "You don't mind?"

Ray wanted to kiss away her frown, but he wouldn't— not in front of her mother. Instead, he'd be patient and follow Michelle's lead. "Not at all."

"I just wish—*Oh!*" She gave him a sudden smile, looking around the street. "Art galleries."

"Art galleries?" he repeated, feeling a sinking sense of dread. He couldn't imagine anything more tedious than wandering around looking at incomprehensible paint splatters or lumps of clay.

Michelle opened her mouth to answer, but Eleanor returned to take hold of Michelle's arm. "So! Where are we going?" she asked cheerfully, smiling up at Ray. "I want to see everything."

Of course you do, he thought, smile never faltering, and led them down the road, heading for the nearest pub.

———

"So, how did you two meet?"

Much as Michelle had expected the question, it made her wince all the same. The last thing she wanted was to have her mother ferret out the particulars of her relationship—especially not what had happened last night.

"It was a mix-up," she said, turning to smile quickly at Ray. They were seated on the same bench. "He usually stays at Valhalla's Rest."

Ray nodded. "I knew the previous owner."

"You're local, then?" her mother pressed.

"I spent my childhood holidays here." He shot a glance at Michelle, his expression almost guilty, and added, "Valhalla's Rest used to be my grandparents' house."

Startled, Michelle asked, "What?" His grandparents' house? He'd never said a word about that, had he? No, she would have remembered. He'd only told her that he'd been coming to Scilly for family vacations all his life.

"After my grandmother died, I sold the property to Liam." Under the table, Ray's leg pressed against Michelle's; both his hands were wrapped around his pint glass. "He'd always wanted to open a bed and breakfast, and the property is in an ideal location. Land is so hard to come by here, I gave him a fair price in exchange for room and board whenever I needed to come home."

She tried not to sound accusatory when she said, "You never told me. You let me charge you for the room."

He gave her a faint, apologetic smile. "I should have mentioned it, but you've been looking at the business through professional eyes. I didn't want sentiment to influence whatever you told your friend."

"Very admirable," her mother said. She got that look in her eyes—that dangerous, sly look Michelle had learned to dread—as she continued, "Not to mention *very* romantic, you two meeting at a special place from your childhood, Ray."

"Mom—"

"I can't wait to see it! It's gorgeous from the outside."

"You were there already?" Michelle asked, stomach

dropping. She should've realized that her mother's impulsive visit meant she hadn't thought ahead to make a reservation elsewhere, at a proper hotel. Her mother wasn't the bed and breakfast type. When she'd traveled to New York, she'd never spent even one night at Anchor's Cove. So why did she want to stay at Valhalla's Rest?

So much for having any private time to get to know Ray better.

Her mother continued as if she hadn't heard Michelle's question. "And the landscaping. Everything is just breathtaking! All these flowers. How do you have such gorgeous weather in the North Atlantic? I mean, you have *palm trees* here."

"Technically, it's the Celtic Sea. It has to do with wind and water currents," Ray explained when she paused for breath.

"Well, it's just *lovely*. It must have been wonderful growing up in such a warm, inviting home. I hope the rooms are as nice as the outside," she said, confirming Michelle's fears. Turning back to Ray, she relentlessly continued, "When Michelle told me Vicky had called with this offer, I just knew it was perfect for her. She's been searching for her path ever since she lost her old bed and breakfast. And while I'm so sorry she had to come to this one through tragedy—my condolences for your loss—I'm certain this is right where she's supposed to be. That's how the universe works, you know."

Poor Ray seemed to be listening with every sign of interest, but Michelle knew it was only a matter of time before his eyes glazed over. Not that her mother would ever notice. She'd just charge headlong into the conversation and run right over anyone in her path. And she was genuinely oblivious to the chaos that surrounded her as she sailed through life. Sometimes, Michelle wondered if she hadn't taken up yoga as an antidote to her mother.

Worse, though, Ray's presence gave her mother something to latch onto. She'd never had faith in Michelle's ability to find a relationship—not that her mother was any better, with her track record of divorces. But she was well-meaning, always looking out for Michelle's best interests, in her own way. Once she realized Michelle was really interested in Ray, she'd probably decide that she could help Michelle "catch" him.

There was no way out of it. Her mother had flown five thousand miles to get here. All Michelle could do was grit her teeth, take things one day at a time, and hope to get out of this with her dignity intact—unlikely, given how much her mother loved telling childhood stories.

For now, though, her mother was more interested in Ray than in interrogating Michelle for the details of their relationship. "So! What do you do now?" she asked, fixing him with her sharp gaze.

Unfazed, he returned the smile and calmly answered, "I'm in private security."

"That sounds exciting. In London?"

"Virginia, actually."

"Virginia!" She shot Michelle a grin. "Chelly's always loved the East Coast."

Please, don't help, Michelle thought, though she didn't dare say it. She even hid her glare, knowing that her mother would only take it as a challenge.

"It's beautiful," Ray agreed. "I've lived there for years now, since leaving the Royal Marines."

"The Royal Marines," her mother said thoughtfully. "My last ex-husband was military. He was a pilot in the Air Force."

"The last—"

"Sorry, before I forget..." Michelle interrupted before Ray could make the mistake of asking about the "dreaded exes," as she called them. "Did you make those dinner reservations?"

He gave her a polite, curious smile at the interruption but thankfully took the hint. "Let me go confirm them. If you'll both excuse me?" He left the table, taking out his phone as he went toward the pub door.

As soon as Ray was gone, Michelle turned on her mother, demanding in a low, fierce tone, "What are you doing here? Really, Mom!"

"It's exactly as I said," her mother dismissed, taking a sip of her whiskey. She'd tried to order a pomegranate martini, but the bartender—too polite to openly be horrified—had talked her into trying the local spirits instead. "I had some spare time, and I couldn't pass up seeing such a gorgeous destination."

Trying to gather her composure, Michelle took a sip of her pint without tasting it. "Okay. Look, Mom, do me *one* favor? Please?"

Her mother beamed at her and reached across the table to pat her hand. "Anything."

"*Please* go easy on Ray." Bracing herself, Michelle admitted, "I like him."

Her mother glanced at the door, eyes narrowed in thought. "I don't think that one needs gentle handling, Chelly."

"*Mother!*"

Laughing, she said, "That's not what I meant—at least, not intentionally. But you can't have known him for more than a few days. Do you *really* like him that much?"

Michelle should have expected the question, especially from her nosy mother, but it still took her by surprise. "I might," she said cautiously, "but I can't tell until I get to know him."

"Is that so?" she asked without a hint of innuendo or humor in her voice, as if she knew something Michelle didn't.

Michelle frowned, turning her glass in her hands. Sometimes, on very rare occasions, her mother could be surprisingly perceptive. Was this one of them? "It's only been a few days, Mom. I hardly know him."

"You already know more than *you* think you do. But you've never been one to trust your instincts, have you?"

After wondering about Ray for all this time— wondering and hoping—and thinking about everything that had gone wrong with Dana, the jab hit home, unintentional as it was. For the last year, Michelle had second-guessed every decision.

More to the point, she'd refused to let herself get close to anyone. To *trust* anyone, other than Vicky.

Her mother pulled Michelle's hands away from the glass to clasp them tightly. In the same gentle tone that had soothed childhood nightmares and comforted teenage heartbreak, she asked, "Chelly?"

Michelle took a deep breath, squeezing her mother's hands. No matter how exasperating her mother could be, no matter how they'd fought and clashed, Michelle had always loved her and she always would.

"I'm sorry. Yes, I like him," she made herse... much as she wanted to add "I think" to the words. ... she *did* like him. She just wanted to get to know hi... better to make sure that liking him was a good idea. "So please—"

"Say no more," her mother interrupted. She released Michelle and gave an expansive wave. "If you like him, *I* like him. Now we just have to make him realize that he likes you, hmm?"

—⁓—

Almost three hours later, Michelle and Ray walked out of the hilltop restaurant, blissfully alone. Her mother had wanted a drink or two at the bar, and she'd insisted, much to Michelle's relief, that she'd find her own way back. Michelle looked up at the stars—bright even here, in town—and sighed, lacing her fingers with Ray's.

Somehow, they'd survived dinner, thanks in part to some well-timed questions about her mother's business as an artist's representative. She could talk about art for hours, whether it was her latest artist discovery or a successful gallery show or gossip about the buyers who frequented her social circles. All Ray and Michelle had to do was politely nod and prompt her to continue, and they'd made it through the entire meal, dessert included, without a single embarrassing story from Michelle's childhood.

Michelle had no illusions that her fortune would last, but at this point, she'd take what luck she could get.

"You're certain you wouldn't rather stay at the bar and take a taxi back with your mother?" he asked, giving her hand a squeeze.

efinitely not. She'll be fine, and I could use the
ak." Michelle leaned against Ray's arm. Only when
e twitched away did she remember his stitches. "Sorry!"

"It's nothing." He let go of her hand so he could wrap
his arm around her shoulders, pulling her close. "Your
mother's very excitable, isn't she?"

Excitable. That was one way to put it. "The wine
at dinner kept her calm. You should see her after her
morning coffee," Michelle said wryly.

"Consider me duly warned. I'll just sneak down for
my tea first thing—and to do laundry, if you don't mind.
I can't recall if I asked."

"Not a problem," she said, frowning, feeling somewhat distracted. Her mother's unexpected appearance
had left her disoriented. She knew she was forgetting something.

"I know the bloke who runs the boat tours," Ray said
tentatively. "Should I ring him up and see if I can shift
our tickets to later in the week?"

"Shit." Disappointment hit all over again. So much
for a romantic sail around the islands. "Probably,
yeah. Mom will expect to spend at least a couple of
days with us."

"We also could bring her along."

"Yeah, right." She laughed, trying not to sound bitter,
and forced a smile. "Because all good pirates bring their
mothers along on—on outings," she said, refraining at
the last moment from saying *dates*.

Ray hugged her close. "We could always strand her
on Tresco."

"I wouldn't do that to the... What are they called,
Trescans? Trescites?"

He laughed long and loud, and some of her dis pointment cracked and fell away. He wasn't runnir away. He'd survived dinner with her mother, which was more than *any* boyfriend ever had. After a while, Michelle had stopped trying. There was no sense in inviting them over just to have her mother tear them apart with her sharp tongue and quick wit.

But the thought of those dinners at home jogged Michelle's memory. She frowned and started walking more quickly, hooking her fingers in Ray's belt loop.

"Are we in a hurry?"

"I forgot, I'll need to make up a room for Mom," she admitted. And she'd have to do laundry soon, too. Her sheets and Ray's needed changing, and she should probably do a load of towels, too.

"Would you mind a suggestion?"

"I'm not going to let you help," she scolded. "You're still technically a guest."

"Just a suggestion." Without slowing their steps, Ray leaned down and kissed the top of her head. "Put her in the Jane Owen suite."

There was only one suite in Valhalla's Rest, a two bedroom with a private bath, up the stairs and to the left. "At the opposite side of the building from the Serica room," she said, giving Ray a sly smile. "Good plan."

"I'm a professional security consultant," he reminded her. "It's far easier to handle one determined mother than a hostile force looking to kidnap a client."

"Don't say that until you get to know my mother," she warned, feeling much better about this visit.

"Ah, it could be worse, love," he said with a laugh. The endearment, casual as it was, warmed her to her toes.

"How's that?"

"Back home, Preston is playing host to his extended family for the entire week so they can meet his brother's fiancée. Your mother is nothing compared to the whole Fairchild clan."

"If there are enough of them, we could always go hide in their midst. Mom can get kind of feisty." Feeling better, she stopped and tipped her face up.

He took the hint and gave her a kiss, quick and light. "Or we could send your mother there instead. She'd probably be brilliant at wedding planning."

With an exaggerated shudder, Michelle whispered, "*Never* say the *W* word around her."

"Have all those divorces left her against that sort of thing?"

"Worse. She thinks she's an expert."

"Oh, this is *charming*," her mother sang out delightedly, looking around the foyer as she dragged her smallest suitcase inside. She had her purse over one arm. Everything else—two suitcases, a small trunk, and a garment bag—she'd left on the porch.

"Why don't I get your bags?" Michelle muttered as her mother abandoned the suitcase and went into the sitting room. After Eleanor had given the taxi driver an extravagant tip, he'd offered to help bring her bags inside, but Michelle had foolishly let him go. Looking between the luggage and the long stairway, she wondered if she hadn't spoken a bit too soon.

Her mother turned, in the middle of the sitting room, and smiled at Michelle. "Where's your bar?"

"There *isn't* a bar, Mom. This is a bed and brea[k]
not a hotel."

"Oh. Well, you must have *something* to drink."

"Mom—"

"Don't worry, dear. I'll find it," her mother declared
airily, giving a wave. "You can just take care of those.
No need to trouble yourself." She swept into the dining
room, turning on every light as she went.

Don't trouble myself. She was very tempted to just
push everything out the front door and leave it for the
wild puffins to scavenge. How often did puffins have
the chance to get their beaks on Louis Vuitton luggage?

But amusing as the thought was, she was too much of
a professional—even when it came to her mother. She
started hefting the bags, aware of her mother's habit of
over-packing. Her mother was never one to let weight-
based luggage fees get in the way of fashion.

At the sound of footsteps, she looked up to see Ray
coming down the stairs, staring at the luggage in surprise. "So we're taking up smuggling after all, Captain?"
he asked, barely hiding his laughter.

Her mother had disappeared into the kitchen. Quietly,
Michelle said, "Welcome to life with my mother."

"Let me help," he offered, going right for the two
largest suitcases.

"No, don't. Your arm," she protested.

He lifted the suitcases with ease. "It's no trouble."

"If you're sure," she surrendered, picking up the
garment bag. She folded it over her arm and picked up the
trunk, only to nearly drop it. What did her mother have in
it, rocks? Pretending the trunk didn't outweigh her, she
picked up the carry-on and braced herself for his protest.

didn't say a word. Instead, he led the way up the
s, asking, "Is she staying for the rest of the summer?"

"Ten days, unless she changes her mind." Privately,
Michelle was hoping that St. Mary's, with its quiet,
peaceful atmosphere and lack of exciting nightlife,
would prove deathly boring to her mother. London was
a matter of hours away and far more suited to her taste.

"Ten days?" He looked significantly at the two suitcases he was carrying.

"Mom," Michelle explained, shrugging her left
shoulder. The right wasn't going anywhere until she
dropped the trunk.

At the top of the stairs, Ray turned left and followed
the balcony overlooking the sitting room. There was a
single door at the end of the landing, with the words
The Jane Owen Suite painted above a picture of a ship's
figurehead. "It's unlocked," Michelle said. "I set up the
back bedroom for her, if you don't mind..."

"No trouble at all." He pushed open the door and
went into the suite, thankfully not offering to carry the
rest of the bags for her.

Together, they found room for the luggage in the
cozy bedroom. Michelle considered unpacking for her,
but one look inside the trunk made her shudder and
change her mind. "If she needs more room, there's a
whole other bedroom for her shoes."

Ray shot her a wary look. "How many bloody shoes
did she bring?"

In answer, Michelle nudged the trunk with one foot.

"My God," Ray said, staring at the trunk as if it were
a venomous snake. Then he frowned, carefully asking,
"How many pairs did *you* bring?"

She burst out laughing and took his hand to lead out of the room. "Not even half as many, I promise. O. suitcase, one carry-on, one tote bag. I know it's extravagant, but not all of us can live out of a backpack."

Ray grinned and stopped in the suite's tiny sitting room. He tugged Michelle close, glancing over her head at the open doorway. His stolen kiss gave her an illicit thrill, and her heart raced as she wrapped her arms around him and surrendered.

"Chelly!"

The shout floated up to them, breaking their moment of shared, secret pleasure. She dropped flat to her feet and let her head fall against Ray's chest, solid and strong. Then she took a deep breath and regretfully pulled out of his arms. She left the suite and went to the railing, calling more gently, "Yes, Mother?"

Her mother appeared in the sitting room, looking up at her. "You've got nothing decent to drink, so we'll have to go shopping tomorrow. For now, I'm making some kava tea, only I can't find the kettle."

"It's—" Michelle began before realizing her mother had probably never used an electric kettle in her life. Or a gas stove, for that matter. In Arizona, she had a ceramic glass cooktop. Michelle shot Ray an apologetic smile and quickly rushed for the stairs. "I'll take care of it!"

"Thank you, dear." She smiled up toward the suite and waved. "Ray! I was wondering where you were hiding. Did you want a cup of tea?"

Michelle quickly answered, "He needs to go to sleep, Mom. We were up early."

"Another morning person?" Her mother didn't roll her eyes, but her tone said more than enough.

Perhaps tomorrow," Ray said, smiling down at them th. "Good night, ladies."

"Sleep tight!" She gave him one more wave as she headed for the kitchen.

Wishing she could have one more good-night kiss, Michelle gave him an answering smile. *Tomorrow*, she mouthed silently at him.

He nodded, smile turning sly. *Tomorrow*, he promised and then headed for his bedroom, leaving Michelle to go rescue her mother from the unfamiliar kitchen.

Chapter 12

Wednesday, July 10

EARLY THE NEXT MORNING, RAY WARILY MADE HIS way downstairs, listening for any sign of life. He doubted Eleanor did anything subtly or quietly, no matter the hour, but Michelle could sneak around like a mouse. He hadn't heard her moving around that very first morning, when he was still fresh from the Peshawar mission. Either that or his subconscious had trusted her from day one.

Now, everything seemed quiet and peaceful. Though he'd grown accustomed to sharing the house with other tourists on these infrequent holidays, he had to admit he rather liked having it all to himself. Or *mostly* private, he amended, thinking of Eleanor.

He crossed the sitting room and went to the game board by the front window. Michelle's three white double-kings were where she'd left them after capturing his last pieces. He picked up one white piece and tossed it on his palm. Her competitive streak had come as a pleasant surprise. She didn't play coy at losing or letting him make decisions thinking she had to save his "fragile" ego. Even when she did look to him to decide something—local tourist attractions or restaurants, for example—it was because of his knowledge.

Mutual respect, he thought as he put the game piece

own. That sort of thing never happened in one-
stands, except on the most superficial level. It was
ce change.

He turned and walked through the dining room into
the kitchen. The coffeepot was untouched, and the dish-
washer lights were still on. Michelle hadn't unloaded
it. Hoping to catch sight of another early morning
yoga practice, he went to the back door, but the garden
was empty.

Biting back a disappointed sigh, Ray went back
upstairs to get his dirty clothes. He really had waited
too long to do his laundry. Yesterday's clothes were still
in the bathroom. He brought them out to the bedroom
and opened his drawer, remembering he'd need clean
clothes after his run.

"Bugger," he muttered. One pair of black dress socks
sat at the bottom of the otherwise empty drawer. He was
wearing the T-shirt he'd worn on the plane, running
shorts, and his last pair of white athletic socks.

Maybe he'd do laundry first and go for his run after
his clothes were in the dryer. That or he'd have to resort
to the bachelor method of laundry: go to Hugh Town
and buy a fresh change of clothes.

When he opened his backpack, he found himself
staring not at dirty clothes but at a stuffed animal. The
reminder of the Peshawar mission was momentarily
jarring. He took a steadying breath and moved the fluffy
toy out of the way, to the foot of the bed. Then he shoved
his dirty clothes into the backpack and left the room.

Only when he was downstairs, in the laundry room,
did he remember that Eleanor was in the Jane Owen
suite, which meant that Eleanor was sleeping right above

the laundry room. He had no idea how much noise, if any, would transmit through the floor. But the industrial washing machines were powerful and loud. He couldn't take the chance of waking Eleanor after her flight almost halfway around the world.

Frustrated, he dropped his backpack on the counter beside Michelle's yoga mat. What *else* would go wrong this morning?

He needed tea. No, he needed a run first, and *then* he'd have tea, and to hell with the laundry problem. Absolute worst case, he'd send Eleanor and Michelle out to play tourist alone while he got himself fit for human socialization after his run.

He'd taken to leaving his water bottle in the kitchen after his runs, so he could wash it and let it dry on the rack. As he was filling it at the sink, he heard a faint click from somewhere inside the house. Not upstairs, he guessed, but up front. The manager's office. *Michelle.*

She walked into the kitchen a moment later, confirming his guess. She was barefoot and fresh-faced, wearing an oversized T-shirt and yoga pants. She'd knotted her hair at her nape, and she looked absolutely adorable.

"Morning," he said, turning off the faucet so he could greet her properly.

She walked right up to him and, as soon as he put down the water bottle, wrapped her arms around his waist. Smiling, he ducked to kiss the top of her head and then hugged her close. He liked that she didn't wear perfume to tickle his nose or, worse, make him sneeze.

"Going for a run?" she asked quietly.

"Just a short one. Will your mother be sleeping in this morning? She might need to adjust to the change in time zone," he said thoughtfully. Arizona was one of the few places in America that didn't shift with Daylight Saving Time, which meant it was…seven hours behind? Eight?

She shrugged and stepped back, reaching for his hands. "She didn't mention what time her flight left Arizona. Would you mind if we played tourist locally today, just to be safe? There are more than enough galleries and artist studios here to keep her happy for a little while, at least."

"Sounds lovely," Ray lied, dreading the idea of having to trudge through a day's worth of art galleries. Hadn't he mentioned that yesterday, right after they'd stumbled upon Eleanor? Perhaps he'd just been thinking it. Emphatically.

Then he remembered his laundry crisis. *Perfect*. He'd go for his run, and by the time he came back, the morning would already be well underway. He'd send Michelle and Eleanor to go to art galleries on their own while he took his time sorting lights from colors, cold from hot. If he got desperate to delay, he could even break out the ironing board.

Michelle laughed. "You're a terrible liar."

Sheepishly, he pointed out, "To be fair, I haven't had my morning tea."

Grinning, she flattened her palms on his chest and leaned in close, rising up on her toes. She kissed his cheek, lips soft against his stubble. "If we call her a taxi, will the driver know some good galleries or studios?" She laughed wickedly, adding, "Are you sure Malcolm only works nights? She thought he was nice, remember? She'd probably love to spend the day with him."

"Nice, but quite happily married."

"That's never stopped her from flirting."

He could just imagine Eleanor Cole versus Helen Stewart. That fodder would last the gossip mill for *years*.

"His wife drives during the day, though I suppose I could call and see if he'd do us a favor," Ray said with a mischievous grin.

"Well…" Michelle's fingers twitched over his shirt, tugging at the fabric. She rose up again, leaning her slight weight against his chest, and whispered, "If he'd be willing to get her started on her tour of St. Mary's art community, we'd have a little time alone."

A thrill of anticipation coiled through Ray, and he nodded. "Absolutely," he promised, determined to do whatever was necessary. "I'll just give Mrs. Stewart at the taxi company a call before I go on my run, shall I?"

Michelle's smile turned impish. "You do that. I'll see if I can find an insulated mug, so Mom can take her coffee to go."

"Brilliant plan," he approved, thinking he'd best take it easy on his run.

After giving Ray a toe-curling kiss good-bye, Michelle filled a glass of water and wandered innocently to the patio door just so she could watch as he broke into a run across the yard, heading for the trail. The muscles in his legs were beautifully defined, and the back view in running shorts was just as entrancing as the photo she would never admit to having saved on her phone. His stride was easy and balanced. He was a man at home in his body, without a hint of awkwardness.

He was a panther, she decided, sighing regretfully as

he finally passed out of sight. Definitely a panther, dangerous and gorgeous and graceful. Her fingers itched to stroke his black hair and pet those sleek muscles. Would he purr for her? She suspected he would.

She laughed wickedly. That thought was *so not her*, but she had to admit, she liked the idea all the same. Maybe she'd suggest it for later, after she got rid of her unexpected mother.

She finished her water and went into the laundry room to fetch her yoga mat, only to find Ray's backpack on the counter. It was stuffed so full that it stood upright. Curious, she lifted the top flap enough to see dirty socks.

Right, he needed to do laundry—which reminded her that she needed to change out the sheets and towels.

Yoga could wait. Thinking it best to take care of business before Ray got back from his run, she went to the linen closet and gathered an armload of towels and sheets. Liam had stored most of his linens with sachets of dried flowers; only one cupboard had been left unscented for guests who had allergies.

Wreathed in a fragrant floral cloud, Michelle carried everything upstairs. She paused to listen for any sign of life from her mother's suite, but all was quiet.

As was apparently his habit, Ray had left his room unlocked. Michelle let herself in and softly closed the door. Then she turned—

And she blinked in surprise. On Ray's bed was a floppy-eared stuffed dog with curly lavender fur. For one moment, she wondered if he'd bought it as a gift to surprise her. But then, as she moved closer, she realized the dog was worn and fraying—a well-loved treasure.

Had it been Ray's? She couldn't imagine a man like

him would carry a stuffed animal around with him. Even more confusing, he'd just come back from a job in a war zone. Why would he have a stuffed animal with him there, especially when room in his backpack was so scarce?

Touched by the mystery, she set the stuffed dog gently aside on the dresser before she went about stripping the bed. Old sheets and pillowcases, she piled on the floor. Once she had the new ones in place, she arranged the pillows, spread out the duvet, and smoothed everything neatly in place. On laundry day at Anchor's Cove, she'd sometimes put a cut flower or seashell on the bed as a surprise for her guests.

Here, the front yard landscaping was overgrown, going wild. There were more than enough flowering bushes to make up a dozen bouquets. She was momentarily tempted to go and cut fresh flowers, but Ray didn't seem like the flowers type.

Then again, he didn't seem like the stuffed animal type, either, but the evidence was right there on the dresser. After she finished with the bed, she picked up the dog, rather than moving to the bathroom to replace the used towels with fresh ones.

The lavender dog was lumpy, its stuffing compressed from years of cuddling and handling. The seam across the bottom was ragged where it had been repaired with heavy, clumsy stitches. Michelle couldn't keep from smoothing down the fur, though she knew it was an intrusion of Ray's privacy—the sort of professional violation that she'd rarely committed.

Finally, she set the dog carefully back down, this time placing it in the middle of the pillows. Ray would know she'd tidied his room; there was no point in trying to hide the dog. And if he knew she'd seen it, she'd be able to ask about it later.

By the time she was done switching out Ray's towels, she heard sounds of life from the other end of the B and B. She gathered up the dirty linens and towels and carried them into the hall just in time to see her mother emerge from the suite, neatly dressed in light layers of pastel cotton and linen. For some odd reason, she was carrying a bright green reusable grocery bag, stuffed full.

"Good morning!" her mother sang, wedge sandals clattering loudly as she bustled over to Michelle. After bestowing a perfumed kiss on each cheek, she tried to take away some of the towels, saying, "Here, let me help."

Michelle shook her head; she was used to navigating stairs with an armload of laundry. The last thing she needed was her mother tripping and breaking a leg—a likely outcome in those sandals. "I've got it, thanks," she said, knowing her mother expected her to refuse. "Do you want breakfast?"

"Oh! I have these wonderful breakfast bars. You crumble them up on top of Greek yogurt," Eleanor answered, brandishing the grocery bag before heading down the stairs.

Michelle followed, hiding a sigh. *That* was what she'd forgotten: grocery shopping. "We don't have any Greek yogurt."

Eleanor paid her no mind, continuing, "And I brought a new type of green tea that's just delicious. And so healthy, full of antioxidants. Or would you prefer coffee? Before leaving, I bought a pound of organic fair trade Sumatra that you'll adore."

Was it even legal to bring coffee, tea, and breakfast bars into the UK? Michelle had no idea. She was just glad she hadn't received a phone call from the Border Agency saying they'd detained her mother.

"Mom, we don't have Greek yogurt," she repeated when she caught up with her mother in the kitchen. "Breakfast-wise, we've got eggs, pancake mix, and bread."

"Oh, Chelly," her mother scolded, clucking her tongue. "What kind of diet is that?"

Michelle bit back her retort—*A normal one!*—and instead said, "It's all local, Mom. The eggs are organic. That's why they're in a basket on the counter and not in the fridge." She looked at the fridge, trying to remember what other food they had. They really did need to go grocery shopping. "I think there are still some vegetables in the crisper drawer. The cheese is also fresh from the deli."

"Huh. Well, that's all right, I suppose," her mother said skeptically. "Were you going to do your yoga first?"

"Not this morning. I have too much to do around here. Maybe later." She dumped the towels and sheets onto the counter. She'd need to go to the manager's apartment to get her own linens. For now, though, she opened the cupboard to take stock of supplies; the brands were unfamiliar, but Liam had stocked the cupboard well. She started skimming labels.

"Did you want me to make you some breakfast, then?" her mother offered.

"That'd be great," Michelle said, pleased to have

something to distract her mother. Besides, before her mother had started her health food kick, she used to make a fantastic omelet. Hopefully she hadn't lost the knack.

Heading right for the fridge, her mother asked over her shoulder, "So where's that gorgeous Royal Marine of yours? Still in bed?" In a mock-scolding tone, she asked, "Chelly, did you exhaust him?"

Thankfully, Michelle had her back turned, because she knew she was blushing—which was absurd. She was a grown woman, not a teenager caught making out on the porch at the end of a date. Hell, she'd never even been that teenager. Her Saturday night study dates had actually resulted in better grades, not high school heartbreak.

Worse, had their places been reversed, her mother wouldn't have been blushing at all. Michelle knew that fact all too well, given how often she'd gone down to her mother's kitchen in the morning, only to be introduced to her mother's latest boyfriend—a different one every time—enjoying a morning-after cup of organic fair-trade coffee.

"He's gone jogging," Michelle said as her eye fell on Ray's backpack again. She tried to calculate how much he had in the way of clean clothes remaining. It couldn't be much.

The linens could wait, she decided. She only hesitated for a moment before she started taking Ray's clothes out of the pack. He wouldn't take offense, she thought. Otherwise, he would've left the pack upstairs.

"You really didn't tire him out last night?" Her mother let out a disappointed sigh.

"No, Mom. We're not sleeping together," she answered, though a smile played at her lips. Her answer might well be different tonight, depending on how things played out today. Assuming, of course, she could find a way to get rid of her mother.

"My God, why not? You've only got…what, twelve days left until your flight back home? Don't tell me you forgot condoms, Chelly. You *always* used to carry them."

Exasperated, Michelle dumped Ray's unsorted laundry on top of one of the dryers and went to the doorway. "Are you going to be like this the whole vacation?"

Her mother turned, holding the knife she'd been using to chop vegetables. "Like what?"

"Like…*you*!" Michelle felt a stab of guilt at her mother's wounded expression, but continued, "Yes, I like him. And not a…one-night-stand sort of 'like.' So can you *please* not try to rush everything along?"

Her mother set the knife down on the edge of the cutting board. She circled around the kitchen island to and walked to Michelle, studying her the whole time. "This isn't like you, Chelly."

Michelle sighed. "I know. That's why I *need* to take this at my own pace, Mom. Okay?"

"I'm sorry." She brushed a hand over Michelle's ponytail, smoothing it down the way she used to, when Michelle had been younger. "If I'd known you had someone special, I wouldn't have come."

Smiling wryly, Michelle answered, "Yes, you would have."

"Well, yes," she admitted. "But only to make sure you didn't make a mess of things. You know how you get when you're nervous."

"Why would I be *nervous* around him?" The question slipped out before Michelle remembered the fierce, dangerous man who'd shown up on her doorstep in the middle of the night.

"Oh, please, Chelly. I mean, have you *seen* him? He's gorgeous."

Michelle hid a smirk. "True."

"Royal Marines..." her mother said thoughtfully. "Do you think he's got a commanding officer, maybe an older friend? Not *too* old, but a senior officer would be nice."

"*Mom!*"

Focused on his timing, Ray ran long enough to feel exhilarated without tiring himself. He needed to be back at Valhalla's Rest before Michelle's mother thought of something else to do—something involving all three of them. Hopefully, Michelle wasn't waiting for him to get back before sending Eleanor on her way. Any of the island's taxi drivers would be happy to get Eleanor started on her artistic discovery of the island. Hell, most of them would probably love to hire out to her for the day and play tour guide.

There was a thought. At the height of tourist season, there were plenty of walking tours of the island. Eleanor seemed to be the active lifestyle sort, like her daughter. Assuming she'd be willing to go without Michelle, a walking tour would keep her out of Valhalla's Rest for hours at a time.

He made it back in just over ninety minutes. Only when he let himself into the kitchen did he realize that his brilliant plan to avoid the day through dirty laundry had one flaw: he was out of clean clothes.

"Bloody hell," he muttered, raking a hand through his hair. It had grown out longer than he normally liked—far longer than he'd ever had it in the Royal Marines. Dirty clothes, hair too long, and he hadn't shaved that morning. It was a wonder that Michelle hadn't thrown him out.

Laundry, a shave, and a hot shower all moved to the top of his priority list, even ahead of seeing Michelle. He went right for the laundry room, only to hear the rumble of the commercial washer and dryer. Just his luck. Michelle was probably doing the linens. With another muttered oath, he went to find one of the bathrobes Liam kept stocked for guests in need.

New plan. Shower, shave, *then* start laundry, and try to avoid allowing anyone to see him until he had clean blue jeans and a shirt, at the very least.

Robe over one arm, he went back for the stairs, only to grin when he saw Michelle at the top. She was carrying the basket Liam had used for cleaning supplies. "How was your run?" she asked, smiling down at him.

He ran up the stairs two at a time. "Better, now that I'm back." He didn't try to kiss her—not with him in need of a shower and her mother possibly lurking nearby.

"Mom's gone to town. You just missed her."

In that case… He leaned in for a quick kiss, one she returned despite his post-running condition. Her smile never faltered. When the kiss ended, he stepped politely back and said, "If you don't mind, I need to do laundry, once you're done. After I shower, that is."

She darted a quick look over the railing and down

into the sitting room. "Actually, I did your laundry before I started the linens. I figured you might need clean clothes, with so little luggage," she said hesitantly.

"That's…" Ray faltered, unsure of what to say. He wasn't used to someone else taking care of him unless he'd been injured on duty, and that was generally limited to bringing him take-out food or driving him to the doctor's office. The last time anyone had done laundry for him it had been Preston, and that only because Ray had hidden his clothes in the laundry basket before swimming laps in Preston's new pool. "That's very kind of you. I appreciate it, really."

Her smile brightened her whole face. "Happy to help. I just put your clothes in the dryer. Want me to get you anything?"

He shook his head, suddenly feeling guilty and uncertain. What had started out as a professional, though unexpected, relationship had crossed over into something more, something undefined. And while he didn't mind having his room cleaned or sheets changed in a regular hotel, the thought of Michelle doing all the work while he lounged about… It was *wrong*.

"I'll take care of it. Is there anything you need to do around here?" he asked, eyeing the basket of cleaning supplies.

"No, I just wanted to dust before Mom got back. Dust makes her sneeze, but she swears she has no allergies." She rolled her eyes, smiling fondly.

"Since you were kind enough to save me from a bathrobe, let me shower, and then we can walk up to the Garrison for lunch. We can even call your mother and invite her to meet up with us, if you'd like."

She tipped her head, smile turning sly, and shifted the basket from one hand to the other. "We've got plenty of time before we need to think about lunch." She licked her lips nervously, cheeks slowly darkening. "After your shower... Maybe you'd like to join me in my apartment instead of going out?"

All thoughts of taking things slowly because of Eleanor—of taking things slowly at all—vanished. "I'd love to."

Chapter 13

Wednesday, July 10

THOUGHTS RACING, MICHELLE WENT THROUGH THE office and into her apartment, leaving the doors unlocked for the first time. Her heart was racing almost as fast as her thoughts. What was she doing? This wasn't her.

Not that she didn't want Ray, because she did. And there was no sense in screwing around and taking things slowly, now that her mother was here. Her mother would end up dropping her version of "subtle" hints that Ray should notice Michelle, and that would only serve to embarrass them both. Better to take matters into her own hands. This should be *their* decision, not her mother's.

Still, it was strange to think that her mother's presence made her feel free to push her budding relationship with Ray to the next step that much faster.

And really, there was no way he could have mistaken the intent behind her invitation. The manager's apartment was a spacious studio with nothing in the way of guest furniture. There was a single recliner instead of a couch and a tray table to eat dinner in front of the old television in the corner. Even the bed was small enough that she wondered if it wouldn't be wiser to go to Ray's room instead, with its more generous double.

But no. She'd just be self-conscious and distracted trying to listen for her mother's footsteps on the stairs.

At least down in the manager's apartment she didn't have to worry about creaking floorboards.

She had no idea how long Ray would take in the shower—hopefully more than a quick five minutes. She hurried to the bathroom and started the hot water running, then stripped out of her clothes. Back at Anchor's Cove, by eight in the morning at the latest, she'd be done with yoga and ready to greet her guests with breakfast, coffee, and a cheery, professional smile. Now here she was at almost ten, with her still in her yoga clothes, hair barely brushed, stinking of cleaning chemicals.

What was she thinking, inviting Ray here now?

Take advantage of Mom's absence. Right.

She got in the shower while the water was still cool. She spared time for only one quick shampoo and then put the floral, locally made body wash to good use. The smell of lavender and chamomile helped to relax her—until the thought of Ray upstairs, showering, introduced a whole new sort of tension.

In so many ways, he was like no one she'd ever dated before: strong, handsome, charismatic. But he was witty and smart and polite, too, and obviously loyal to more than just himself. A perfect balance, really, of what she wanted in a man and what she'd never expected she could have.

She braced one foot on the edge of the tub, trapping the shower curtain under her toes, and ran her hands down over her thigh and calf. Thankfully, she'd shaved her legs yesterday morning. She put her foot down and straightened up, running her hands over her bikini line. There was no real stubble there, but she circled her fingertips anyway, closing her eyes as the image of Ray's powerful, callused hands came to her mind.

Lost in her imagination, she smoothed one hand up over her breasts while the other dipped between her thighs. She hadn't had a steady boyfriend since losing Anchor's Cove, and no matter how many designer vibrators Vicky sent her for her birthday and Christmas, she missed the feel of a real man's body.

Not that she'd ever even gotten near a "real man" like this one. Just imagining all those muscles turned the tingles to a slow-burning heat. Ray was strong and powerful and more than she'd ever imagined. Why fantasize about something she'd never hope to experience? Or so she'd thought, before Ray.

The pipes rattled, jolting her out of her thoughts. A change in water pressure. Had Ray finished his shower, or was the washing machine refilling? Either way, she had no time to linger.

Breathless, heart pounding, she rinsed off as quickly as she could, with barely a shiver as she splashed water between her legs to get rid of the last soapy residue. Then she turned off the water, got out, and wrapped up in a towel. She dried off with a second towel and wrung most of the water out of her hair. Did she have time to blow-dry? Or should she put on makeup first? And what should she wear? She wasn't Vicky, with a wardrobe of lace and satin. Had she packed *anything* more seductive than white cotton with a little lace trim?

She *really* hadn't thought this out. Excitement turned to anxiety as she rifled through her toiletries bag. She'd unpacked only her makeup and hairbrush, which she put to use with one hand to get rid of the worst tangles. With her other hand, she dug through emergency first aid supplies, nail clippers, a spare comb, lotion—Aha! She found the three condoms she always carried, just as her mom said. She carried them not because she expected to have sex whenever she traveled but because it was her way to always be prepared.

A quiet knock made her jump. She looked up, into the foggy mirror. Her reflection was less than reassuring: no makeup, hair brushed flat, wearing a white towel tugged high over her breasts. Nothing about her screamed *seductive* or *sexy* at all. *Scatterbrained* was more like it.

"One minute!" she shouted, rushing out into the studio, condoms in hand. She dropped them on the nightstand, made it two steps away, then turned back to hide them in the drawer instead. Less obvious that way.

As if her answering the door in a towel wasn't obvious? Why hadn't she thought this through?

Only after knocking on the office door did Ray consider that he should have given Michelle more time. She'd been hard at work all morning, doing not just his laundry but the linens as well, and then she'd straightened out his room, made his bed, dusted, and cleaned. She needed the chance to relax and unwind, not rush through a shower because he was an impatient barbarian.

But while he'd been showering, his mind had been consumed with thoughts of her, beautifully naked save for water trails and soap suds, and he'd showered as efficiently as he could, needing to get her in his arms. His only stop had been at the laundry room, where he'd dressed in clothes still warm from the dryer. Michelle was shy about her mother's presence; if she came home early from playing tourist, he'd give her no reason to suspect anything had happened in her absence.

When Michelle opened the door, wrapped up in a towel, wet hair dripping, Ray felt one single momentary pang of guilt. Then it was lost under the spell of seeing her, stripped of all artifice. No makeup to hide her natural beauty, no clothes to conceal her body, not even perfume to distract him from *her*.

"I'd say I'm sorry, but I'm afraid I'd be lying," he admitted quietly, lifting his hand. He wanted to pull away the towel, but he restrained himself. Instead, he touched her cheek, tracing the blush that rose under her skin.

She ducked her head, pressing against his fingers, and inched back. "Come in."

With a nervous smile, she led him past the desk and filing cabinets and into the manager's apartment. It had been years since Ray had been there, but nothing had changed, except that the curtains and windows had been flung open, filling the room with sunshine and sea air.

After a few steps, she stopped and turned to face him. Her gaze skittered down from his face to his clothes and back up, never quite meeting his eyes. "I'll, uh—"

Before she could suggest getting dressed, he interrupted, "There's no need, unless you'd rather. You're beautiful just like this. You have a gorgeous body."

She looked down at herself, avoiding his eyes. "You're one to talk."

He gave a dismissive laugh. "I have to take care of myself for work. You... You're exquisite. I could watch you move for hours," he said, closing the distance between them. "You're like a dancer, strong and graceful. All I wanted was to watch"—he touched her face, running his finger along her cheekbone—"and touch"—he slipped his finger down to the corner of her mouth—"and kiss every inch of you."

"I don't…"

"Shh," he said, touching her face again. He tipped her chin up so their eyes met. "Relax, love. We'll do nothing you don't want. *Do* you—"

"Yes," she interrupted. This time, her laugh was more genuine. "Yes, I do. It's just…been a while."

Something inside Ray purred in contentment at that thought, as if it made her that much more *his*. He hoped his answering smile was reassuring and not fiercely possessive, though he couldn't be certain. Desire had taken the reins.

"We'll go slowly," he promised, leaning in to kiss her. She surrendered to the kiss with endearing shyness, holding her towel in place with one hand as the other drew soft lines up and down his arm. He nearly asked what she liked, but he suspected he wouldn't get a clear answer. Better to read her body language and tease out her preferences than to start a conversation that might well embarrass her.

Step by step, they moved deeper into the apartment, the sound of her bare feet a whisper against the quiet slap of the sneakers he now regretted wearing. He stopped before they drew too near the bed and ran his hands down her arms, keeping his touch as innocent as he could manage. When she pulled away, he straightened and cupped her face between his palms.

Deliberately, he kissed her again, though he kept the kiss brief and tame. "May I touch you?"

Her lips parted, though she said nothing—only nodded, wide eyes fixed on his face.

For long seconds, she held him entranced. He let his eyes take in her bare skin and the curves only hinted at beneath the towel. Drops fell from the ends of her hair, soaking into the towel, drawing sparkling trails down her shoulders and arms.

Ray slid his hand under the cool weight of her wet hair, cupping her nape. She shifted, raising her head for a kiss. "Shh. Patience," he said, rubbing soothing circles with his fingers. Her muscles were tight, pulse rapid against his fingertips.

She took a deep breath, breathing from the stomach, and he felt some of the tension bleed from her body. He eased his touch until his fingertips barely skimmed her hair and watched the way she shivered in response. When he stroked down her spine, just to the edge of the towel, she sighed. She was skittish but so beautifully responsive. He gentled her with his calm, reassuring touch until she allowed her eyes to fall closed.

"Let me make you feel good," he whispered, leaning down to brush her lips with his, silencing her quick gasp. Her answering nod was just a twitch. "Remember, only what you like."

A bit breathless, she said, "That won't be very difficult."

At least one of them felt confident, he thought. Hiding a smile, he asked, "Why's that?"

"Because it's you."

Ray laughed, pulling her hair back to bare her shoulders and throat. "Let's see if there's more to it, shall we? Close your eyes."

She gave him one quick, delighted look and then closed her eyes. Her smile never wavered. "Can I trust you?"

"Do you?"

Her smile softened. She licked her bottom lip. "Yes."

The honesty in her voice touched him. He leaned down to kiss her lips, her jaw, her throat, feeling the warmth of her soft skin. *Every inch*, he had said, and he meant it. She let her head fall to the side, baring her neck for him, a sweet invitation he couldn't refuse. In no hurry, he kissed down her neck from ear to shoulder, allowing his lips to linger on her skin.

She lifted her hands to his waist and started to embrace him. He caught her wrists and said, "No. Let me."

After a moment, she allowed him to guide her hands back to her sides. "But what about you?" she asked, blinking her eyes open to give him a puzzled look.

"All I want," he said, kissing her again, "is for you to enjoy what I'm doing. Will you do that for me?"

She smiled, head tipped to one side. "If you say so."

He ran his hands up her arms to touch a finger to her lips. "Close your eyes."

When she did, he lowered his head and resumed his exploration of her throat, kissing down to her shoulder. He stepped to the side, holding her in place when she would have turned to face him. Gently, he moved her hair aside, so he could kiss her shoulder blade, circling behind her until he was at her spine.

He let her hair fall and ran his hand forward, around the top of her towel to where it was tucked back in on itself above her breasts. Her breath hitched. Instead of pulling away, though, she leaned back against him. Cold drops of water soaked through his shirt.

Slowly, he worked his fingers under the terry cloth, giving her every opportunity to object. She didn't. He tugged the corner free and let the towel fall open. She swayed forward, freeing it from where it was trapped between their bodies, and then leaned trustingly against him once more.

"My God, look at you," he whispered, pressing his cheek to her hair as he stared down the length of her body. Her breasts were small, nipples taut from the slight chill in the air. He could see the gently shadowed definition of her muscles, softened by the slight curve of her belly. Below, he could just see her dark hair, neatly trimmed, and his fingers itched to touch.

"Ray," she breathed, lifting her hands. Then she let them fall to her sides, fingertips curving back to touch his legs.

Her hands were nowhere near his cock, but his arousal spiked all the same. The heat of her body seared right through his clothing. His hands rested lightly on her shoulders; if he touched her intimately now, he'd need more.

Instead, he petted her, exploring the contours of her arms and shoulders and back with light, soothing strokes. She shifted and sighed and allowed him to touch as he pleased. He discovered that she was ticklish high on her sides but not low, near her waist. The small of her back was sensitive enough to draw a quiet moan when he touched with his fingertips, a gasp when he kissed down her spine. He went to one knee behind her, loving the opportunity to feel the powerful muscles in her legs.

When he moved lower, brushing his fingertips over the silk-soft skin behind her knees, she let out a yelp and jumped away. Laughing, he rose to steady her, but she caught her balance unaided.

"That tickles!" she scolded, looking over her shoulder to smile back at him.

He rose and turned her around, stealing a quick glance down the front of her body before he pulled her close. "Sorry," he lied, determined to surprise her again sometime, just to hear that bright, unfettered laugh.

"Uh-huh," she hummed skeptically, tugging at his polo shirt. "I think it's my turn. Don't you?"

"Anything you like."

At that very moment, she wanted nothing more than to indulge in the sight of him, stripped as bare as she was. She pushed his shirt up, hands roving over hard muscles that burned against her palms. She let out a quiet, admiring breath as she flattened her palms against his solid, powerful chest. Only a few old white scars marred the perfection of his lightly tanned skin.

Every inch, he had said, and she found herself in full agreement with his desire. She'd always been more attracted to a sharp mind and compelling personality, but she suddenly understood the appeal of a hard, sculpted body.

He pulled the shirt off and dropped it aside, drawing her gaze up to his broad, muscular shoulders—and down his left arm, to the wound on his biceps. It was no small cut, as he'd implied, but a gash as long as her finger, closed with black stitches and short pieces of corrugated translucent tape. All around it were other cuts, healed into scabs and pink scars, and faint yellow bruises.

He followed her gaze. "It's nothing."

"Nothing?" She pushed him back so she could see the wound more clearly. "The last time a Brit said 'it's nothing' to me, Vicky ended up with pneumonia."

He allowed her to her take hold of his arm to look more closely. "It really is. I got cut with a bit of glass, that's all." He gently tugged at her wet hair until she looked back up and met his eyes. "I'm perfectly healthy. And you're getting distracted," he said, leaning down to brush his lips across hers.

Her practical mind railed at her to *do something*—to cover the wound so it wouldn't get wet or something— but…maybe she didn't need to. Ray was a soldier, entirely capable of taking care of himself.

As soon as she pushed her worry to the back of her mind, the reality of Ray's hot, bare skin hit her like a thunderstorm. She'd never even seen a body so beautifully sculpted. Certainly she'd never *touched* one.

When she reached for the waistband of his jeans, he released her hair and dropped his hands to his sides. With shaky fingers, she unbuttoned and unzipped, then spread the denim apart, revealing tight gray boxer briefs. A tiny spot of moisture had soaked through where his cock, hard and thick, pulled the fabric taut. As he toed off his sneakers, she pulled down his jeans and crouched, helping him step out of the denim.

She looked up, and their eyes met, and the raw desire in his gaze, barely restrained, captured her. She ran her hands up his legs and over his boxer briefs to the waistband. Slowly, she eased it away from his body and down, refusing to look up until she'd pulled off his briefs and helped him out of his socks.

Then she rose, staring down at his body, now exposed to her sight. Her throat went dry as her gaze fell on his cock, standing thick and hard, surrounded at the base by neat black curls. She ran her fingertips down the hard planes of his abs, along the shadowed valleys between his muscles, to the soft, pale hollows of his hip bones.

Ray's breath caught. Hitched. She drew her fingers closer together, combing through his curls. Turning her wrist, she cupped her hand to feel the weight of his cock, the velvety soft skin hot against her palm.

His quiet laugh was tense. "Are we rushing things along, love?"

Heat surged through her as she thought of just how she could do that. All she had to do was curl her fingers. Press tightly. Move slowly. Or she could lower herself to her knees and take him into her mouth. She was no expert, but he wasn't hiding how deeply she affected him. She'd be able to read what he liked. She *wanted* to know what he liked.

The idea was absolutely thrilling.

He gave her no chance, though. He pulled her close and kissed her breathless, leading her, step by step, toward the bed. *Yes*, she thought, following him down onto the narrow mattress. She sprawled atop him, spreading her legs as she rolled her hips, pressing against the hard length of his cock.

The touch seared through her. They gasped together, arms and legs entwining as Ray rolled them over. He propped up on one hand; the other cupped her breast, fingers teasing at her nipple. Lightning shocks of pleasure spread from his hand, waking her skin to new heights of sensitivity. Heat turned to aching emptiness. She bucked her hips up against him, a wordless demand she could more easily make with her body than her voice.

With a quiet groan, he moved down her body to capture her nipple with her mouth. Hard suction drew a sharp cry from her. "Ray!"

He pressed hard with his tongue, licking up over her nipple. "Rushing, then?"

"Yes." She scratched down his back and pointed in the direction of the nightstand. "In the drawer."

Thankfully, he understood. When he moved away to reach for the drawer, she rolled onto her side, kissing carefully up over his arm to his shoulder, where a curve of black caught her eye.

He had a tattoo—a small infinity symbol, no bigger than her thumb, high up on his shoulder blade. She traced the curve with her fingernail and asked, "What's this for?"

He stilled for a moment. "Loyalty," he answered. Then he turned away from the nightstand and gave her a slow, seductive smile. "Ask me again some other time."

Her curiosity crumbled under the scorching flame of his smile. She nodded and allowed him to guide her onto her back. Weight braced on his elbow, he skimmed his hand down her body, a slow drag of strong, callused fingers that left her trembling. His fingertips combed through her curls, dipped lower.

She arched up with a cry of need, and his finger slipped inside. Self-conscious of her reactions, she bit her lip and tried to hold still, but he crooked his finger and made her groan. Had a man's touch ever affected her so much? So deeply? Not like this.

"Please, Ray," she whispered.

"I've got you, love." He slid his finger out, then back in, finding that spot inside her once more.

She shook under his touch, heart pounding against her ribs as his finger moved. He leaned in, lips against hers, capturing her gasps with soft sweeps of his tongue. Tingling heat spread beneath her skin, a rising pressure that gathered deep within her until she saw nothing but the brilliant blue of Ray's eyes. Beneath his intensity, she shattered, flying apart in waves of absolute bliss that she felt all the way down to her toes.

When she could finally open her eyes again, she saw him smiling down at her. "All right, then?" he murmured, brushing her hair back from her face.

She hummed, returning the smile. "Yes," she said, feeling her cheeks go hot, though she couldn't bring herself to really care. At the moment, she felt too deliciously sated to be embarrassed.

He kissed her, slow and lingering and hot. She wound her arms around his shoulders, holding him close as the kiss ended. He looked down at her from inches away, and his smile turned absolutely wicked. "Ready for more?"

Excitement fluttered through her. She licked her bottom lip and nodded. "Oh, yes."

Leaning down to touch his lips to hers, he settled his body between her legs. She was almost too sensitive to bear the touch of his cock. Her gasp made him laugh softly.

"Go slowly?" she asked, lifting her hips. She

wrapped one leg around his, loving the feel of their intimate embrace.

"As slow as you like, love," he promised. "Why don't you help me out?"

It took her a moment to realize what he meant. Then she reached down between their bodies to take his cock in her hand. She wanted to ask when he'd put on the condom, but it was too embarrassing to think she'd entirely missed the sound when he'd torn open the wrapper.

She steadied him, and he allowed her to set the pace as she guided the head of his cock into her body. The stretch was almost too much. Her hand twitched, and he stilled with a soft, tense exhale.

Imagining how he would feel, buried all the way inside her, made her groan. "Ray," she said brokenly.

"Easy, love." He moved, a slow shift of his hips, and heat—the promise of pleasure to come—sparked through the ache.

Her hand went to his hip, holding him steady. He pushed further in, just another careful inch, and her heart lodged in her throat. It had been too long for her—this was too much—but she bit her lip to keep herself from telling him to stop.

He eased inside her slowly, though, giving her body time to relax. "God, Michelle. You feel *perfect*."

Encouraged by his tone, she rolled her hips, gasping at the shift of pressure inside her body, and wrapped her legs around his hips. "Just—Just let me—"

"Yes, right," he muttered, holding himself very still, except for his deep, steady breaths.

She slid her hands up his back to curl her fingers over

his shoulders. "Ray." Experimentally, she shifted her hips beneath him, and the building pleasure stole her words. She let out a cry and tightened her legs, and Ray drew back just enough so he could thrust inside once more.

"Too much?" he asked, voice strained.

At once, she shook her head. "More."

"With pleasure," he said, his voice full of wicked promise.

She tried to think of a response, but then he moved, and tingling heat sparked through her body. For all his power, he moved with gentle strength, flowing into her. Every smooth thrust brought pleasure upon pleasure, building within her like a sand castle rising one grain at a time.

Then he changed the angle of his body, pressing against her clit with each thrust, turning the rising pleasure into an inferno. Her chest went tight. Her breath lodged in her throat. Her skin sparked with life. Heat. Ecstasy that rose up and filled her, leading her deeper into her body and out into a brilliant heat to rival the sun.

She cried out, arching and trembling beneath Ray, who called her name, and pushed deep inside her. He silenced her with a kiss, hard and demanding, and held her through the last aftershocks of pleasure that racked them both.

Slowly, Ray withdrew and moved off her, gathering her into his arms. Michelle curled up against him, closing her eyes. Her heart rate slowed, and she turned enough to press a kiss to his chest.

"Thank you, love," he said, his low voice rumbling through her body.

She smiled, content, and whispered, "Ray."

Chapter 14

"YOU KNOW WHAT I WANT?" MICHELLE ASKED, HER voice beautifully rough with lazy pleasure.

Ray smiled at the sound of it, not bothering to open his eyes. He'd left the bed once, to clean up and to bring her a glass of water that she'd insisted they share. Then they'd both been content to lie together under a fresh, soft bedsheet that still smelled of flowers.

"What's that?" he asked, running his hand up the curve of her spine to toy with the ends of her hair. It hadn't fully dried, and it was heavy and cool in his hand.

"Promise you won't laugh?"

"If you put it like that, I bloody well promise I *will*," he teased.

She lifted her head enough to narrow her eyes at him. "What happened to chivalry being part of your heritage?"

"You don't think knights laughed?" He grinned. "They made their horses wear tablecloths, love. And they wore tights. If the lot of them weren't laughing, then they were all mad."

Her eyes lit up, and she snuggled back under the sheet, breath ghosting softly over his chest. She'd ended up pressed against his left side. Even her slight weight pulled at his stitches, but he would have endured far worse to keep her in his arms.

"You're an awful person," she accused, turning to press her lips against his chest.

"And possibly mad, given my heritage. You'd best tell me what you want before I take it upon myself to start guessing."

She tried to hold back a laugh. "A cheeseburger. And that doesn't mean you get to bring me one of those. I just changed the sheets."

"But if I wanted to, I *could*," he declared confidently. "I know exactly where to find you the best cheeseburger on St. Mary's. With proper rashers of bacon, if you'd like."

She groaned against his skin. "Now you're being a *terrible* person. I don't want to get out of bed."

Ray smirked. "I thought you wanted a cheeseburger."

"I do."

"Then up, love. I'll fetch it for you. Did you want chips with it? That's 'french fries' to you—"

"Colonials. Yeah, yeah, I know." She lifted her head again, looking gorgeously mussed, her hair framing her face in a wild tangle.

He grinned at her.

Suspicion flared in her eyes. Slowly, she looked up, brows rising. Then she twisted up and out of his arms, trying to flatten down her hair. The effort was futile.

"Ugh, why didn't you tell me?" she demanded.

He sat up and wrapped his arm around her, holding her still so he could press a kiss to her shoulder. She tasted of soap and sweat, and when she shivered, he turned to kiss her throat next. Then he nipped as gently as he could, making her groan again, though this time with pleasure, not exasperation.

"You're gorgeous," he whispered in her ear. For good measure, he pressed a kiss to her earlobe as well.

"I look like I lost a fight with a wind tunnel," she complained, trying to sound fierce, though it came out breathless and soft.

"You're *gorgeous*," he insisted, "and if you lie back down, I'll see about proving it to you."

Laughing, she let her head fall back against his shoulder and kissed the side of his jaw. "Do that and it'll end up being a bacon and chili cheeseburger, with extra 'chips.' I'm seriously *starving*."

Ray gave an exaggerated sigh and eased his hold on her, though he didn't let go. "All right, all right." He stole one more kiss, this one just behind her ear, right on the spot that made her shiver so beautifully. "Care to let me scrub your back?"

She ducked her head, charmingly shy, but then caught hold of a tangle of hair that slipped over her shoulder. "It's going to take an hour for me to work out the tangles."

"Let's see if we can rush that along, shall we?" he suggested, shifting around her so he could get out of bed.

"Because you have so much experience detangling long hair?" she asked.

He held out his hands to her and tugged her to her feet. "German shepherds," he said, realizing only too late that she might take offense to the comparison.

"Excuse me?" She let go of his hands to wrap her arms around his waist.

With a mental shrug—she did have a good sense of humor, after all—he explained, "Preston has two German shepherds. They shed like mad every spring, when they lose their winter coats. Who do you think ends up bathing and brushing them?"

"Really? You like dogs?"

"I always have. It'd just be cruel to have a big dog in an apartment, and I'm not a fan of little dogs."

She smiled, head tipped thoughtfully to the side. "I've always wanted a dog. I promised myself, someday…"

He braced himself for that sinking feeling that always came when a woman mentioned the future. But this time, instead of panic, all he felt was curiosity. As he took her hand and led her to the bathroom, he asked, "How do you feel about German shepherds?"

―⁓―

As soon as Michelle had her hair slathered with conditioner, she switched places with Ray and indulged her desire to explore his body without the urgent need that had filled her earlier. *All mine*, she thought as she ran soapy hands up his chest to his shoulders. And if the moment was made bittersweet by the thought of their unintentionally shared vacation ending, she pushed it out of her mind. She'd enjoy the days she had and not worry about afterward—not yet, anyway.

"So, your tattoo," she said when he turned to rinse, presenting her with his back. The view was as good as from the front, and as she soaped over his shoulder blades, she leaned in to kiss his spine.

"It symbolizes loyalty. Did I say that already?"

"Yes." She scratched her nails down his back, lightly drawing stripes through the lather.

"That's nice," he muttered, melting under her touch, head falling forward, and arched his back. She took the hint and scratched harder, grinning when he groaned as though purring. When she stopped, he looked back. "You stopped."

"Keep talking," she prompted, scratching again.

He laughed and surrendered, pushing insistently against her hands as he said, "It was a couple of months after the mission where I met Preston. He and his troops ended up in the UK, and we all went out drinking. At some point, we apparently all decided to get tattoos—not that I precisely recall making that decision."

"I'm surprised you ended up with something so unobtrusive." Flattening her palms, she let her hands rove down to the small of his back and lower, over the taut muscles of his too-perfect ass and thighs.

"Oh, we didn't go that night. We're not *quite* that stupid. But when we went the next day, Preston knew straight away what he'd wanted. I just got the same thing," he said, reaching up over his shoulder with one hand. His fingertips just covered the tattoo. "Only after the fact did he bother to mention he got it because the girl he was going to marry wore it on a necklace."

"Awkward," Michelle said, giving him a wry smile as he turned to rinse his back. "Weren't you a little…"

"Mad?" He shook his head. "That's when he offered me the VP role in his company."

She laughed and hugged Ray, thinking she really did want to meet this man who was so important to him—just like Vicky was to her.

Assuming, of course, that she and Ray didn't go their separate ways at the end of this vacation.

Don't think about that, she scolded herself. Instead, she switched places with him again and tipped her head back to rinse out the conditioner. When she went to comb her fingers through her hair, he took over. He was so strong, with such powerful hands, but his touch was so gentle, she barely felt the least tug.

"Vicky tried to get me to get a tattoo," she admitted, closing her eyes to better luxuriate in his touch. With his hands on her, she felt so safe, so *cherished*.

"I can't see you with a tattoo."

She frowned, blinking her eyes open, and lifted a hand to wipe at the droplets clinging to her eyelashes. "Why not?" she asked neutrally, though the answer was obvious, at least to her: she was far too *boring* to get a tattoo. She only had pierced ears because her mother had got them done when she'd been a baby. Vicky had tried to talk her into far more daring piercings, too.

But instead of brushing off her fears—or, worse, confirming them—Ray cupped her face and leaned in close to kiss her. "Because you don't need one. Your skin is beautiful as it is."

The heat of the shower covered the blush she felt rise in her cheeks. She laughed, saying, "Tell that to Vicky. She's still disappointed."

He smiled and went back to combing his fingers through her hair. "I'd call her right now, but I'm rather happy right where I am."

"Mmm. You can do that for about forever, you know," she hinted.

"I thought you were starving. And you can't properly eat a cheeseburger in the shower."

Something in his tone made her crack open one eye to give him a skeptical look. "Don't tell me you're talking from experience."

He grinned. "I'd never admit to that."

"Nice, evasive wording there."

"I rather liked it," he said, nodding proudly.

———~~~———

There was a rhythm to relationships that Ray had never mastered. Given that they were sharing the same roof, this one in particular was potentially very awkward. After spending a wonderfully satisfying summer afternoon together…what next? Did she expect him to ask if he could stay with her? Or, more likely, to invite her to stay with him, given that his room at least had a double bed and hers had a single.

Or did she want her privacy? Did he want *his* privacy, for that matter? He had no idea.

And all of that was before factoring in the presence of Eleanor.

He finally decided to let Michelle dictate the terms, as long as Eleanor was about. By the time they drew close to the end of their vacation, he'd hopefully have a better idea of what he wanted. If he was lucky, he'd have an idea of what Michelle wanted, too.

While she was doing esoteric things with makeup and her hair, he excused himself to go get the rest of his laundry out of the dryer so he could put it away. The best cheeseburger on the island, in his opinion, was at a harbor-side restaurant right on the beach. Every room at Valhalla's Rest had a guidebook with local phone numbers and addresses; he found the restaurant's listings and called to make reservations for three, just in case Eleanor caught up with them. The first dinner seating was at six, so they had some time to coordinate with her, and much as he wanted to have Michelle all to himself, he didn't want to come between mother and daughter.

After he hung up, he took the time to shave and changed his T-shirt for a lightweight sweater. As he was trying to tame his hair into a semblance of his usual neat, short look, he heard a tap at his door.

He stopped himself from shouting a greeting at the last instant. He dropped his comb and went to get the door instead. "Isn't this backward? I thought you're supposed to take more time than me," he said, looking her over as he stepped aside to invite her in.

Under a denim jacket, she wore a peach-colored top. Her lightweight white skirt had a pattern of little bronze shapes matching her wedge sandals. She was probably making some sort of fashion statement, but the details didn't matter. She looked absolutely adorable, and he was glad he'd changed out of his T-shirt.

"Old college habit," she said, going to the chair where he'd been keeping his backpack. "Being ready first gave me the time to do everything Vicky and Dana forgot—get the car, find out where we were going, that sort of thing."

"Sounds like you'd make a good officer." He went back into the bathroom to check his hair one last time. "I didn't know if you wanted to invite your mother tonight. I made reservations for three, just in case."

"Thanks. I should probably text her. Who knows where she'll end up if left to herself?"

Ray grinned, finally giving up on the comb. He dried his hands, saying, "Fortunately, we're on an island. There's only so far she can go before she ends up back here."

She had her phone in her hands. When he went back into the bedroom, she looked up from the screen and said, "Again, you don't know my mother. It wouldn't surprise me if she ended up on a whole other island somehow. Where are we going and when?"

"Have her meet us at Porthmellon Beach, between five and half past," he suggested. "Anyone she asks will know where to send her. We can start with drinks. Our reservation's not until six."

"Perfect. She's never on time. Always an hour early or two hours late," Michelle said with a little huff of irritation. She tucked the phone into her little purse and stood, stepping right into his arms. Her kiss tasted of lip gloss and mint toothpaste.

"We've got a couple of hours," Ray said, wondering if he hadn't been premature in getting dressed. "What shall we do until then?"

"Actually..." She looked toward the bed, and he felt a spark of interest shoot through his body. But then she asked, "Maybe you can introduce me to your friend there?"

He blinked in confusion. Then he followed her gaze to the pillows, where she'd left the stuffed dog when she'd made the bed. "That's from my last mission."

"Oh. I thought... It looks old."

Ray took a deep breath and sat on the edge of the bed, tugging Michelle down beside him. He reached back to pick up the stuffed dog, looking at the worn fur without really seeing it. "It belonged to a little girl named Fauzia. We—Samaritan—had a team in Peshawar, Pakistan, less than two hundred miles from Kabul."

Michelle put her hand on his arm, the touch as light as a bird's wing. "That's not exactly a safe area."

Ray shrugged. "It was supposed to be a quick job. Bodyguard a civilian contractor in the area to negotiate for a business contract. Only it turned out he was *also* there because he'd fallen in love with an aid worker who was trying to organize a girls' school outside Jalalabad, over the Afghanistan border. Her school was attacked, and he got himself trapped in a war zone trying to save her. We saved the lot of them, in the end."

"How?"

"Negotiation, good timing, and luck," he said bluntly. He gave her a reassuring smile and said, "Maybe if we'd known before going in, we could've taken steps, but I doubt it. We probably wouldn't have taken the job at all. We're a security force, not a bloody army."

"And the girl—Fau…"

"Fauzia." He smiled faintly and put the stuffed dog in Michelle's lap. "In rather good English, she told me the dog's name is Laramore, after the soldier who gave it to her, and that he'd been with her long enough. She said he'd keep me safe until I got a real guard dog."

Michelle stroked a hand over the old, worn dog and turned to kiss his shoulder. "Looks like he did his job, if he got you out of there mostly in one piece."

He grinned, relieved that she hadn't asked for more details. "I'm fine. I keep meaning to take out my stitches."

Her eyes narrowed suspiciously. "You mean, you're going to a doctor to have them removed, right?"

"Well, yes," he lied cheerfully, making a mental note to take them out himself, rather than asking her to help.

"In any case, that's the tale of Laramore the dog." He got up and held out his hand, thinking he should probably hide the dog in the dresser or something.

Instead, she took his hand and let him help her up. Then she put the dog on top of the dresser, turned to face the bed. "There. He can keep an eye on you when I'm not around. I get the feeling you need full-time supervision to stay out of trouble."

"You know me so well already," he said and kissed her to keep from asking if she wanted the job for herself.

—◆◆◆—

An hour later, Michelle leaned back and looked unseeing toward the harbor. Ray's simple, abridged story of Fauzia and Laramore the dog had captured her imagination. Her heart swelled as she pictured him carrying this little girl out of danger, shielding her with his own body, a modern-day knight on a rescue mission. She knew it was probably unrealistic—he'd gone in with a team, for one thing, and he hadn't mentioned anything like a gunfight—but she knew that he would have braved any danger to save that little girl.

It was touching and terrifying all at once.

"Here we are," Ray said, joining her at the little table. He set down two mugs of milky tea and a plate with two small biscuits and little bowls of jam and what looked like butter.

"This looks suspiciously like breakfast," she said, though she picked up one of the biscuits. It was denser than she expected, and when she tore it in half, it crumbled, revealing light, fluffy air pockets.

"It's cream tea. If you ate four of these scones, it would be breakfast. You said you're starving, remember?"

"Very," she admitted, smiling at the memory of why she was so hungry. She picked up one of the knives and reached for the butter, but Ray stopped her.

"Jam first, then clotted cream."

"Clotted cream?" she asked hesitantly. She was willing to experiment with food, but she had her limits.

"It's like butter, only you'll never enjoy butter again once you taste it," he said, enthusiastically preparing his scone. "Did you hear from your mother?"

Mirroring his actions, she spread a thick layer of jam over half the scone and nodded. "She finally texted. She said she'd be here soon." She refrained from mentioning that her mother had asked if they'd put their "alone time" to good use.

He nodded, spooning a dollop of clotted cream on top of the jam. It was too soft to be butter, too thick to be whipped cream. "She wasn't upset at being left to her own devices?"

Michelle took an experimental bite of her scone. The clotted cream added a smooth, nutty flavor to the tart jam. Her stomach rumbled as if to encourage her to take a bigger bite. "Oh, this is good," she said as soon as she swallowed. "Delicious, in fact."

Ray grinned. "Told you."

She sipped her tea to keep from wolfing down the whole thing. "Anyway, a year ago, Mom would've been upset. Since I've been living with her this whole time, we've…come to appreciate a little distance."

He raised a brow skeptically. "Five thousand miles too much, then?"

"Oh, Mom's not an idiot." Michelle used her scone to point toward the beach, where about a dozen people, mostly women, were clustered around a sleek, long boat. "My being here is just the perfect excuse for her to come 'visit.' Dinner, maybe a couple of tourist things... She'll probably want to take me shopping. Other than that, she'll hopefully be happy to go out by herself."

Ray tried to hide his relieved sigh by taking another bite of his scone, but Michelle caught it. She considered warning him about her mother's matchmaking, but something held her tongue. Maybe it was an inherited sense of mischief, or maybe she assumed he had to have guessed by now. Either way, he'd figure it out soon enough.

After their cream tea, Ray and Michelle walked along the beach and watched as the sun crept down toward the horizon. When Ray's phone beeped to remind them of their reservations, they went up to the restaurant. There was no sign of Michelle's mother.

True to form, she showed up late, after Michelle and Ray had been seated long enough to order wine and a seafood starter plate. Michelle's mother swept in, preceded by a cloud of floral perfume, and Michelle turned in time to get a kiss on the cheek and an armful of brilliant pink, white, and magenta flowers.

"You wouldn't *believe* what I found," her mother declared, descending on Ray, who froze in the process of politely standing. He got a lipstick smudge on the cheek for his troubles, though no flowers. Instead, her mother put down a large rectangular package, wrapped in butcher paper, on the empty chair beside him and then went to sit down next to Michelle.

"Painting?" Michelle guessed, wondering what she was supposed to do with the flowers. She eyed the empty corner of the table across from her mother, but Eleanor's immense purse landed there instead.

"The most *gorgeous* painting," her mother agreed. "There's this little gallery not far from here. They do cats and beach scenes. Absolute realism, but the use of natural light is just stunning. You can almost feel the sun."

"That's…good," Michelle said, finally squishing the flowers down so she could wedge them under the table; thankfully they were dry. "New clients?"

"I'm tempted, but I don't do realism. I picked up some samples to send to Julian, in San Diego. He's allergic to cats, but he loves natural scenes with personality, so he'll just have to get over it." Beaming at them both, she asked, "So what did you two do today?"

"Laundry," Michelle said innocently. It was true, after all. "Tomorrow, we have tickets to go to Tresco. There's a garden there, with a collection of shipwreck memorabilia."

"We'd love to have you join us," Ray added with believable sincerity.

"That would be wonderful."

"Let me make another quick call. I should be able to get us tickets on the boat over there. Excuse me," Ray said before leaving the table.

Michelle took a sip of her wine, concealing her smile. He was strong and smart and dangerous—really, her instincts that first night had been almost completely accurate, given his profession—but he was so *nice*, too.

He came back a few minutes later, saying, "We're all set."

"Lovely. So, a garden? Phoenix has a huge botanical garden, but it's all cacti."

Ray laughed. "I think you'll like this one. If nothing else, it's safer."

"Nothing in Arizona is safe," Michelle said, remembering too many close encounters with cacti and thorny trees. "Why don't you tell Mom about the shipwrecks?"

"I'm no expert, but it has to do with ocean currents. The same currents that bring us such a mild climate blew all sorts of ships off course here, to get wrecked on the rocks around the islands. The Valhalla Collection is a museum of those ships' figureheads. That's where all the room names come from: Father Thames, Jane Owen, Serica, and so on."

As Michelle listened to him charm her mother, she realized that she really did trust him. This felt completely natural, the way a first meeting between her mother and her boyfriend was meant to be. Was that what he was? Her boyfriend? Her friend, yes, and her lover, but was there more to it?

She hoped so.

When the waiter came to take her mother's drink order and to ask about dinner, Michelle let go of the bouquet of flowers and slid her hand across the edge of the table. Ray met her eyes, and one corner of his mouth lifted. His crooked smile was all it took to fill her with happiness. When his fingertips touched hers, it was as though an electrical circuit had been completed.

Judging by the way his eyes lit up, he felt it, too.

—◆◆◆—

"I'll brave the crowd," Ray offered as Michelle and her mother settled at the table he'd managed to claim. "What can I get you both?"

"A cosmo, please," her mother said.

"Nothing for me, thanks." Michelle gave him a rueful smile. "And I'm never eating again. I'm stuffed."

He leaned down to kiss her cheek. "Best cheeseburger on the island. I told you."

She groaned theatrically and gave him a little shove. Laughing, he slipped into the crowd, moving gracefully despite his size. Tall, broad shoulders, powerful chest... Sated and happy, Michelle didn't even realize she was staring until her mother laughed.

"You've got it bad, don't you?" her mother asked.

"Mom..." Michelle couldn't put any real irritation into the word. She looked down at the flowers—pinks, they were called—and grinned. "Maybe."

"Maybe?"

"All right, *yes*." Michelle lifted her gaze and said, uncertainly, "This is supposed to happen the other way around."

Eleanor knew exactly what she meant. Waving a hand, she said, "Only on the surface."

"You married Richard after knowing him for seven hours in Vegas."

"*Dick*," her mother said grandly, "was a fling. I'd never been married in Vegas, so I got married in Vegas. Plus the honeymoon was just to die for—all twelve hours of it."

Michelle rolled her eyes. "And Ray and I met on Friday night. It's only Wednesday—"

"Oh, Chelly, no." Her mother took Michelle's hands from the bouquet, letting the flowers fall to the table. "I don't go marrying for a lifetime. Why do you think I'm still friends with all my ex-husbands? Well, except Dick, but he's not a real ex-husband. What's an annulment make him? An ex-boyfriend?"

"Or it makes you a serial ex-wife," Michelle teased.

Instead of taking offense, her mother laughed. "That's going on Twitter." She squeezed Michelle's hands and said, "Ninety-nine percent of your decisions are made after enough thought and consideration and deliberation to try the patience of a monk. But that one percent..." She let go and pointed at Michelle's heart. "That other one percent comes right from there, Chelly. Right from the heart."

Michelle's smile faded. "That'd be my one percent's worth of bad decisions?"

Her mother shook her head. "That would be you quitting piano lessons, after I bought you that piano, because you liked singing more. Or you taking your business degree and opening a bed and breakfast instead of that office job in Manhattan," she said gently.

"Yeah, *that* turned out well," Michelle snapped, frowning. "What are you getting at?"

Her mother looked at her steadily. "You were *happy* running Anchor's Cove, Chelly. Happier than you've ever been. You made the decision on impulse and then spent six months doing a financial analysis before you cosigned the papers with that...*Dana*. Your *one percent* decision was to run a B and B. Your ninety-nine percenter was to bring Dana along as a safety net."

Michelle opened her mouth to protest but stopped herself. She clearly remembered the day she'd made her "one percent decision," as Eleanor called it. In that moment, she'd felt the whole course of her life change.

"Don't get me wrong. You make good decisions when you think about them, Chelly. Better than I ever have," her mother admitted. "But when you follow your heart"—she pointed at Michelle's heart again—"that's when you make the *best* decisions."

Michelle licked her lips, feeling as if the world had suddenly shifted around her. Her mother was impulsive and flighty—not so unexpectedly wise. She turned away from her mother's intent gaze, and she found herself searching the crowd for Ray.

"So, what's that heart of yours say about him?" her mother asked softly.

"Yes." Michelle smiled, warmth rushing through her, stealing her breath and making her heart race. She'd never fallen for someone this hard and fast. Because she'd never allowed it, or because no one had been right for her? It didn't matter. Everything inside her *knew*, in defiance of rational thought, that Ray was so much more than a vacation fling or casual boyfriend. Blinking back tears of happiness, she repeated, "Yes."

Her mother patted her hands and sat back. "I'll go with you two to that other island tomorrow, but after that, I think I'm going to go explore. Maybe I'll go to Ireland. I've never been there before."

"Ireland!" Startled, Michelle turned back to her mother. "But you just got here."

"And you don't need me here," she insisted. "You just promise me you'll bring him to Arizona. You were at two of my weddings before I eloped. If you even *think* of not inviting me…"

Michelle's calm, sensible, rational self almost protested that it was more than a little premature to even think about that sort of thing. She wanted to consider and take her time and move slowly.

Ninety-nine percent.

But…the thought of letting go of that caution—the thought of trusting her heart—felt *right*. Ray was everything she wanted, and everything she'd never known she wanted. And the thought of building a future with him filled her with an elation she'd never before felt.

"You know," she said thoughtfully, grinning as Ray came into sight, "I think you might be right. Thanks, Mom."

"Of course, I'm right. I'm your mother. Now you trust your heart—and don't you dare forget to ask if he's got an older friend. Just—"

"Not too old," Michelle interrupted, laughing. "I promise."

Chapter 15

Thursday, July 11

RAY COULDN'T REMEMBER WHEN HE'D LAST VISITED Tresco Abbey Gardens or even Tresco Island itself. That was one more thing to thank Michelle for—getting him out of his usual routine on St. Mary's. Not even a week, and she'd turned everything upside down in ways Ray had never expected.

The garden was as beautiful as Ray remembered, but he hung back, preferring to watch Michelle instead. She moved from one floral display to the next like a hummingbird, bright and small and beautiful. Her mother followed in her wake, though not without a few sly glances at Ray, as if she knew Ray had been intimate with her daughter. He hadn't felt intimidated by a parent for twenty years, but this time he wasn't in danger of being beaten by an overprotective father. No, this time...

"So, Ray," Eleanor cooed, sidling up to him as Michelle disappeared around a corner. "How are you and my daughter getting along?"

This time, he thought, it was a mother who accepted no boundaries.

"Very well," he answered as casually as he could, keeping his eyes fixed on the spot where Michelle had disappeared. "I think the Valhalla Collection is this way."

Eleanor's hand clamped around his arm, forcing him

to keep his steps slow. "She's not scheduled to leave the island for, what…another week?"

Remembering his resistance-to-interrogation training, he limited his answer to a brief nod.

"You two haven't known each other long at all," she mused. "Most of my daughter's boyfriends, she knew for months. Years, even."

Here it comes, Ray thought.

"And yet," Eleanor said smoothly, "she seems very attached."

"Mrs. Cole—"

"Eleanor," she corrected.

"Eleanor—"

"*Unusually* attached," she interrupted, tipping her head to look over her sunglasses, meeting Ray's eyes. "Is that attachment reciprocated?"

Ray's thoughts went not to answering but to disengaging, because there was no safe answer. Say yes and risk having Eleanor drag him and Michelle into a conversation he, at least, wasn't ready to have; say no and get shredded by an overprotective mother.

"We're taking things slowly," he answered as evenly as he could manage.

She sniffed and glanced around. "Hmm. 'Slowly.' Sounds boring."

Ray blinked, wondering if he'd chosen the wrong answer.

"My daughter happens to be a wonderful girl, Ray." Eleanor's smile put Ray in mind of a shark. A hungry one. "You should consider yourself very, very lucky to have met her."

"I do." That, at least, was an honest, complete answer.

Eleanor stopped at the corner where Michelle had disappeared. "Then you understand that if you hurt her feelings, Ray, I will do everything in my power to drag you to Arizona and make sure the last creatures to see you alive are the coyotes and—"

"*Mom!*"

Michelle rushed into sight and put herself defensively in front of Ray, bristling angrily. Startled, Eleanor backed away. "Chelly—"

"No," Michelle interrupted. "I told you to stay out of this."

"I'll just go…" Ray said, plotting escape routes.

Without looking away from her mother, Michelle nodded. "I'll catch up with you in a minute."

Ray hesitated. He wanted to offer Michelle some reassurance or support, but this moment between mother and daughter was too private, too personal. He brushed his fingers over her shoulder, feeling the soft nap of her battered denim jacket, and then left silently.

—◦◦◦—

Michelle wasn't one to give in to anger. She believed in tranquillity. Balance. Even little emotional glitches, like the other night, weren't normal for her. She'd only caught the last part of her mother's eloquent threat, but that was enough to have her seeing red. She stalked at her mother, driving her three steps back into a little gazebo decorated with sparkling white, blue, and yellow mosaics.

"I was only looking out for you," her mother explained, holding up her hands.

"I asked you *not* to interfere," Michelle snapped in a harsh not-quite-whisper.

"We were just talking!"

"Oh, really? Is that some new sales technique you learned in the art world? Do you always threaten the people you talk to?"

Her mother sat on the bench, took off her sun hat, and leaned against the wall. "Come sit, Chelly."

The last thing Michelle wanted was to have a heart-to-heart with her mother, but storming away would be childish. So she sat down, shoulders tense, and looked toward the path where Ray had disappeared. "What, Mom?"

"I'm sorry," her mother said insincerely, patting Michelle's hand. "But I'm leaving tomorrow, and I just wanted him to know how important this is to you."

Michelle sighed, letting her head fall back against the wall. "I appreciate your help," she lied, "but I don't need it." That part, at least, was true.

"But you know how you are with men."

"Really? How 'am I' with men?"

Her mother pulled off her sunglasses and gave Michelle a sad smile. "You're…sweet. You don't assert yourself. You're too *nice*, Chelly."

"Too nice?" Michelle asked in disbelief. "Not predatory, you mean."

"Predatory," her mother scoffed, waving her hat dismissively. "It was my idea to marry your father. If I hadn't gone after him, you wouldn't even be here."

"You got married because you were pregnant!"

"And I was pregnant because I went after him."

It took all of Michelle's willpower to keep from rolling her eyes. "Mom, I'm not you. I'm not even like you."

Her mother pulled her hands back, shooting her a wounded look.

Michelle sighed and shook her head. "I don't mean that in a *bad* way. You and I... We're just different people. I'm not comfortable rushing into anything."

"You're leaving in a week."

Michelle flinched, looking away. She was all too conscious of the deadline looming ahead of her. "I know. Believe me, I know exactly how long I have. But rushing isn't the answer."

"But a week..."

"A week, and then I'm going back to the States. Ray lives in Virginia, Mom, not on Mars. It's not like I'll never see him or talk to him again."

Her mother sighed and patted her hand again. "You're right. There's plenty of time. I'm sorry," she said, rising smoothly. She brushed her hair back before she put her hat back on. "Let's go find him."

Relieved, Michelle got to her feet and kissed her mother's perfumed cheek. "Thanks, Mom. I know you're just trying to help."

Her mother beamed at her before putting her sunglasses back on. "It'll be fine," she said, taking hold of Michelle's arm. As they started to walk, she added, "Besides, I can tell you're sleeping with him. That counts for something."

"*Mom!*"

It was nearly eleven before they returned to Valhalla's Rest, tired, footsore, and sated from a wonderful dinner on Tresco Island. Ray had pulled in a favor and arranged for a late ship back to St. Mary's. By the time Michelle unlocked the front door, Eleanor was hiding yawns. In the foyer, she stopped just long enough to kiss Michelle's cheeks, then Ray's, and then said, "I'm going to turn in. Make sure I'm awake early enough to have breakfast before my flight, will you, dear?"

"Yes, Mom. Sleep well," Michelle said, shooting Ray a quick, questioning glance.

"Good night," he said, watching Eleanor head up the stairs.

Michelle remained silent until her mother's door closed. Then, with a relieved sigh, she turned and leaned against Ray's chest. "I forgot how exhausting she is," she muttered, her breath warm through his shirt.

Ray laughed, wrapping his arms around her. She felt wonderful, fitted close to his body. "Too exhausting?"

"Mmm, ask me again after I take a long, hot bath."

Ray almost offered company, but there wasn't a single bathtub in the inn big enough for him, much less the two of them. "Mind if I watch?" he asked instead.

Michelle's cheeks went rosy. She ducked her head and said, "Why don't you get us some wine? I'll start the water running."

"Brilliant plan, love." Ray claimed a quick kiss before he let go of her. She went into the manager's office while he went to the kitchen, absently rubbing at his arm. He'd taken off the surgical tape that morning, and the stitches kept catching on his sleeve.

He went past the liquor cabinet to the laundry room where he knew Liam had kept a toolbox. A quick search yielded needle-nose pliers, but he couldn't find a razor-knife or small shears. Thinking Michelle might have something he could use, he pocketed the pliers and went back into the kitchen to look over the selection. He chose a nice cabernet sauvignon, which he opened before taking down two glasses.

He'd felt the subtle friction between Michelle and her mother all day, but tomorrow Eleanor would be gone. Ray and Michelle could get back to normal... whatever *normal* was. He certainly didn't know, and judging by what Eleanor had said earlier, Michelle was no expert at relationships either. They'd just have to find their way into this relationship together and see what happened.

Quietly, Ray let himself into the manager's office and locked the door against the possibility of maternal interference. He could hear the water running in the bathtub, and he wondered if Michelle had already stripped or if she'd let him help. He toed off his shoes, then carried the wine and glasses to the bathroom. Michelle had left the door cracked, so he nudged it open with one arm.

"You changed," he said, eyeing the belt to her bathrobe. One good tug, and it would fall open. "What's underneath?"

Michelle smirked and took the glasses from him. "I'll show you later," she promised as she set the glasses on the counter. She examined the bottle and approved, "Good choice."

When he poured, the stitches twinged, reminding him to ask, "Do you have cuticle scissors?"

She sipped the wine and nodded. "Sure. Want me to take a look?"

He almost asked for help before thinking she might not approve. "Ah, no, that's all right."

"Are you sure? After four years with Vicky, I got very good at giving manicures," she said wryly as she dug through her travel toiletries kit.

"I'd much rather help you out of that robe," he offered.

She handed him the scissors and shooed him back out of the bathroom. "You go fix your nails. I need a moment's privacy."

"I get to take off the robe," he said as she closed the door.

Her answer was muffled. "Deal."

In the kitchenette, he unbuttoned his shirt and then hung it over the back of a chair. He moved under the light, then worked the scissors under the first stitch. It cut cleanly; the scissors were as sharp as he'd hoped. A few more snips, and he had all the stitches cut.

The bathroom door opened a crack. "Ray?"

He went back into the bathroom, where he found Michelle sitting on the edge of the bathtub, wineglass in hand. "Thanks," he said, holding up the scissors. He dropped them in the toiletries kit.

"Everything okay?"

He took the pliers from his pocket. "Fine. Just dealing with the stitches," he said, taking hold of the first knot and giving it a slow, steady tug. It pinched, but the thread pulled cleanly free, leaving only two tiny spots of blood.

"What—Are you—*Ray!*"

"It's time they came out," he said as she stood.

She put the wineglass on the counter and tried to take the pliers away. "And you can't wait until tomorrow, for the clinic?" she scolded.

He kept hold of the pliers and assured her, "It's fine, love. I've done this before. Besides, I've already cut the stitches. No choice now but to take them out."

She blew out a frustrated breath and relented. "You've done this before. Of course you have," she muttered, returning to her seat on the edge of the tub.

"I haven't always had the luxury of a hospital or clinic," he said as he pulled out the rest of the stitches and dropped the threads in the wastebasket. He put down the pliers, picked up her wineglass, and turned to offer it to her. "See? It's healed."

Eyes narrowed skeptically, she beckoned him to kneel beside the tub so she could examine the wound. "You're *never* doing that again," she muttered, then leaned in and kissed him.

He set the glass down on the floor so he could untie her bathrobe. "I'm afraid I have quite a few bad habits."

"Do you?" she asked, glancing down as he pushed the robe open.

He looked up into her beautiful, dark eyes. "Too many to count," he said softly. Honestly.

She lifted her hands to his face, running her fingertips over his skin with a featherlight touch. "Maybe we can work on those bad habits of yours."

He knelt up and let her pull him into a kiss, just as light as his touch. When the kiss ended, he whispered, "Maybe we should. Starting now?"

Her eyes lit up with her smile. "Maybe tomorrow. Tonight, we have other plans, don't we?"

"Yes," he said with a soft laugh. "Yes, we do."

—ᨆ—

Friday, July 12

The narrow bed in the manager's apartment wasn't comfortable to share for too long. In the early hours of the morning, Ray went back upstairs for a couple of hours of sleep. After a too-short nap, Michelle got up, woke her mother, and then went to make breakfast and coffee on autopilot. If she was going to stay awake long enough to make breakfast and see her mother off to the airport, coffee was a medical necessity.

Ten minutes later, the smell of coffee and toast filled the kitchen, and the only sounds upstairs came from the far side of the building, where Ray had apparently just left his room. Her mother, she guessed, had gone back to sleep.

Grumbling to herself, Michelle took her phone out of her pocket and sent her mother a quick wake-up text. Ray came into the kitchen, looking far too awake on such little sleep.

"Morning, love," he said, catching her around the waist so he could pull her close for a quick kiss.

"Ugh," she answered insincerely.

He laughed and went to take mugs out of the cupboard. "Why don't we go to the café in Old Town? This way, you don't have to cook breakfast."

Saved, Michelle thought, and gave Ray a more thorough kiss. "You're a genius."

"You know, I keep telling Preston that, but the bloody bastard refuses to give me a raise."

"I'll write you a note," Michelle offered. "I'll even sign it, if you pour me some coffee."

"At my lady's service," he teased and turned to get the milk from the fridge.

Michelle finished her first mug and half a piece of toast by the time her mother finally came downstairs. "Good morning!" her mother called cheerfully as she swept into the kitchen. "I left my bags outside my room. What's for breakfast?"

Michelle considered throwing the other half of the toast at her mother, but Ray came to the rescue. "We're taking you out to a café in Old Town," he said, allowing her mother to leave a lipstick print on his cheek.

"Sounds lovely, as long as I can make it to the airport on time. There's only one flight today that can accommodate my luggage. If I miss my flight, it could take up to a week to ship my bags."

Michelle glanced at Ray and saw the resolve in his expression. "We won't be late," Michelle promised.

"In fact, I'll go arrange for a taxi right now," Ray offered.

"Did you want to get rid of me that badly?" her mother asked just as Michelle took a sip of her coffee.

Ray answered before Michelle could swallow: "I wouldn't want to deprive you of your luggage. All those shoes."

Michelle's mother laughed. "Oh, he's a keeper, Chelly. Not many men understand a woman's priorities."

Michelle watched as Ray took his phone from his pocket and left the room. She had one more week with Ray—one more week to decide if this would be a lovely vacation or something more. "I'll keep that in mind," she promised, thinking that "something more" was sounding better each day.

Chapter 16

THE GORGEOUS, SUNNY WEATHER HELD INTO THE FOL-
lowing week, allowing Ray and Michelle to explore to
their hearts' content. For seven days, since her mother
had left for Ireland, they'd walked every trail, visited
all the islands, and even gone snorkeling, and still had
plenty of time for windy nights out on the hillside to
watch the stars.

Michelle woke up in Ray's bed—their bed now, she
supposed—with Ray nuzzling at her nape. As soon as
she made a quiet, contented noise, Ray's deep voice
growled in her ear, "Good morning, love."

She rolled over, shoving her hair out of her eyes. She
kept trying to go to bed with it neatly braided, and he
kept "accidentally" pulling off her hair bands. He loved
playing with her hair, and he indulged now, stroking it
back from her face with a soft, gentle touch.

"Morning," she said, trying to turn away to spare him
her breath. He insisted, capturing her for a brief kiss that
tasted like mint. "You were up already?"

"Only to use the loo."

She snickered and wriggled free of his hold. "My turn,
then," she said, shivering as she slid out from under the
blankets. His body was like a furnace, keeping her warm
through the night despite the open windows. She dove

quickly into the bathrobe she kept beside the bed for mornings like this and then let herself into the bathroom.

Five minutes later, she was feeling human, all except for her Medusa-like hair. Since her hair was Ray's fault, she felt under no obligation to tame it. Instead, she went back into the bedroom, abandoned the bathrobe, and snuggled up under the covers once more.

He didn't complain at her cold skin—not even when she shoved her feet between his calves, trying to warm her toes. He just wrapped his arms around her and kissed her properly, a long, slow kiss of heated breath and tongues. His lips were chapped; she gently bit his lower lip and felt him smile. When she opened her eyes, she caught him staring at her with blue eyes gone dark with wide pupils.

The playful morning caught fire. Last night, he'd teased her for what felt like hours, kissing and licking every inch of her skin until she'd pleaded for more. He'd made love to her the same way, with smooth, fluid thrusts, a slow build of sensation that left them both trembling and exhausted.

Now, impatience seized her. She wanted him now. This very instant. She wanted to take him, to claim him, to destroy his self-control not with patience but with overwhelming pleasure.

She rolled on top of him, loving the feel of his hard, hot body beneath hers, and ducked her head to demand a kiss of her own. His fingertips swept over her back, lighting sparks up and down her spine. His hand dipped low, cupping her ass, holding her in place as he pushed his hips up. She spread her legs without thinking, and her clit pressed against Ray's cock.

"Ray," she groaned, lifting her head to look at the wicker nightstand where they were keeping the condoms.

His fingers dug into her hip, pinning her in place. Another thrust, and his cock slid over her clit again. Heat gathered low in her body. With his free hand, he pulled open the drawer and dug around. The lamp rocked unsteadily, and she thought about moving so she could stabilize it, but she ground down against Ray instead.

This time, they both groaned.

He ripped open the condom and got his hands between their bodies. His fingers pushed through her curls. One slid over her clit and down further.

In a rough voice, he started to say, "Slow—" but she silenced him with a kiss, bucking her hips down. When his finger slipped inside, she bit his lip again.

"Now," she whispered into his mouth.

She felt his hands move. Then he shifted her hips up enough to guide his cock between her legs. The head slid over her clit and she gasped again.

And then, with a roll of her spine and a thrust of his hips, his cock breached her body. The pinpoint sparks of sensation centered on her clit. Pleasure flared through her in a tidal wave as she slid down, taking him deeper. Even after a week, his girth left her breathless. Her body clung tightly, nerves turning to channels of molten fire that spread into every inch of her body.

She pushed up on her knees and settled her weight onto his hips. The blanket slithered off her back. Cold air licked at her body. When he slid his hands up to cup her breasts, fingers toying with her nipples, she let her head fall back and gasped.

Every shift of her weight brought new nerves to life

inside her. Why hadn't they done this before? He felt incredible beneath her, inside her, in all sorts of new ways, as if this was their first time all over again.

Then he dropped one hand, drawing a ticklish line over her abdomen. His hand teased through her curls to brush over her clit. "Gorgeous," he whispered, pressing hard, rubbing one small circle.

Her world exploded, shattering into raw pleasure with every beat of her heart.

—᳁᳁—

Ray had never seen anything so beautiful, so captivating. There was no artifice to Michelle's pleasure—no calculated seduction, not even a sense of mutual give-and-take. Only a pure, raw need that spoke not of selfishness but of trust that Ray would give her anything she wanted, without hesitation. He wanted to grasp her hips, dig in his heels, and thrust up into her, but he didn't. He stayed perfectly still except for his fingers, rubbing at her nipple and clit in slow synchronicity, lightening his touch as the tremors of her body eased.

When she finally went boneless, lowering herself to lie against his chest, he moved his hands to hug her close. The shift of his cock inside her was maddening, urging him to *take*, but he still held back.

It took all of his effort to sound calm and controlled when he asked, "Good?"

She gave a short laugh, breath warm against his chest. "*Too* good," she mumbled.

"No such thing, love."

She buried her face in the hollow of his shoulder. "I'd *planned* to do more, but I don't think I can move."

"Mmm, I think I can manage for a bit, if you'd like," he said, giving a shallow thrust of his hips, barely moving inside her.

She gasped all the same, and he froze.

"Too much?"

After a moment, she shook her head. "More," she whispered.

He obliged with pleasure, finding a slow, easy rhythm to guide her down from her unexpectedly powerful peak and slowly back up again. At first she lay compliant atop him, hips barely shifting, holding him back by her position. But then she propped herself up, palms resting on the bed by his shoulders, and began to move. She was slender and graceful but strong. Her momentary pause was just that, nothing more than her need to catch her breath.

Soon, she knelt upright and took control once more, hands flat on his chest for balance. Ray had to stop moving, not just to give her this, as she wanted, but because the sight of her was almost too much. She glowed in the diffuse early morning sunlight; her tangled hair gave her a wild edge so unlike her usual composed self.

This was a side of her that belonged to him. He suspected no one had ever seen her quite like this before, brazen and uninhibited. The thought that he had somehow incited this abandon turned the building pleasure into a raging brush fire.

Casting all good behavior to the wind, he thrust up into her, catching her by the hips. She cried out in surprised pleasure, opening her eyes wide. Her lips were parted, her expression unguarded. He thrust up again, bracing his feet on the bed, using her ragged breath and hitched moans to guide him.

She went tense, grinding down against him, and threw her head back as her body clenched tight. Her nails scraped against his chest, scoring sharp, stinging lines across his skin.

He had time to take just one breath, time to whisper her name, before she pulled him over the edge with her.

~~~

After making breakfast, Michelle went into Liam's office to finish her report, leaving Ray on the patio, alone with his thoughts.

Three days. Today, tomorrow, Friday. She had a reservation to fly to Newquay, with a connecting flight to London. He'd delayed making any plans at all, as was his habit. Normally, he preferred to keep his options open. Now...

Now, he didn't want to think about leaving at all—not leaving St. Mary's, but Michelle.

He walked out onto the lawn, remembering watching her do her yoga out here for the first time, almost two weeks ago. He sat down on the bench, and all he could think of was her sitting there beside him, watching the tide roll in.

What now?

He could stay here. She'd already offered to leave him the keys. She'd even gone so far as to clear it with Vicky. He could stay here in his childhood summer home as long as he liked, and the thought of staying for one *minute* without Michelle felt...wrong.

Slouching down on the bench, ankles crossed, he dialed and put the phone to his ear.

Preston answered, saying, "Really, Ray? Five in the damned morning?"

"It's a weekday. You're up," Ray said.

"Boundaries, Ray. How do you know I don't have anyone here with me?"

"The only female in your bed is Moneypenny, and that's because she wants to steal your pillow as soon as you're out of bed."

"Dogs are like that. What do *you* want?"

Ray sighed. "Hell if I know," he admitted. He had just a few more days left with Michelle. He should have been content. He'd had a wonderful holiday, which was all he'd wanted, at first.

In a calm, neutral voice, Preston asked, "Is this your way of telling me you're quitting Samaritan so you can buy your grandparents' old place?"

"No." Ray took a deep breath of cold sea air and closed his eyes for a moment, trying to clear his thoughts. "Michelle's leaving in three days. I figure I'll start toward home then, too."

"Michelle," Preston said thoughtfully.

Ray waited, but Preston said nothing else. Finally, Ray asked, "What about her?"

"You tell me."

It was Ray's turn to fall silent. How could he possibly explain his feelings to his best friend if he couldn't even explain them to himself? Preston was an avowed bachelor, just as Ray was. Or had been. Or maybe still was, though by circumstance rather than choice.

"I don't know," he finally admitted.

"And I'm supposed to diagnose you from three thousand miles away?"

"You're supposed to… I don't know. Be sympathetic. Tell me to get my head out of my arse. Something like that."

"Right." Preston sighed, and Ray heard him moving around. "Can you wait until I'm out of bed?"

"Should I call back?"

"Not you. Moneypenny. Now there's fur all over my pillow."

"She wouldn't shed if you'd brush her."

"She hates it when I brush her," Preston complained. "She misses you."

Ray smiled grimly. "Is that a hint to come home?"

"I didn't know I needed to hint. Or are you back to thinking about quitting Samaritan to take up the hotel business?"

"No," Ray answered without hesitation. "It's about time I said good-bye to Valhalla's Rest. Maybe even go somewhere new, next time I go on holiday."

"Okay," Preston said, thoughtfully drawing out the word. "What brought that on?"

"Michelle."

"Go on."

"She's…" Ray faltered. Words seemed inadequate to capture who Michelle was. What she'd come to mean to him. How he felt her absence like an ache, even knowing she was just twenty yards away.

How much would it hurt when she was two thousand miles away? After Friday, he had no idea when—or even *if*—they would ever see each other again.

"Ray?" Preston asked, his voice quiet. Worried.

"Sorry." Ray pushed a hand through his hair. It was nearly long enough to fall in his eyes. He never had made it to a barber. "I just... I don't know what she plans to do after this. Go back to Arizona, I suppose."

"And you haven't asked her...why?"

Ray huffed out a laugh. "I'm not going to bring that up if she hasn't. Not once has she said a bloody thing about what happens after this holiday's ended."

"Have you?"

"Of course not. I don't want to"—he hesitated uncomfortably—"to pressure her."

Preston's only answer was a deep sigh.

Ray stood and looked down at the grass. He kicked at it with his bare foot. "So you're saying I *should* ask her?"

"That depends."

"On?"

"On what happened to this being a fun vacation fling?"

"*Michelle* happened, obviously." Ray kicked at the grass again and then paced to the edge of the flower bed and back to the bench. "She's..."

"Fucking hell, Ray. You're going to have to eventually complete that sentence."

"She's more than I thought she would be," Ray finally said.

"More, how?"

"How the bloody hell am I supposed to know?"

Preston laughed, the bastard. "Maybe because you've spent almost two weeks with her?"

"Almost two weeks," Ray muttered.

"You want more."

Ray glared out at the sea. He wasn't supposed to

want more. He was fine with what he had now. The challenge of his job. His simple life. His friends and colleagues.

More meant change. Compromise.

More meant he might have to lose something to make room for what he'd gain.

"Ray?"

"Yes." Ray blew out a breath and closed his eyes for a moment. "Yes, I want more. But at what bloody cost?"

Warily, Preston asked, "What's that supposed to mean?"

"Just that. She lives with her mother in Arizona now. She wants to run a hotel. Where the hell is there room for *my* life in all that?"

Preston sighed. "Ray…"

"What?"

"You're a fucking idiot," Preston said, exasperated.

Taken aback, Ray asked, "Me?"

"Yes, you. Fucking idiot. You're in love with her."

"It hasn't even been a fortnight."

"So?" A hint of bitterness crept into Preston's voice. "I knew how I felt about Lilit before she'd finished giving her intelligence briefing."

"Preston—"

"Tell me I'm wrong," Preston challenged. "Tell me that just thinking about her leaving—about never seeing her again—doesn't hurt more than a gunshot. Tell me that looking ahead at a life without her isn't like drowning."

Ray's chest went tight at the thought.

More softly, Preston said, "That happens once in your life, Ray, and only if you're very, very lucky."

"Fucking hell," Ray said softly. He rubbed a hand over his shoulder, remembering the sting of the tattoo needle inscribing a permanent reminder of friendship and loyalty into his skin. "I won't leave Samaritan."

"Did you ask if she'd even want you to?" Preston countered. "If she feels the same about you, I'll bet she wouldn't expect you to."

Ray turned and looked toward Valhalla's Rest—the building that had once been his home but was now so much more. It was where he'd found Michelle.

Where he'd fallen in love.

"Right, then," he said as a wave of calm swept over him, as if merely thinking the word had banished the last of his doubts.

"Which means what?" Preston asked.

Ray laughed and started for the porch. "I'll be home by Monday at the latest, hopefully not alone. That or I'll call and keep you updated."

"I'm not hiring another VP. And Ian expects you to be an usher at his wedding."

"Bloody hell, what did I do to deserve that?"

"You wore a tux to that military veterans' fundraiser last year, and our mother saw the pictures. And if you're not back by Monday, I'll make damned sure Cecily pairs you with Amelia, who's one of the bridesmaids."

"Do that and I might just have a critical mission in Australia that weekend," Ray threatened, walking up the porch steps. He went to the table where he'd left his half-finished mug of tea. He eyed it thoughtfully but decided he'd rather make a fresh cup. "Give Moneypenny a kiss for me."

"It's five in the morning, Ray. I'm not starting the

day by kissing the dog. Bad enough I had to fix my idiot best friend's love life at this hour."

Ray laughed. "Yeah, thanks for that," he said, hanging up.

"Should I be jealous?" Michelle asked from the kitchen doorway.

Ray turned and grinned at the sight of her. "Sorry?"

"You and 'Moneypenny.' Isn't that a little cliché?"

He shoved the phone in his pocket, abandoned the mug of tea, and crossed the patio so he could pull her into his arms. "Well, yes, but she does adore me."

"Oh, really," she asked archly, giving him a poke in the ribs. "If you tell me she's your secretary…"

Ray laughed and kissed her cheek. "She's Preston's dog."

"He named his dog Moneypenny?"

"Moneypenny and Bond. No one ever accused him of originality."

Michelle rolled her eyes and wrapped her arms around his waist. "I suppose it's better than Rover and Daisy or something."

"Of course it is. What would you have picked?"

"It depends on the dog's personality." Michelle leaned up on her toes, demanding a proper kiss.

He complied happily, wondering just how he could admit his feelings to her. Should he just say it bluntly? Was he supposed to arrange some sort of romantic occasion, or was that limited to engagement? Should he even be *thinking* things like engagement at this early stage?

"Hmm, you seem distracted," she accused, stepping back. Her hands slipped from his waist to grasp his, and she gave him a little tug toward the kitchen. "Lunch?"

Reprieved for the moment, he nodded. "Sounds good. Shall we go out?"

"We have leftover roast beef from last night. Can I trust you to slice some for sandwiches without starting a fire?"

He laughed. "How could I possibly start a fire with a knife and a cold joint of beef?"

"That's exactly the sort of mystery I don't want to solve," she said, poking his ribs again. "Mostly because if anyone could burn down the kitchen that way, it'd be you."

———

"Hey, Vicky," Michelle said, leaning back in the office chair. "I hopefully just emailed you my analysis of the B and B's books, a prospective business plan, and what it'd take to keep the business running. I had to—"

A beep interrupted her. She glanced at the phone and sighed, hanging up on the voice mail to take the call. "Hi, Vicky."

All in a rush, Vicky said, "Sorry, just saw you rang. I was getting off the tube. Reception's spotty."

Michelle smiled. That was Vicky, living life at faster-than-light speed. "No problem. I just emailed you my report on Valhalla's Rest. I had to do some magic to get it from the computer to my phone. If it didn't go through, I'll send you another copy from the deli."

"From the deli?"

"Where else would there be Wi-Fi available on the island?"

"Oh, naturally. So, just skip to the summary then. What do you think?"

"I think it could be an excellent business or secondary revenue stream. You could hire a few locals to take care of it—"

"Chelly…"

Michelle shook her head, running a finger over the edge of the age-worn desk. "No, Vicky," she said gently. "Thank you, but it's not for me."

Vicky sighed. "It'd be lovely having you only a few hours away. We could visit all the time. Think of all the weekend road trips. All the castles you wanted to see. Your ex-Royal Marines boyfriend…"

"I don't belong here, Vicky. Besides…" Michelle glanced at the office door. She'd closed it most of the way, but she no longer bothered to latch it, much less lock it. Lowering her voice, she said, "I think I might just look into somewhere in Virginia."

"Oh, *really*?" Vicky asked slyly. "So does this mean you have *plans* with Captain Gorgeous?"

Michelle rolled her eyes, knowing Vicky expected it even if she couldn't see it. "It means, *Ray* and I have some things to talk about, as soon as I can figure out how to bring them up. We haven't exactly talked about the future. It's only been two weeks."

"What happened to 'like mother, like daughter,' then?"

"Genetic aberration." Michelle smirked. "Look, I don't want to ruin our last few days together with expectations. I won't drive him away by moving too fast. I figure I'll bring it up slowly."

"Oh, please," Vicky scoffed. "If he's going to panic at the very thought of commitment, best to know now. Plus, he'll sense it the second you go sniffing around plans for next month, much less ten years down the line. And if you're *too* subtle, he'll never notice. Men aren't exactly perceptive, you know."

"Ray's different."

"I know. I sent you the photographic evidence, remember?"

"The real-life view is even better."

Vicky laughed. "That's my girl! So, what's your plan, then? Shag his brains out, then catch him while his guard's down?"

"I was leaning toward a sensible conversation at our favorite restaurant."

"Where's your sense of adventure?"

"He wasn't complaining this morning."

"Oh? Do tell," Vicky invited.

"Sorry, no time. I need to shower and change," Michelle said cheerfully. "We have dinner plans."

"Chelly! Don't you dare—"

"Talk to you soon, Vicky. Bye!" Laughing, Michelle hung up and then set her phone to silent.

"I think you should know, it was incredibly unfair to get me addicted to this stuff," Michelle complained as she tore open a scone.

Ray grinned, leaning back in his seat to watch her. "The worst part is, you can't get decent clotted cream in the States."

She tipped her head down to glare at him over her sunglasses. "Incredibly unfair," she repeated, spreading jam on both halves of her scone. Then she went for the clotted cream.

"Just consider it incentive to come back here and visit," he said casually.

She licked her lips, studying him. Between her hat and sunglasses, she knew he couldn't see her eyes clearly. Maybe it was cowardly, but she needed to hide, at least a little bit, while she tried to come up with just the right words.

She was running out of time.

"I think I will," she said slowly. "It's nicer here than it is in London."

"It is," he agreed, turning to look out at the harbor.

She took a deep breath, trying to steady herself. Should she suggest they both come back to visit? She didn't want to wait a year. Besides, she doubted he could make plans that far in advance—not if he was a trouble-shooter as well as an executive at his company.

She could suggest a trip to Arizona. But it was July, and it was hot as hell there. It wouldn't be *nice* in the Estrella Mountains, where her mom lived, until October.

Was it too soon to suggest she visit him in Virginia?

"Do you travel often?" he asked while she was still fumbling for words.

"I'd like to. It's not as if I have a lot to do." Only after the words slipped out did she realize she sounded like a vagrant sponging off her mother. "At least, not until I make a decision about another B and B."

"You're thinking of running one, then."

She nodded, finally taking a bite of her scone. The flavors melted on her tongue. She swallowed and washed it down with a sip of tea. She usually didn't like her tea with milk and sugar, but she was getting used to it.

"But not Valhalla's Rest?" he asked, idly turning his mug in his hands.

"No." She gathered her courage and said, "I want something on the East Coast."

He glanced at her. "If you don't have your heart set on New York, there are some gorgeous areas in Virginia. The coast is nice, but the Shenandoah River Valley... There's lots of tourism there."

Her heart skipped; according to the map she'd pulled up on her phone, Samaritan had its headquarters in the northern part of the Shenandoah River Valley. If he was inviting her there, that was a good sign.

"I think I'd like a change from New York," she admitted. She sipped her tea again. "And getting away from the coast would keep me from constantly worrying about hurricanes."

"Do you like snow? Winters can be... Well, anything's more than you get in Arizona. But you'll also get tourists looking to ski."

"I love snow." As casually as she could, she added, "Though there's only so much shoveling I could take. I might need help."

He looked at her, one corner of his mouth twitching up. "A little thing like you could get lost under a heavy snowfall. I could always help out. Save you the trouble."

She smiled, hope blossoming in her chest. "I'd like that." She put down her tea and slid her hand across the table. He reached out and laced his fingers with hers. "Maybe you could show me around while it's summer? I mean, while it's still nice?"

His hand tightened, fingers twitching. "I'd love to."

She couldn't hide a laugh of relief. "Ray…" She looked down, feeling dizzy with happiness.

"If it's not too forward of me," he said, shifting his chair closer so he could take her hand in both of his, "we could travel there together. We'd have to delay until Monday, though."

Elation hit, mingled with just a tiny bit of confusion. She'd delay for a month if it meant she could stay with him. "Why?" she asked curiously.

"I spend most of my time in the office or at Preston's. His guest room is bigger than my whole flat. His brother and soon-to-be sister-in-law are going back to Manhattan on Sunday. By Monday, the maid will have the house squared away."

For one moment, she considered protesting. She'd rather have privacy in a tiny studio than share a luxury house with anyone who wasn't Ray.

But then, as she opened her mouth to say so, she realized exactly what he was saying. He wanted her to meet his closest friend in the world. More to the point, he wanted them to get to know each other, rather than have one brief, supervised meeting at a restaurant.

"I'll call Vicky and let her know," Michelle said, smiling at Ray.

He nodded, shifting his chair even closer. "Michelle…" He took a deep breath, taking hold of her other hand. "I'm rubbish at words, but you should know… It's only been two weeks, but…" He stared down at their joined hands.

In the silence that followed, she could hear what went unspoken. She wanted to take off her sunglasses, to look

into his eyes, but she didn't want to let go of his hands.
"Me, too, Ray."

His head came up.

She nodded, blinking tears away. "I love you."

He let out a sharp, ragged breath and released her
hands, only to cup her face and pull her close for a kiss.
"Michelle," he whispered against her lips. He kissed
her again—her lips, her cheek, her forehead—and then
wrapped her in his arms. "I never thought—I never
imagined I could be so happy."

She pulled off her sunglasses and dropped them on
the table. "Ray," she said, burying her face against his
neck, feeling his stubble against her cheek.

"I love you," he said roughly. He tugged her close,
and she ended up in his lap. His voice dropped to a thick,
strained whisper. "God, Michelle. I love you."

Two weeks, she thought, holding him tight. She'd
always thought that love was something meant to be
built in slow, careful measures made up of things like
respect and affection and attraction, but she'd been
wrong. Love was unexpected and terrifying in its power,
appearing from the darkness with no warning at all.

Two weeks ago, she hadn't known Ray Powell
existed. Now, she couldn't imagine sharing her life with
anyone else.

Chapter 17

Monday, July 22

RAY'S DEEP VOICE EASED MICHELLE AWAKE. "Michelle? We're almost there, love."

She sat up, yawning, and blinked at the darkness. It felt like it should be getting light out, but she could no longer trust her body clock. The digital display on the truck dashboard showed it wasn't even midnight—just about three hours after their plane had landed.

"Sorry, you should've woken me earlier," she said, trying not to yawn again.

Ray turned the pickup truck onto a driveway with trees crowding close on both sides. "I slept on the plane, remember?"

"Ugh. How you could sleep with that turbulence..." Rubbing sleep out of her eyes, she flipped the visor down so she could take a look in the mirror. She had dark shadows under her eyes and her lips were dry, but at least her hair wasn't a mess—except for where she'd been sleeping against the window, flattening her hair against the side of her head.

Ray laughed, sliding a hand up her back while she bent over to get her purse. "I've slept on military transports. A passenger jet is a luxury, no matter how bumpy the ride. At least the seats have springs mostly intact."

She shivered, thinking how much worse it could've

been in economy. Ray had gotten them an upgrade, using miles. He'd offered to upgrade to first class, but Michelle had caught sight of the cost and put her foot down, refusing the ridiculous expense.

"Where are we?" she asked, looking at the old growth trees that surrounded them. "And don't just say Virginia," she added, poking Ray's arm with her lip gloss tube.

He laughed. "Virginia. *Specifically*, Preston's house."

Her chapped lips stung as she applied the lip gloss. "He lives in the trees? That's very Tarzan of him."

It was Ray's turn to poke her arm. "I knew you should've had coffee on the flight. You get stroppy when you're tired."

"Stroppy?" She burst out laughing. "Did you just call me *stroppy*?"

He shot her a quick, wary look before he went back to steering the truck around a sharp curve. "Depends on whether or not you're upset over it."

She hummed thoughtfully as she flipped the visor back up and put away her lip gloss. "I think I'd rather be stroppy than a wuss. So—"

She cut off as the headlights illuminated a blocky Colonial house.

After two weeks on the charming Isles of Scilly, the house was an eyesore with its geometrically aligned small-pane windows, three brick chimneys, and absolute lack of character. Only the landscaping redeemed it at all, with a sweeping lawn and hedges covered with flowers edging the foundation.

"That's very—" She struggled to find something polite to say.

"Hideous?" Ray pulled into a round driveway and parked at the front door. It had been painted a deep forest green that clashed with the grass.

"Now who's getting stroppy?"

Ray grinned and turned off the engine. "It *is* hideous. Preston bought it as a restoration project, thinking he'd have the time to work on it himself. Took him six months of living with sheet plastic over the windows and bare wall studs to give in and hire contractors."

"I know he's your best friend, but is he...crazy?"

"I'm sure of it." Ray leaned over the center console and kissed her cheek. "Let's go introduce you."

She slung her purse over her arm, pushed open the door, and jumped down from the raised truck. Her heartbeat picked up, and not just because she was exhausted. Preston was Ray's closest friend—the most important person in Ray's life. What if he didn't like her? What if he felt like she was going to come between them? Telling herself she was being ridiculous didn't work, either. Preston and Ray were both confirmed, lifelong bachelors—at least until she'd come along and stolen Preston's best friend.

The front door opened, stopping her in her tracks. She caught a glimpse of a tall, broad silhouette, and her heart skipped as she remembered when Ray had appeared on the doorstep at Valhalla's Rest.

And then two huge German shepherds bounded out. Michelle wanted to crouch down and pet them, but she held still, not knowing their training.

Not that she'd needed to be cautious. One of the dogs leaped at Ray, barking wildly, spinning in mad circles.

The other sniffed at Michelle, from feet to abdomen, before trying to stick its head in her purse.

"Did you intentionally pick a later flight so you could get out of the Monday morning meeting?" asked the man in the doorway. He had a deep, pleasant voice and a distinctively East Coast accent, sharp but lacking the nasal tones of New York or Boston.

"Bloody right, I did," Ray said, ruffling the dog's fur with one hand. He put his other arm around Michelle's waist and told her, "That's Bond. And this is Moneypenny, who likes me more than she does Preston."

Michelle laughed, extending her hand for the dog to sniff, though he skipped that part and went right to licking. "They're beautiful."

"Don't introduce me. It's fine. So much for your legendary British courtesy."

"We've been traveling for two days now," Ray complained. "Courtesy can wait until tomorrow morning."

Shaking his head, the man stepped into the porch light. He was a couple of inches shorter than Ray, with a lean build that reminded Michelle of his German shepherds—all muscle without an ounce to spare. He had blond hair cropped in a short military haircut and sharp features, with high cheekbones and a square jaw. His eyes were a startlingly deep green.

"Preston Fairchild. It's good to finally meet you," he said, offering Michelle his hand.

She reached for him and then hesitated when she remembered the dog's enthusiastic licking. "Sorry."

Grinning, Preston clasped her hand anyway. "You get used to it with these two around. I hope you're not allergic."

"Nope. I love dogs, actually."

"Good. Ray, get her bags while I give her the ten-cent tour."

Ray stuck to Michelle's side. Cheerfully, he said, "Sod off, mate. You're the host. Make yourself useful."

"I am. I'm trying to get Michelle alone so I can talk her out of saddling herself with you."

"She *likes* me."

"Temporary insanity."

Affection for both men rose up inside Michelle. She burst out laughing, hugging Ray close for a moment, though her laugh turned into a jaw-cracking yawn. "I'm sorry. I'm all turned around from the time zones."

"The guest room should have fresh sheets," Preston said. "You can have the tour tomorrow while Ray goes in to the office. He's got two weeks' worth of paperwork to catch up on."

"Or *I* can give her the tour after sleeping in, and *you* can go to the bloody office instead," Ray countered, hugging Michelle close.

"You've had your vacation," Preston said, and though he was trying to look stern, Michelle could see the smile in his eyes. "Now you have paperwork."

"Which is hardly incentive to get out of bed."

"And don't forget a doctor's appointment," Michelle said helpfully.

"Doctor?" Preston asked sharply, looking to her. "What did he do to himself this time?"

"Nothing!" Ray protested.

Michelle huffed. "Except take out his own stitches using nail clippers and needle-nose pliers."

"The cut healed," Ray insisted. "I didn't need the bloody stitches anymore."

Michelle shot him a look.

Ray sighed dramatically. "There, see?" he said, turning to Preston. "I can't come to the office tomorrow. Apparently I have to make a bloody doctor's appointment."

Preston laughed. "Nice work, Michelle. It's good to have you on the team."

"Why are you helping him?" Ray asked plaintively, looking down at her.

"Like I said, she likes me," Preston answered on her behalf.

"She likes me more," Ray said confidently. "I warned her about you."

"Or I can leave you both here to fight about it, while the dogs show me the way to the guest room," Michelle said, grinning at them both. She slid out of Ray's grasp and called, "Come here, babies!"

The dogs swarmed at her, ignoring the two familiar, boring men in favor of their new playmate. Michelle led them to the porch, where she turned back to look at the two men. They would never be mistaken for brothers, but everything about them, from the way they stood side by side to the casual-chic way they turned jeans and T-shirts into fashion statements, spoke of their close friendship.

"Don't forget the suitcases," she added, giving a little wave toward the bed of the truck. Then she told the dogs, "Let's go inside. Good dogs!"

—⁂—

The king-size bed was a welcome change after the cozy—meaning crowded—double at Valhalla's Rest, but Michelle still ended up cuddled close to Ray's side. This time, it was because two German shepherds were taking up half the bed and then some, and she didn't have the heart to kick them off.

Besides, Ray wasn't complaining.

"Preston's invited us to stay here as long as we like, so we don't need to go to my flat," he said, combing his fingers through her hair with slow, lazy strokes.

"I don't want to be any trouble."

"It's no trouble. He has the whole house to himself. I've lived here more than once, between flats."

"That's kind of him. I really didn't think this through. I don't do this, you know."

"I should hope not—at least not more than this once," Ray said, hugging her close.

She smiled against his chest, but only briefly. "Really, Ray. I just…picked up and came here, without any sort of plan."

"Did you want to go back to Arizona?"

"No. Absolutely not." She turned to kiss his shoulder. "I don't want to leave you. I just… I have no idea *where*. Other than a couple of Civil War battlefields and the interstate to Florida, I've never been anywhere in Virginia."

"There's no rush, love," he said reassuringly. "We have time."

Michelle sighed, thinking of how much she had to do—more to the point, how much they needed to discuss. "I lived at Anchor's Cove," she said slowly. "There's so much to running a B and B, especially if you don't hire a lot of staff, it's easier to live on-site."

"I know. Liam lived at Valhalla's Rest, remember?"

Michelle nodded against his shoulder. "I was thinking about it in the tub. Maybe a farmhouse with a barn. The farmhouse would be a perfect bed and breakfast, and we could convert the barn into a house for us—if you wanted to...to live together, that is," she said, courage failing her at the last moment.

Ray's arm tightened against her back. "You're stealing my lines," he accused. "I'm supposed to ask you to live with me, only I'm not sure a goldfish could live with me at the moment. And I'm damned well not inviting you to live with Preston *without* me."

She laughed wickedly. "Oh, I don't know. The two of you are both awfully handsome. A sort of matched set. Day and night."

With a deep sigh, Ray complained, "And here I just got comfortable."

"What?"

"Now I'm going to have to go shoot him," he said, trying to get out of bed.

Laughing, she tugged him back down and rolled on top of him. The two dogs promptly claimed the foot of space she'd vacated. "Or we could just take him up on his offer to let us stay here and maybe start house-hunting tomorrow?"

"All right." He slid his hands down her back to her hips. "Michelle... I don't have much, other than my truck—"

She shook her head, interrupting, "Ray, it's fine. I'm the one who wants a bed and breakfast, remember?

I have my share of the insurance settlement from Anchor's Cove."

He laughed softly. "Love... It's not that at all. In truth, I've got more money than I know what to do with. I've been drawing a salary from Samaritan for years and spending almost none of it. We can buy any farm you'd like. If *you* want to, that is."

She went cold inside, chest tightening at the thought of *sharing*. "I..." she began, shaking her head.

His smile vanished. "Or not. Whatever makes you happy."

"It's just—" She licked her lips and swallowed, thinking...no, wondering what she'd been thinking, actually. She'd realized Ray had money; Scilly was too remote to be a very affordable holiday destination even once, much less every couple of years. He'd booked his trip on impulse, paying a premium for last-minute travel. And then his offer to upgrade them to first class...

She twisted off him and got out of bed, bracing instinctively for a rush of cold air that didn't come. The summer night was mild, with just enough of a breeze to stir the warm air, filling it with the scent of trees and grass. When unpacking his backpack, Ray had put the stuffed dog on the nightstand. Michelle picked it up absently and paced to the window, tugging down her oversized T-shirt.

"I know, love." He pushed away the blankets and sat up on the edge of the bed. "After what happened, I wouldn't trust anyone, either."

She flinched. "It's not...*trust*, exactly. I trust you." She laughed sadly and turned to look at him. "I really do trust you. This is just something I need to do."

There was no hint of anger in Ray's expression—just

a calm, steady thoughtfulness that helped her to breathe more easily.

"Right, then," he said, glancing over his shoulder at the dogs, who were slowly claiming more of the bed. "A remodeled barn and a farmhouse. Should be simple enough. You buy the farmhouse and do as you like with it, and I'll buy the barn and handle the cost of the remodeling, though you'll have to deal with the architects and contractors."

She blinked. "You're not offended?"

"It's perfectly logical, isn't it? Besides, you don't want me running a bloody B and B, dealing with guests and"—he grinned—"cooking breakfast."

She let out a nervous little laugh. "If you go near my kitchen…"

He held out a hand. "Sounds all right, then?"

There were nuances that she'd want to work out, for her own peace of mind, but she really did trust Ray. "All right," she agreed, taking his hand. "It sounds pretty close to perfect."

He drew her down beside him. "How can we make it perfect, then?"

Smiling, she put the stuffed dog back on the nightstand and looked over her shoulder. Moneypenny had wormed under the blankets. Bond was sprawled across the foot of the bed, legs outstretched, head thrown back.

"First, we're going to need another bed."

―⁓―

Friday, August 30

"You're not peeking, are you?" Ray asked as the truck slowed down.

Michelle rolled her eyes, though she kept them closed—not that Ray could see them behind her sunglasses. "I'm not peeking," she said, bracing herself against the armrest as the pickup truck jolted over rough terrain.

"All right. Keep them closed. I'll come around to get your door."

Feeling ridiculous, Michelle unlatched her seat belt and sat quietly. Ray turned off the engine and opened his door. His seat creaked, and the pickup rocked gently as he got out.

They'd been driving for almost an hour, the last ten minutes of which she'd spent with her eyes closed. Stubbornly, he hadn't even given her a hint about what they were doing here—wherever *here* was.

Her door opened. He reached in and took hold of one hand. "All right, duck your head. I've got you," he said, moving his other hand to her waist to help her down.

Gravel crunched under her sneakers. She took a step away from the truck so he could close the door. Sniffing the air, she caught the smell of horses and freshly mown grass. She couldn't hear any vehicles, so they weren't close to a highway or busy road.

Had he found a farm he wanted her to see? Her stomach gave a nervous little flip at the thought. They'd been living in a rental house while she searched for just the right property to turn into a B and B. And while she was happy to go scout property with him, she wanted— *needed*—the decision to be hers first. It was irrational, she knew, but she'd explained it to him anyway, and he'd been fine with that.

Until now?

Trying not to feel resentful, she let him take her hand and lead her away from the truck. She might be wrong. She'd give him the benefit of the doubt. At least, that was what she told herself.

Michelle heard the sound of approaching footsteps. "Mr. Powell?" a woman asked. She didn't sound very young, and she wasn't familiar at all.

"You can open your eyes," Ray quietly told Michelle.

She blinked against the bright summer sun and found herself, as she'd feared, in front of a barn. But this barn was occupied by horses, floor strewn with hay. Off to one side was a modern little house, but there were also other outbuildings that she could see as her eyes adjusted to the light. Nothing about this property even hinted at being a good site for a bed and breakfast.

And the woman who approached didn't look like a realtor. She looked to be in her forties or early fifties, with sun-bleached hair and a friendly, weather-worn face. She wore boots, blue jeans, and a flannel shirt with the sleeves torn off.

Ray offered her his hand. "Ray Powell. This is Michelle Cole."

"Laney Anderson," the woman said, shaking his hand, then Michelle's. "You're a couple minutes early. No trouble finding the place?"

"None at all."

"Good. Come on back. Watch your step—the horses like to leave surprises," she said, turning to head into the barn.

Michelle shot Ray a curious look, wondering what was going on. He gave her that crooked smile that he knew she couldn't resist, then took her hand and went after Laney.

Michelle let Ray lead her through the barn, past stalls not just with horses but mules and even an old-looking cow. Some of the animals looked dangerously thin, even though the barn was well-appointed. Apprehension flickered through Michelle. What kind of farm was this?

They went through the other side of the barn, where a half-dozen pygmy goats ran up to a nearby fence to bleat at them. "Don't mind them," Laney said, heading right for a fenced-in porch at the back of the house.

"Busy place you have," Ray said casually.

"Oh, we get all sorts. Don't turn anyone away, either." Laney opened the porch door and held it from them. "Come on through. Just to warn you, the momma might try to jump. She's awful friendly."

Momma? she wondered.

They stepped into a small living room, where a skinny German shepherd, fur shaved almost bald over much of its body, twisted up from a nest of pillows and rushed at Laney. The dog was in pitiful condition, though it wasn't cowering. After one leap at Laney, the dog bounced between Ray and Michelle, tongue darting out at their hands. As soon as Ray stooped to offer affection, the dog climbed up onto his bent legs and licked at his face.

"That's a good girl," Laney said affectionately. "Just a month ago, she would've been hiding in the corner, poor thing."

"What happened?" Michelle asked.

"Puppy mill." Laney huffed angrily. "Bonny here isn't even two years old, and this is her second litter.

Maybe third. Come on, let's introduce you to the pups. All four of them made it and look to be in excellent health."

Michelle's heart leaped. She looked at Ray, who grinned proudly as he gently eased the dog off his lap.

The dog followed them to the kitchen, which was fenced off with a sturdy baby gate. Shredded newspapers were scattered all over the floor, along with an assortment of stuffed toys. As soon as Laney unlatched the gate, a furry mass in the corner of the room separated, and four squat, round puppies barreled at them on stubby, uncoordinated legs.

"Oh, Ray," Michelle said, taking one step inside the gate before she knelt down. The puppies were attacking Laney's boots, ignoring her for the moment.

Ray followed her in, and Laney latched the gate. Stepping carefully around the puppies, Ray suggested, "Why don't you get to know them, love?"

Patiently, Michelle waited for the puppies to notice her. One finally did, tottering over to try and climb up onto her legs. Michelle gave the puppy a hand, carefully scooping it up, and was rewarded with licks and nibbles at her chin.

"They'll need some more socialization and training," Laney said, "but I've taken them out to the barn to get them used to noises and other animals. Pa was by only yesterday for deworming and the first battery of shots. If you need a vet, I've got some of his cards."

"Preston's already given me one," Ray said.

"That's right. How are his two doing?"

Ray grinned. "They generally keep him in line."

As they chatted, a second puppy noticed Michelle and

started gnawing on her sneaker. Hands full with the first, Michelle couldn't stop the second from untying the lace. Laughing, Ray rescued her, lifting the second puppy.

"What do you think?" he asked, grinning, as he sat down next to her. The puppy he was holding immediately jumped out of his lap and attacked the nearest sheet of newspaper.

Irrationally, she wanted them all, but she knew she couldn't properly give them the attention they deserved. She'd never had a dog of her own; she wasn't even confident with the idea of taking two. "Do they need to go in pairs?" she asked Laney, thinking of Preston's dogs.

"No, they'll do fine alone. All they need is love, patience, and attention." Laney distracted the other two puppies with a squeaky toy and then let herself out of the kitchen. "You two take all the time you need," she said, latching the gate.

"Preston vouched for us as adopters," Ray said. His hands were full, so he nudged her with his shoulder. "If you don't want, we can—"

"Don't you dare finish that sentence," Michelle scolded, kissing his arm, which was all she could reach without sending the puppies tumbling.

Ray grinned. "What do you think of that one? He seems to have chosen you."

"He's adorable," she said, hugging the puppy to her. He got his paws over her shoulder and started chewing on her hair. "Did you want to hold him?"

"And come between you two?" Ray leaned over and scratched gently down the puppy's back. "Do you like him?"

Michelle closed her eyes for a moment and nodded,

chest going tight with love for Ray and his surprises. She should have known he wouldn't make a decision about something as big and important as real estate. And while this was just as important, this was the sort of surprise she could treasure.

"Yes. He's wonderful."

Ray gave the puppy one last scratch and then got to his feet. "Stay here. Play with them for a bit," he said, letting himself through the gate. "I'll go talk to Laney."

Fifteen minutes later, Michelle held the puppy while Ray got her seat belt buckled in place. "We need to stop by the pet store on the way home," she said, trying to keep the puppy from wriggling free to explore the interior of the truck.

Ray grinned and stayed leaning over the center console to ruffle the puppy's fur. "Preston's already gone for us. He picked up food, toys, everything we need."

Michelle smiled, constantly amazed at how thoughtful Ray could be. "You two thought of everything, huh?"

"Logistics and mission planning. We're professionals, love, remember?" he asked, lifting his face.

She obliged with a kiss—and so did the puppy, shoving his head right between theirs. Laughing, they both recoiled from the wet nose and wetter tongue. "Uh-huh. Then why did I end up cooking dinner for you two almost every night? You would've starved without me."

Ray started ticking points off on his fingers. "First, you like cooking. Second, Preston doesn't go grocery shopping. Third, you told me if I ever went near the kitchen again, you'd try to have me deported."

"Okay, I'll give you that," she said agreeably. "We'll at least need to think of a name for him."

"No need. I have the perfect name already," Ray said as he started the engine. The puppy looked up in surprise; Michelle soothed him with gentle petting.

"Oh?" she asked when she had the puppy distracted.

"Stormageddon."

Michelle blinked. "Sorry, what?"

"Stormageddon." Ray shot her a look. "Don't you watch *Doctor Who*?"

"No, sorry."

He huffed. "Colonial. We'll fix that. Trust me. Stormageddon."

At the moment, Michelle couldn't deny Ray anything—not even a silly name. "Stormy for short?" she offered as a compromise.

"If you must," he said with a sigh. "You'll understand soon enough. We'll start watching it this weekend, once the telly's hooked up."

Michelle grinned down at the puppy. "Stormageddon. The name's bigger than he is."

"Only for now. He'll be as big as Preston's two soon enough. Preston ended up going through three collars each before they finally stopped growing." Ray glanced at her as he stopped at the end of the driveway. "Speaking of which, there's a collar and lead for him in the glove box."

"Sneaky," she accused, hugging Stormageddon so she could open the glove compartment. She drew out a tangle of leather. "You really did think of everything, didn't you?"

"Again, love, logistics and—"

"—mission planning, I know," she finished, straightening everything out. The leash was thin brown leather with a small matching collar. She saw something hanging off the collar ring and thought for a moment it was an ID tag tied into place with a white ribbon, but it caught the light, sparkling brightly. Stormageddon helpfully attacked the collar, chewing on it ineffectively.

It took some effort to wrestle the collar free. Michelle straightened it—

And gasped when she saw that it wasn't an ID tag at all. It was a delicate gold ring with two small diamonds flanking a large central stone.

"Ray," she said softly, looking over to see that he'd put the truck in park.

He was watching her, smiling a bit nervously. "So that's where that got to," he said in a falsely casual voice. "I thought you might like it."

Tears filled her eyes. With shaking hands, she tugged the ribbon to free the ring. Stormageddon immediately pounced on the collar.

Ray took the ring from her hand and held it up for her. "So, I know you hate sudden decisions—"

"Yes," she whispered.

His smile lit up his eyes. "Yes, you hate sudden decisions?" he teased. "Or yes, you'll marry me?"

Laughter burst free as her heart soared. "Yes, I'll marry you."

He slid the ring onto her finger and then lifted her hand to his lips. "Thank you," he said quietly, releasing her hand so he could brush at her tears.

She ducked her head, blinking to try and clear her eyes. Stormageddon gave up on chewing the collar to lick her face instead, making her laugh. "We should get him home," she said when she could speak again.

Ray nodded, though he didn't put the truck in gear again. "Are you happy?" he asked instead.

She nodded, tears stinging her eyes again. They'd discussed renting their house and buying property together, but neither of them had said a single word about marriage. After watching her mother marry and divorce so many times, Michelle had spent years wondering if she'd ever feel comfortable with the idea.

Now, she realized just how natural it felt. She loved Ray more than she'd ever imagined loving anyone, and she knew he felt the same.

"Yes," she said, swallowing against the lump in her throat. She hugged the puppy close and turned to look at the man she loved—the man she wanted to have beside her for the rest of her life. "Yes, I am."

Acknowledgments

The Isles of Scilly are a gorgeous hidden treasure, and the people who live there are equally wonderful. Thank you to Harbour Master D.J. Clark, Zoe at Churchtown Farm, and Canon Paul Miller for answering my questions. One day, I hope to visit Scilly.

Thank you to the wonderful authors Jo Leigh and Diane Duane, for answering questions about the mysterious process of writing; to my agent, Jen at Donald Maass, for encouraging me to bring Eleanor to life; to Cat, my editor at Sourcebooks, for her feedback; and to my expatriate husband, who answered my questions about British language and culture.

And thanks especially to all those who have encouraged me to continue writing for the last forty-plus years, from my first grade teacher, Mrs. Liebner, who taught me about run-on sentences, to every last person who's dropped me a comment or kind note on my works. I write because I must, but I share my works for you!

The Longest Night

by Kara Braden

Two fiery personalities living together in a remote cabin...

When a car accident leaves gorgeous but prickly genius Ian Fairchild with a debilitating injury and an addiction to painkillers, this city boy has to find a safe place to recover. He escapes to the remote Canadian wilderness, as far from the lights of Manhattan as he can get—and in the company of a woman he has no reason to trust.

Will they make it through the winter?

Former Marine Captain Cecily Knight prides herself on being self-sufficient. Her nearest neighbor is miles away, she has to fly to town for basic necessities, and she can go weeks without seeing another soul…and that's the way she likes it. But when she's called on to repay a debt, she agrees to allow Ian to stay with her in her isolated cabin, on one condition: just because he's invading her privacy doesn't mean she's willing to open herself up to him, even if he is as tempting as sin.

But as they spend day after day in the wilderness together, Cecily and Ian's wary friendship turns into a love these two lost souls needed more than they ever knew.

For more Kara Braden, visit:

www.sourcebooks.com

What to Do with a Bad Boy

The McCauley Brothers

by Marie Harte

USA Today Bestselling Author

What is with Mike McCauley?

Every time Delilah Webster runs into Mike McCauley, he practically bites her head off. The rough-and-tumble contractor clearly has baggage. Del knows she's better off keeping her distance, but a man that seriously sexy is hard to ignore.

There's something about the strong-willed mechanic that sets Mike's motor running--and scares the hell out of him. Mike has loved and lost and will never hurt like that again, even if that means walking away from a woman who makes him feel alive for the first time in years.

When a simple kiss turns hot and heavy, Mike discovers he can't stay away...

Praise for Marie Harte:

"Charismatic characters and sexual tension that is hot enough to scorch your fingers." —*Romance Junkies*

For more Marie Harte, visit:

www.sourcebooks.com

About the Author

Kara Braden believes in fighting fire with fire. As she spends her days in the desert outside Phoenix, Arizona, she combats the heat with endless cups of hot coffee, setting her kitchen ablaze once or twice a week, and writing smoldering romance. Her hobbies include incessant reading and writing, video games, and hiking whenever it's not too hot outside.

A Single Kiss

A Sweetest Kisses Novel

by Grace Burrowes

New York Times and *USA Today* Bestselling Author

The first in a powerful contemporary romance series from Grace Burrowes

Hannah Stark set her sights on corporate law, but to support her daughter, she accepts a temp position in a small firm's family law department. After growing up in foster care, it's the last place she wants to practice, but the boss—Trent Peckham—is charming and the law school loans are overdue.

Trent is attracted to his new associate counsel, but is Hannah ready to build the solid foundation she never had?

Praise for Grace Burrowes:

"Grace Burrowes weaves her magic with eloquent, revealing words, and subtle humor." —*Long and Short Reviews*

"Burrowes has a knack for giving fresh twists to genre tropes and developing them in unexpected and delightful directions…" —*Publishers Weekly*

For more Grace Burrowes, visit:

www.sourcebooks.com